The Past Attacks

Part 2 of Eight's Warning

Book 2 of West's Ghost Ranch Series

A Novel by **Aidan Red**

To a great IP whose passion gave me the love of aviation and whose knowledge and patience taught me the skills necessary to fly and survive in an airplane, my dad.

My many thanks to my editors.

Content Editing by Trenda London,
http://ItsYourStoryContentEditing.com

Copy Editing by Amy Jackson,
Copy Editing and Proof Reading, http://AmyJacksonEditing.com

Cover by
Aidan Red and David Lundblade

The Past Attacks

After seeing her picture in an aviation article, and knowing that people knew she looked like the missing Emli Collingsworth, Charlie's fears rose to new heights. Glen hired a software and internet communications expert from his own past and together they searched for clues to Howard Collingsworth's activities.

They began to follow Howard's emails, his plans and intentions, learning what they could, while Charlie threw herself into supporting Glen and the ranch and making preparations for the upcoming fly-ins. But nothing they did prepared her for her biggest challenge yet; that moment when she unexpectedly found herself face-to-face with the other lookalike; Emil's sister. Recoiling from the encounter, Charlie suddenly found herself caught in the net cast by Howard's henchmen...

Chapters

Fourteen
Sunday, May 7

Howard was in a miserable mood when he returned to his downtown office from lunch. His morning had started foully, fed by the lingering taste of Monte's disagreement with him for asking for a complete list of investor's assets. Then he got to the office and problem phone calls from both of his current development projects had filled his time until noon. At lunch he ignored his phone, hoping to sidestep any new, unwanted problems for that short interval, but he knew it would not last.

He returned to his office, poured himself a cup of coffee, and sat down at his desk. With a deep sigh of resignation, he turned to his computer and scrolled through his emails.

His heart stopped! There in the list was one he did not expect to see; the name was Voster and the URL was "gov.za," and he knew it was not good.

Howard opened the email, denied the sender's request for notification when he opened it, and slowly read the text:

> Mr. Collingsworth.
> Being that I have not heard from you since our most recent communication in the fall, I find it necessary to provide you with another reminder.
> I am certain you realize your contract extension only has twenty weeks remaining. And as was explained at the time this one was granted, it is the last one that I can consider. They cannot be granted to extend the terms of the original contract beyond ten years and therefore, in this case, a new,

replacement contract must be negotiated.

I must also reiterate that I am not in any position to consider negotiating a new contract, seeing as you have requested and been granted two extensions on the present contract. You have received our considerations and support in return for your promises to supply certain additional assets of value. Since those assets have not been delivered, and the fact that I have not heard from you, forces me to prepare for the possibility that you cannot supply the one named asset, your younger daughter Emli, by the agreed date, September 30. If you do not deliver, I will not hesitate to enforce the termination rider in the penalty clause attached to your present extension.

In the sincere hopes that I have misinterpreted your silence, I look forward to your response and will make arrangements to meet you and your daughter in Pretoria / Tshwane in September.

Best Regards, Elrich Voster, Deputy Minister of State Security, Pretoria, South Africa.

Howard slowly sat back in his chair, staring at the computer monitor, rapping his fingers on the edge of the desk. He vividly remembered the addition of the "rider" and did not have to be reminded that it was his termination it referred to. Now all he had to do was to find the elusive Emli—or a suitable lookalike.

Tuesday, May 16
Ten Days after the Alamosa, Colorado Fly-in

"Hey, come in," Norman said when Celia knocked and pushed his New York apartment door open. He smiled at her straight-from-work young attorney look: white blouse and gray above-the-knee skirt with a matching gray jacket, black shoes, and scarf.

"Nice." Celia closed the door and she looked through the kitchen to the dining area at the front of the apartment and then took in the living room that filled the area beside the kitchen. She smiled at him when she spotted the fireplace and the picture on the mantel. Then she turned her gaze to the hallway leading away from the living room.

"A hall bath for guests." He followed her quizzical look and gestured as he went. "Large bedroom with a master bath, full glass outside walls with room-darkening curtains on the south and west."

"This would be comfortable for a couple," Celia agreed with a sheepish smile. "Mine is a studio with my bed in half of the living room. Single bath where your hall bath is and no master anything beyond that. No glass walls, either. This is very nice."

"Thanks. Drink?"

"Sure."

He slipped into the kitchen as she sat down on a stool at the kitchen eating counter and watched.

"Would you be interested in a casual dinner in a little bit?"

She nodded.

"There's a great little pizza place around the corner, or if you'd like something more—"

"Pizza will be fine. I admit I liked your doting on me in Colorado, but I don't need any more of those wonderful lavish dinners like you fed me. At least, not on a regular basis."

Norman set her metropolitan in front of her and opened a beer for himself.

"No cocktail?" she questioned as she sipped her drink. "Is this something new?"

"Well, I'll probably have a beer with dinner, so I figured I'd just start now. Cheers." He clinked his bottle neck against her cocktail glass.

He picked up an envelope from a mail holder on the dining room end of the counter, then came around and took the stool next to her. He leaned to her and kissed her gently.

"Sorry, I got my greeting out of order." He grinned at her before he sat back on his stool. "How was your day?"

"My day was normal." She glanced down at the counter. "I was almost late for work, again. Too much daydreaming about our mornings in Colorado. But we won a few cases today. Helped a struggling single mother with three young kids."

"That's great." Norman took another sip.

"What do you have there?" Celia gestured to the envelope.

Norman handed it to her, and she opened the flap and took the letter out. "You've been accepted? To the Colorado Bar?"

"I told you I took the exams," he reminded her. "I have to go back out to Colorado over the weekend and meet with the Bar Association next week, and I think I'll take a few extra days to look at potential office spaces. Sure you can't take more time off?"

"You know I can't, but this is wonderful. It's a lot sooner than I expected, but wonderful."

"Have you decided what you're going to do? I'll look for places to live if you're ready to move, but it would be nice to get your input."

"I guess I better start planning," she admitted, and sipped her drink, "if I'm going to partner with you in that new law office. I better get ready for the Bar Exams myself. When did you say the next exams are given?"

"Mid-July, and the results would be sent out in October." Norman ran his finger along the rim of his beer bottle. "Come out as close to the beginning of June as you can and use the month to study. I have enough saved so you won't have to work, just study. Then, after the exams, there are a lot of things you can do to help us settle in."

Celia nodded. "I have savings too. I'll help. If I give my notice this week, I could be free to move in a week or so, just after Memorial Day."

"That would work nicely. I figure that's about when I'd be ready to move."

"When do I have to apply?"

"May first."

"What?" Celia stared at him. "I've missed it and you didn't tell me?"

He chuckled. "You can pay me back, but I sent your application and the fee in last month. I was hoping. If you decided not to, it'd only cost me a couple hundred to retract the application."

"Thank you." Celia leaned and kissed him. Then she finished her drink and he stood up and took her hand.

"I don't know about you, but I'm getting hungry." He helped her up, slipped his arms around her, and pulled her close. "Please tell me if you're having doubts or second thoughts. If you feel I'm pushing you into something you're not ready for, don't let me."

"You're not." Celia leaned back to look at him. "I'm still trying to accept that you want me to come with you, to be your business partner, to—"

"You mean more to me than a business partner. I hope you know that."

"Are you sure this is what you want?" She held his eyes.

"Yes. If the living arrangements are a problem, I'll be sure you have your own space. Maybe I can find a place with a casita, a guest house."

"That's not a problem." Celia smiled. "Let's go eat and talk there."

"Okay."

Celia and Norman settled on two stools at the wraparound counter just inside the glass wall of the pizzeria. They each ordered two slices and a beer on tap.

Celia leaned close. "I don't think I really thanked you for taking me to Denver and everything we did there."

"I thought you showed me how you felt in a very nice manner," he said, and raised one eyebrow at her. "But if you think that wasn't good enough, I can ask for a do-over."

"That's not what I meant." She punched his shoulder. "But thank you, again. And for going souvenir shopping with me." She stopped long enough to snag a bite of her pizza and a sip of her beer. Then she glanced around to see who might be close enough to hear, and said, "Norman, I know I slept most of the way back from Alamosa after the fly-in, but I don't remember getting back to the Lodge or going to our rooms. Did you have to carry me?"

"Yeah," he chuckled. "I just tossed you over my shoulder and—"

"You did not!" She clouted his shoulder again. "Did you dress me for bed that night?"

"Only partially." He smiled. "You didn't want to sleep in your room and sent me to get your pajamas. When I came back with them, you were half asleep and half undressed. I just helped do what you asked me to do."

"Sorry." She patted his arm. "I hope I wasn't too demanding."

"Not at all. I liked helping."

"You just liked seeing me undressed." She looked at him sideways.

"I like seeing you any way you'll let me, dressed or not."

She took another bite and a sip and watched him eat for a moment. "I've been thinking."

"Me too." He paused to look at her. "What were you thinking about?"

"More of this and the things you said before we went to Alamosa. Us." She let her fingers doodle in the condensation on the beer mug. "But mostly about the newspaper pictures of the airshow. You know they could get pretty wide distribution if what they said is true, about Glen West never taking four airplanes to any one airshow."

"Yeah. They did say that was very unusual."

"The problem I see is the pictures that go with the article."

Norman took a longer-than-normal sip of his beer. "How so?"

"If someone that knew Emli or one of those guys looking for her sees Charlie's pictures"—Celia looked at him, holding his eyes—"they're going to jump to the same conclusion you did and that I would have if you hadn't prepared me. You said Emli's father was behind the searching."

He nodded.

"Well, if he or someone working for him sees those pictures, I'll bet they'll only see Emli and not believe she's Charlie, Glen West's wife."

Norman's eyes widened. "Damn. That could be very bad."

"Yeah. And I don't see how we can do anything to prevent it."

Norman let out a deep sigh. "You'll just have to spend more of your days and nights with me and help me think of something." Levity was the only thing he could think of at the moment.

"This is Howard," he announced when he answered his office phone.

"Howard. Lawrence in Paris," the voice on the other end greeted. "Is this a good time to report?"

"Yes, Lawrence. Are you still at the table or are you back at the hotel?"

"Hotel. The negotiation talks recessed about five our time and William and I had dinner before we called you. We think we're making some headway. We've exchanged energy credits, commercial interests, and even are making some progress in the land-usage clauses and the final price figures."

"But? Where's the rub?" Howard heard the undertones in Lawrence's voice.

"Down-the-road profit-sharing. They've heard of things you've done in the past to make your 'business' deals more like 'family' deals, if you know what I mean. They're fishing."

"Hmm. I don't have the assets to swing that kind of deal."

"If you can figure out how to arrange that sort of a relationship, I think you'd be surprised how quickly the negotiations would reach an agreement."

"You know we've never admitted to anything under the table like that. Do you know which arrangements they've 'heard' about?"

"Only two were hinted at: the arrangement between the Brickets' eldest daughter and Count Lavar's eldest son in the Bolivian Resort deal, and the similar arrangement in financing the Spanish deal about thirteen years ago."

"I see. What's the offer from the other side?"

"With the right arrangement between a suitable, pretty female from an appropriate, aristocratic family, you get what you want, and as is customary, you both split the proceeds from the operation of the finished project."

"Very well, Lawrence. I'll see if there is anything I can do. I'll try to call you tomorrow evening."

"Goodnight."

Howard studied the silent desk phone console for a long moment, then reached out and tapped a speed dial button.

"Monte?" he asked when the call connected.

"Hello, Howard." His voice sounding distracted. "Hold on a minute."

Howard could hear Monte get up and walk across his office and close the door. Then in a moment, he returned to the phone.

"What's up?"

"Just spoke with Lawrence in Paris." He ran his hand over the wooden desk. "The negotiations are being slowed down again." Howard took a minute and explained his discussion with Lawrence and described what he felt was needed.

"So why did you call me?"

"Get me the names of suitable candidates."

"What? Just like that?" Monte's voice was full of dismay. "Is there a catalogue of available wom—?"

"Don't take that tone with me, Monte. You weren't above an arrangement when you were the one that was going to benefit. Just remember you and your father have profited very well under the circumstances, and far more than the original estimates. You've even got a beautiful family to show for it. And I think Cat has actually come to like you some. So don't put any of that at risk."

The connection was quiet for a long moment.

"Now, there are businesses involved in this deal that could benefit handsomely if they are willing to play the game. Get me a list of current associates that have suitable assets and we'll discuss their options. Call me in the morning."

Howard hung up and scowled at the phone console.

"I can't believe Cappie is saying the new hangars will be ready in another month," Charlie said as they crossed the main house's wide veranda to the double front door. It was late and the winds had settled to barely a breeze as the day turned into a peaceful night. "All of the main structure, the roofs, the doors, and the movable ramps are done, and he only has the lights and services to install and the main floor to pour."

"He is a wizard," West said as he stopped in the living room. "Would you like some wine this evening?"

"Sure," She lovingly looked at her husband.

West collected a bottle of her choice from behind the bar. He handed her two glasses and then led her up the stairs to their large bedroom suite. They settled on the balcony loveseat and West poured a glass for each of them.

Charlie clinked her glass with West's and sipped, happy with how her life was turning out. "I know things can't always be this good, but thank you for everything you've done for me, for loving and being here for me."

"It is truly my honor," West said in return. "Thank you for being you. But now you've made it hard for me to bring up some things that I need to talk to you about."

"Oh? I don't mean to make it hard." She winked at him and he smiled at her double entendre.

"Mostly, I just don't like bringing up anything that might be upsetting to you or stir up bad memories."

"Just talk to me. What's up?"

"First, I don't know if you knew it, but your old acquaintance Norman Kent was at the Alamosa Fly-in."

"Yes. I saw him and Celia," she admitted. "I was hoping she would keep him under control, and it seems she did. Maybe they're together now. They were quite the item in college."

"You knew he was there? You didn't say anything and you were okay with it?"

"Yeah. Woody and the guys were trying to keep it a secret, but I do watch around me. I've had to for a long time, and just because we got married, I can't just expect you and everyone else to keep me safe. I have to work at it too."

"And speaking of your safety," he continued, "you should know that Ratchet and I have been collecting information on Emli's dad." He purposely referred to her old name so she would know he didn't think of her as the woman in her previous life. She was his Charlie and no one else. "We feel pretty certain you were right that he's been talking to those that she knew in school, and we think his checking on her trust funds just confirms your thoughts that he's started inquiring again."

She watched him and waited. "You know this still scares the piss out of me."

"Yes, I do. Ratchet doesn't know why I'm looking. Other than the few comments at Reno, he doesn't know much about

Emli."

She nodded. "Will this help us know if Emli's dad starts anything else?"

"Well, we can't tell for certain if he is or is not up to something," he admitted with a sigh, "but I have an idea that might help us keep ahead of him, if you're okay with it."

Charlie inhaled and smiled as she slowly let her breath out. "Tell me what you have in mind, love."

"Many years ago, in my software development days, my staff and I came up with some code that I think can be modified to let me see what's going on in different places in the internet. To move forward, I need to use the special talents of one of my old programmers. She was part of my group that went with the new company when I sold mine, and I think we can use her gifts and insights on a little side job."

She smiled and caught his hand. "I'm okay with using her if you think it's the right move."

"Will you go with me and meet her?" he asked, squeezing her hand as he slipped his arm around her shoulders. "I'd like to see if your instincts agree with me or tell you something different. We can just tell her that I'm collecting information for the ranch's business purposes."

Charlie kissed him gently. "Okay, love. When?"

"I'll call tomorrow and confirm a time," he said, finishing his wine. Then he slowly stood up and extended his hand to her.

"But right now…" he said as he helped her up. When she was standing, he bent and scooped her up in his arms; her arms quickly wrapped around his shoulders and neck. "I'd like to help my Charlotte make some pleasant memories."

Wednesday, May 17

Norman casually took a bite of a huge, overflowing hot dog from a street vendor, still wrestling with his concerns over Glen West's wife. He finished his can of soda, took another bite of his dog, and decided.

He would do it! He would write Glen a clear and concise message and explain his concern in the best manner he could. If he did not hear anything back, or did not see a cloud of smoke rising from somewhere in Colorado, he would write again. And again, if need be, until someone listened or the police showed up on his doorstep.

Filled with resolve and continued worry, he tossed his trash into a sidewalk bin and went back to his apartment to take a stab at composing a suitable message.

Friday, May 19

"Ghost Ranch. *The Lady* is off at oh seven hundred," Charlie said as *The Lady* broke ground and started a cruise climb on a direct course to Austin, Texas. "One hour plus fifty-four block time."

"Safe trip, *Lady*," Belle's clear voice responded.

"Thank you, Ghost Ranch."

The Lady passed over Amarillo at 0731.2 and Lubbock at 0817.1. Ten minutes out, Charlie contacted Austin Executive with Delta, and landed on runway 13 at 0850.

"Looks like *The Lady* has drawn a crowd again." West chuckled, seeing the people peering out of T-hangars and stopping on the ramp as *The Lady* taxied back from the first turnoff and turned onto the Executive's main ramp. "Winds are light out of the southwest and forecast to be less than ten until this afternoon."

Charlie swung *The Lady* into the wind in front of Executive's main hangar. She stepped through the shutdown checklist as he rolled the canopy full open and waved to the line boy that stood at the right wingtip after placing the wheel chocks.

He stepped out onto the wing and waited as Charlie secured the cockpit and stood up. She took his hand as she stepped out and slid the canopy closed to three inches open and released the latch button.

West followed her down the left strut and stopped to talk to the line boy, assuring him they had enough fuel and did not need servicing at that time. Then he gestured to the main hangar and lobby.

He opened the lobby door and Charlie led the way in, stopping when a petite, ginger-headed woman in a light gray business pantsuit got up from a bench by the front windows and walked toward them. As she came closer, Charlie saw she was younger than her business appearance initially implied, and her bright smile was warm and friendly.

Holding Charlie's hand with his left, West stepped forward and extended his hand to the woman.

"Jessie. It's so good of you to come out and meet us." He shook her hand.

"Thank you, Griff," Jessie said. "I was certainly surprised when you called." She looked at Charlie.

"Jess, my wife, Charlie."

Charlie extended her hand. "Pleased to meet you, Jessie,"

"Likewise, Charlie," Jessie said as she took Charlie's hand and her smile widened. "I'm surprised, yet not really. Griff didn't mention that he'd married, but I'm glad he has. It really is a pleasure to meet you."

"That's another thing, Jess. Since I sold and moved, I've taken my dad's first name, 'Glen,' and my nickname, 'West.' I'm known as Glen West, 'West' to friends, and Charlie is Charlie West in public."

"Okay." Jessie nodded slowly. "I'll remember."

He looked around and asked if the pilots' lounge was clear.

"I believe it is." Jessie glanced back at the ramp. "Obviously, you started flying after you left the software world. Nice plane."

"Thanks." He led Charlie to the lounge, noting a table set in a corner niche. He sat Charlie in the back corner, he beside her on one side and Jessie across the table from him.

"And obviously you're a pilot as well," Jessie said to Charlie.

"Yes." Charlie smiled simply. "I am, among other things."

West chuckled, but decided to follow Charlie's lead and skip the explanations.

"Your call asks a lot of questions, Griff—I mean, West," Jessie remarked. "What's going on?"

"You remember when we developed the protection software to find and remove a number of spyware routines that have since turned into market-tracking tools many businesses use?" He took a flash drive out of his flight suit's shoulder pocket. "Well, I have here a software application that does something similar, but is not resident. There is a complete description of the code and the goals, encrypted with my old routine 'K-9' first and then 'G-6' second."

"Wow. You really don't want anyone to know what you're doing." Jessie's eyes slowly widened.

He took his time and slowly gave her a high-level explanation of what he was attempting.

"This is a lot more than just spyware." Jessie looked at him and then at Charlie.

He grinned. "Look at the data on the drive and give me your questions and comments. There's an encrypted URL on the drive that will get you directly to Charlie's and my computer, and I've included our personal phone numbers. If you call, the code is 'ham and cheese.' Then switch to voice encryption."

West sighed and looked at her, waiting as she digested his explanation. Charlie watched Jessie's manner become serious as he spoke.

"I am looking at different companies in association with my current business and its needs. More often than I want to admit, I hear that a company I'm working with, and some of my prospective associates, have an involvement in dealings that could be considered illegal or unscrupulous and I need to be able to verify if that's true or not before we continue or start doing business together. The servers in question are public, though not widely used. I don't want to step over the line and do any illegal prying on our part, but I need to mature this tool to protect myself. I don't have time to create and evaluate new software these days, so I'm asking for your help. Very confidential, of course." He paused a moment, then added, "Who knows—it might be marketable if we do it right and prove it works correctly."

"This has to be kept between the three of us, Jess," Charlie added in a firm and controlled voice. "West says you're the best and we're really counting on that, but you will have questions. When you do, please let us know quickly. West is the software man and I'm more the business side of things. Our time is a bit short and we apologize ahead of time for that."

"Thanks, I'll see what I can do and let you both know."

West asked about the other four from his former company and Jessie gave them a concise update on each, again thanking him for thinking of them when he sold his company.

"You're welcome, Jess." West stood up. "Sorry, but Charlie and I need to get back. I'd ask you to tell the others hello for us, but I really don't want to put you in a position of having to answer a lot of questions. My being here would easily be seen as for only one reason."

"I understand. Are you still as secretive about where you are these days?"

"Yup." He turned to Charlie. "I'll get the weather briefing. You want to get *The Lady* ready?"

"Sure. Nice to meet you, Jess. Thanks for the help."

Then Charlie walked out and started a pre-flight check.

"She's beautiful," Jessie admitted as she watched Charlie walk out to the plane.

"Yes. She sure is." He extended his hand. "In every way. Thanks again. We'll be looking for your questions."

He picked up the handset on the phone console and called Flight Service.

"Any intuitive flags?" West finally asked somewhere near Lubbock.

"No flags. She's younger than I expected."

"Yeah. She was seventeen when I hired her. That makes her about twenty-nine or thirty now, and she's still single."

She let a few minutes pass while she reviewed the details of their meeting in her mind.

"West? Interested in lunch on the way home?"

"Certainly. Santa Fe?"

"Ooh, that sounds wonderful." She chuckled and consulted her charts. "We have the fuel."

"Good trip?" Ratchet asked as Charlie climbed down off *The Lady*'s wing.

"Think so."

"Lenny's bringing the tug. Any squawks?"

She handed him the half-sized clipboard. "Only a couple. Nothing serious. Engine has twelve hours remaining."

"We've got the replacement engine almost ready. Let's think about scheduling an engine change late next week."

"Good. Log it and we'll get it done." Charlie nodded and turned as West stopped beside them.

"Helen said she has something for us," West informed her when she finished. "Can you and Lenny fuel and put her away?"

"Sure," Ratchet happily assured him. "Rosita's up again. You know, she'll be ready to start cross countries before long."

"Very good." West turned Charlie to one of the jeeps. "We better go."

Helen met West and Charlie at the side door. "I printed it out and put it on your desk."

16

"Thanks," West said absently. "Who's it from?"

Helen gently pushed their backs. "Go and read it. Tell me what we need to do when you come down."

West inhaled and looked at Charlie as they climbed the stairs to the second level. He led her into his office and stopped beside his desk chair, staring at the sheet of paper on the desk.

Charlie picked it up and read the header, then gestured for West to sit down. She settled on his lap and together they read the message.

To: Glen West: Private.

From: Norman Kent.

Subject: Mrs. Charlie West's Safety.

Mr. West, I am writing to you with a grave heart and a matter of utmost concern. I hope you will read my message before you remember my terribly disrespectful actions in Reno, and simply discard it.

To properly describe my concerns, I must provide you with a brief piece of history. A little over eleven years ago, I was one of five people at Yale Law School that knew a woman, a student, named Emli Collingsworth. Everything about this woman and our relationship was normal for college friends until the beginning of her third year when she failed to return to school and reenroll. This is a normal occurrence for the start of the third year, but the week following the reenrollment period, representatives of Emli's father arrived on campus and began interrogating everyone that knew her. The five of us were questioned the most, but had nothing to tell. Emli simply had not returned for the fall semester and had not explained why to anyone. Apparently, not even to her family.

Three years later, two of us, myself and Ben Scroles, were contacted again by new representatives of Emli's father and asked the same questions. Then last year, the Tuesday after Labor Day, again.

This brings me to my concern and the cause, as unacceptable as it was, for my behavior when I saw your Charlie at Reno, and I must again apologize for my actions. But with the renewed questions and attention given to Emli's whereabouts, I jumped to an incorrect conclusion when I saw Charlie. Charlie is an identical *twin* for Emli Collingsworth.

Since Reno, Emli's father's henchmen have contacted Ben Scroles, asking the same questions again. When I figured out you were bringing some of your planes to the Alamosa fly-in in early May, I brought a friend of mine with me to the fly-in, hoping your Charlie would also be there. My friend, Celia Gibbings, also knew Emli and she confirmed your Charlie and Emli look enough like each other, they could easily be confused. She agrees they could be twins. This is the crux of my concern and the reason for this message. I have attached a picture I took of Emli when she got her commercial ticket and another we took at Alamosa.

Since Alamosa, the newspaper article of the fly-in and of the Ghost Ranch's generous participation has been picked up by many papers across the country. Ben saw the article in St. Louis and also thought the picture of Charlie was the lost Emli.

It is my heartfelt concern that in the blind searching by Emli's father or his henchmen, they will see the pictures of your Charlie and think they are of Emli. By the nature of their questions and of their manner, I have also been concerned for Emli's safety if they find her, but I believe they will see Charlie's picture and decide she is the missing Emli and I further believe that Charlie will then be in serious danger.

The danger is further increased by Emli and Charlie inadvertently crossing paths, or nearly so, when Charlie, Bassett then, bought the same Cessna 180 that Emli sold to Templeton.

If you've read this message to this point, I must thank you and reassure you that I do not, in any way, mean to pose a threat to you or to Mrs. West. I hope the best for you in this situation and in all the years yet to come. I have seen how happy you two are together and I sincerely wish that blessing continues forever.

The only regret I have is that there is nothing I can do to remove the danger caused by Mr. Collingsworth. Thank you again for your time.

Best Regards, Norman Kent.

"Oh shit!" West whispered, suddenly feeling like he had let Charlie down. "I never thought about the papers."

She lay her head on her arm and against the side of his head, staring at the paper where he had laid it back on the desk. She inhaled deeply. "Well hell! Now he knows what state I'm in."

"I'm sorry, love. Let's see who's picking up groceries and supplies and have them look for a copy of anything concerning the Alamosa fly-in."

"Yeah. It will be nice to see what everyone else is seeing." She squeezed his shoulders. "I know the day is young, but I feel like I'm sinking again."

"I know, love. Me too." He thought about the message a long moment. "Norman must've searched the FAA's airplane records to figure out the airplane switch."

"He had to dig down to the serial number level." She sighed. "I didn't think about anyone going to that much trouble."

West turned his head and kissed her. "Come on. Let's talk to Mom and then go saddle a couple of horses."

"Sounds good. We need to think about all of this."

"Thanks for having lunch with me." Norman held Celia's hand as he finished his beer. "Sorry for taking you to pizza again."

"That's fine. Reminds me of our college days," she expressed with a giggle. "Call me when you get to your folks'?"

"Sure." He squeezed her hand. "I'm scheduled out of Louisville and into Denver Sunday evening. I'll split my time on Monday, half in Denver and half in Colorado Springs looking at office spaces. I'll send you pictures of the ones I look at."

"Any reply to your message to the Wests?"

"No. Don't expect one." He looked at her longingly. "Wish you'd at least take the weekend and come with me to the folks."

"I really would like to, but I have to finish a case this afternoon and then start cleaning and boxing my things up. The weekend will let me get started."

"Okay." He looked at his watch. "I better call a cab. Don't want to miss my flight."

"Better call, then." Celia squeezed his hand in return.

Monday, May 22

Howard looked up from the files on his desk when he heard the knock on his office door.

"Come in, Monte. On your way home?"

"Yes." He stepped up to Howard's desk. "The list you asked for." He laid a thin folder on the desk on top of the other papers.

Howard opened the folder and picked up the single sheet of paper. "Five names? That's actually more than I expected."

"Those are the only ones on this project that have daughters like you asked about."

Howard opened a desk drawer and extracted another file folder.

"If I look at a list of our last three projects"—Howard opened the folder—"I have four additional 'partners' that have suitable assets. Let's see...you have Carolton, Lunas, Newit, Olgana, and Myers, each with one unmarried daughter."

"And your list?"

"Ableman, Dufmat, Gibbings, and Scott. Thank you." Howard studied the two sheets.

"Goodnight, Howard," Monte remarked tersely as he turned and closed the door behind him.

Norman got off the commuter from Denver and walked up the jet way and into the Colorado Springs airport. He waited and collected his one checked bag, then his rental car.

Driving south out of the parking area, he felt a mixture of elation and apprehension, relief and despair. He had finally completed the first step of his plan to leave New York when the Colorado State Bar Association had notified him early the previous week that he had successfully passed the state's bar exam. Now he was working on the next step: to set up his own practice and serve both business clients and family clients. He was not depressed, but he did wish Celia was there to share in some of the decisions he was going to have to make—especially those that would have an effect on her in the future.

To celebrate his moving forward, he decided to spend the weekend with his folks and younger sister Ronnie before going back to Colorado and starting his search for office real estate. The visit turned out to be a wonderful break from his normal reality, and all in all he felt his folks were happy for him and his move to Colorado. They harbored the normal parental concerns when their kids started something new, no matter their age, but that was only natural.

He arrived in Denver Sunday evening as planned and spent the morning with one of the real estate agents suggested in the Colorado Bar Association's "get acquainted" literature, looking at a number of spaces suitable for a solo practice. Then, after a quick lunch, he flew to Colorado Springs and an appointment to look at similar properties. Once he decided on where he wanted his practice located, he'd look for a place to live.

Then he remembered his dinner engagement and wondered if that would help him decide between the two cities.

Norman arrived a few minutes early and waited in Vega's Mexican Bistro's reception lobby. A family of four entered and a waitress led them to their seats before two men in casual business attire stepped in and stopped inside the front door. The taller of the two spotted him and stepped forward.

"Norman? Norman Kent?" he asked, and Norman nodded.

"Yes, I'm Norman."

"Good to meet you. I'm Tom Grant and this"—he gestured to the other man—"is Bill Strong."

Bill and Norman exchanged greetings and Tom checked on their reservations.

A young waiter led them to a quiet booth away from the louder family guests and placed their menus, saying their server would be right with them.

"I believe you said you were going to look at real estate today," Bill opened their conversation. "Did that go well?"

"Looked at number of places in Denver and a few this afternoon here in the Springs," Norman explained. "But I don't know if I know enough to decide which city would be better."

The waitress stopped and asked if they knew what they wanted to drink. Tom and Bill ordered a *cerveza* and Norman stayed with iced tea, then they gave the waitress their dinner orders.

"Thank you for meeting with us," Tom said when the waitress left. "We represent a business that is looking for a new attorney to handle their limited corporation's legal affairs."

Bill explained the general scope and nature of the legal support the business was looking for.

"Is it inappropriate to ask what the business' name is, or what they do?" he asked, glancing from one to the other.

"If the owner likes our report, he will want another meeting with you," Tom explained. "Until then, he requests we keep that to ourselves."

"Sounds mysterious," he admitted. "But if that's the way it is, that's the way it is. What do you need to know from me?"

The waitress returned and served their drink orders.

"The most pressing question I have," Bill started as he sipped his beer, "is what made you decide to pack up and move to Colorado to continue your career?"

Norman shrugged and smiled. "We camped a lot when I was young, mostly in and around Kentucky and the Appalachian Mountains. But one summer, my dad took an extended vacation and we came west. Colorado, Utah, Wyoming. I later found out his extended vacation was because he was 'down-sized,' which is a 'whole 'nother story,' as they say. Anyway, I was hooked on real mountains after that, and during breaks in college and summers, I would come out here to recharge."

"And the other story?" Thomas asked.

"Dad's legal troubles, once he was out of work"—Norman inhaled and slowly began explaining—"caused me to pay more attention than a fifteen-year-old usually did. He connected with a family law attorney in Louisville and I was impressed with how the attorney was able to help us through the minefield. It didn't solve Dad's problems, but his help made them manageable. Remembering that in college when I saw some folks with a similar situation, I added family law to my studies."

They spent their dinner asking questions and listening to his answers and explanations. Norman talked about how he got into studying law and his love for flying and why he had stopped flying. He explained that the work he was doing in New York no longer seemed fulfilling and fed his feeling that he urgently needed a change in his life.

"The woman that was with you when you recently vacationed here," Tom noted, "is she part of your future plans? Someone special maybe, or just someone for the week?"

Norman smiled, admitting they would have to ask.

"Yes. Celia is special to me and part of my future plans," he answered. "I met her at Yale, also business law and family law. We lost track of each other for a few years after she graduated and moved to New York, but we've become close again and I've asked Celia to partner in my practice here. She's planning on taking the Colorado Bar Exams, probably in July. We aren't engaged, yet, but she's still very special."

When Tom and Bill finished asking their questions and Norman had finished answering them, they called it an evening. Bill said one of them would call him around breakfast to let him know what the owner thought.

Fifteen
Wednesday, May 24

West walked into Hangar Five from Four to check on the engine change progress. Ratchet and Charlie had *The Lady* tucked away in a back corner, and by the time he arrived, the old engine was gone and Ratchet was deep in inspecting everything in the resulting hole forward of the firewall.

He stopped, opened the clipboard cover, and looked at the inspection log. He also noted that Ratchet was using an electronic tablet and a scanning wand as he systematically worked his way down one side of the engine compartment.

"Using the new system?" he asked when Ratchet looked up.

"Yeah. We're comparing the new against the old, looking for things we need to add or maybe don't need."

"How's it looking?"

"A couple of hoses are worn and we'll replace them. An electrical harness needs repair, chaffing, and we're adding a bar code tag on each connector and hose connection." Ratchet wiped his hands and stepped out from under the engine mount beams. "Oil system and coolant lines have been flushed and drained, filters checked, and new elements installed."

"Good, good. Where's everyone else?"

"I think Charlie and Lenny are bringing the new engine out of the engine shop and should be here in a few minutes. Not sure where Bump is, and Woody and Rosita ought to be halfway to Boise City. Dual cross-country. Do you need anything?"

"I'll catch Charlie when she's not busy. How's Rosita doing? I missed a report at breakfast."

"Rosita felt embarrassed when we talked about her training at breakfast, and Charlie said we could defer it to a different time," Ratchet conceded. "But she's up every hour she can get away and Woody says she's doing very well. Charlie says her ground school is about done and she should take her next exam sometime next week."

"Very good. We'll transition her into the T206 and the Beaver once she gets her Private," West said with a broad grin. "Then put her in the weekend flight schedules to help her build time. She should like that."

"She'll be ready for her Check Ride by late next week or the week following."

West nodded. "Have you talked to Bobby Hill yet? About his T-6?"

"Called him Monday. He asked me to find out when you needed it."

"We'll let him know as we get closer. Probably about August, after she gets her commercial."

"After her commercial?" Charlie asked as she walked up and stopped beside West. "Something about Rosita, I presume."

"There you are." West smiled at her, then he took a second to steal a kiss. "Yes, something about Rosita."

He glanced past her and saw Lenny and Bump pushing the engine trolley with the rebuilt engine into the hangar from the back passageway.

"Did your phone meeting go well?" she asked softly.

"Yes, I would say so. Bill and Tom were adequately impressed, and with the stipulations you listed over breakfast, we're moving ahead and we'll see how it goes."

"Good," she admitted, and looked back at *The Lady*. "Engine should be in this afternoon and prop and systems hook up tomorrow. Engine starts on Friday, maybe."

Friday, May 26

"I'm glad Chinese takeout is good enough for you tonight," Norman said as he set the cartons on his dining room table and glanced westerly, through his living room at the late afternoon sun. "I'm a little tired from the traveling and I was really hoping you wouldn't want to go out tonight."

"I've told you before," Celia said with a smile, "I eat normal meals. Takeout is great and staying in suits me just fine. Do you have tea?"

"Hot or cold?" He got up and went back to the kitchen to check his cupboard.

"Would hot be okay?"

"Sure. I have Oolong or Shoumei." He started rummaging in his cabinets. "Aah, here it is. For a minute I was afraid I'd already packed the kettle. I'm surprised you weren't going home to see your dad for the long weekend."

"Let's do the Shoumei. Flavor's a little more robust."

He filled the kettle and set it on a burner, and then he collected plates from the cupboard and set them and utensils on the table. She set out the chopsticks and the napkins.

"June went, but I'm staying here to spend as much of the weekend with you as you'll let me. The Colorado trip surprised me too, and I was a lot more than a little lonely while you were gone this week. So I want time with you to help make up for some of that."

"Then I think we should plan on spending all of it together."

"Good. You didn't say how your week went," she continued, more of a question.

"Better than expected, I think." He set cups for their tea on the table and trivets for the kettle and teapot. "I decided on Colorado Springs for an office and took the liberty of renting a place for us."

"Oh? And you didn't send pictures?" She took a seat facing the living room.

"Please allow me the opportunity to surprise you a little." He set two glasses of water on the table. "The hot water is still a few minutes away," he added as he sat down beside her.

He laid his phone on the table and began showing Celia the few shots he had taken of the rental.

"It looks beautiful, Norman, but it's hard to really see how large or how the rooms are situated. Looks like it's furnished."

"It is a furnished rental, and if you like it"—he paused as he got up to retrieve the whistling kettle—"we have six months to convert the rental into a down payment."

"You mean, like buy us a house?"

"Yes. If you like it. I figure in six months you should have received acceptance to the Bar and might be ready for more in a relationship."

"You keep hinting on more," she said, and opened a carton while Norman filled the small teapot to let the tea steep. "When we were at the Lodge, you talked about getting to know each other well enough to share your name and plan a future. Were you being real or just hypothetical?"

"I did?" he questioned with wide eyes, then grinned. "Hmm, I guess we should think about that."

She giggled and they ate in casual, happy camaraderie.

"I had a meeting with a couple of men representing a client that's looking for help in his business," he explained casually.

"A business client?"

"Yes. That client will get us firmly placed and get our practice started."

"So it's a long-term client?"

"I have a retainer to provide counsel and services for the next year."

"You what? A retainer? For a year?"

"That's what I said." He leaned to her and kissed her. "You need to listen more closely."

"I am listening closely." She raised her voice slightly. "You're holding back and not explaining succinctly. Must be a big company to offer a retainer for a year. Who is it?"

"I can't tell you until we're moved." He took a little more food from a carton. "I had to promise."

"They wouldn't know you told." She added a little plea to her voice.

"But I would and you would. Let it be another surprise for the start of this chapter in our lives. Please."

"Okay." She lifted her cup in a toast. "I'll try to be patient. To the start of the next chapter in our lives."

"Thank you." He returned her toast.

She squeezed his hand.

Climbing out of Clayton, New Mexico, on a course to Las Vegas, Rosita was on top of the world with forty-seven hours in her logbook, flying the one-hundred-twenty-four-statute-mile second leg of her solo cross-county. The Cessna 172N was performing well as she leveled at eighty-five hundred feet; the wind was brisk and warm out of the southwest with quite a few thermals, as was normal for the high plains country that time of year. She calculated her ground speed at one hundred and twenty-one statute miles per hour, a loss of nineteen miles per hour due to the temperature and the wind component.

"So be it," she sighed to herself, remembering Woody telling her it was a rare day when you got good tailwinds.

Rosita switched the transmitter and spoke into the earphone mike. "Ghost Ranch, Ghost Seven out of Clayton at eighty-five hundred."

"We have you Ghost Seven. Safe flight," Helen's voice answered.

"Thanks, Ghost Ranch." She happily settled into monitoring landmarks to estimate her drift.

She remembered the breakfast after she had soloed, the first time she had sat with the rest of the pilots and mechanics at the formal breakfast table—no longer serving, but included as part of the 'elite,' as she had always, and incorrectly, thought of them. That was the breakfast when Ratchet had announced that from then on, she was Ghost Seven, the seventh official Ghost Ranch pilot.

Twenty minutes into the leg, she began smelling gasoline. She looked around the cockpit, looking at the doorposts where she knew the lines came down from the tanks in the wings, then at the floor. Everything looked dry, but the odor was getting stronger and she knew a leak would just drain through the openings in the floor at the bottom of the doorposts and into the space beneath. She also knew there were fuel lines under the floor and under the instrument panel and console, and those she could not look at and fly at the same time.

She started a slowly descending turn to the south, knowing she had flown past a country road. The chart said it was New Mexico 120.

"Ghost Ranch, Ghost Seven," Rosita said, keying her mike.

"Ghost Ranch here, Ghost Seven. Go ahead," Belle's clear voice answered.

"Ghost Seven has a strong fuel smell in the cockpit. I'm going to put down on New Mexico Highway One Twenty about fourteen miles south of Highway Fifty-Six and take a look."

"I'm tracking you, Ghost Seven. I've alerted Ghost Six. He will launch in five minutes in *Box Car*," Belle explained.

"Thanks. Gotta go. Ghost Seven out." Rosita quickly returned her focus to the state highway.

Rosita had the floor access panels open and had discovered the loose fuel line connection from the right-hand wing tank when she heard the Beaver roll to a stop and shut down behind the 172.

"Hey, Woody." She stood up and turned to greet him. "I'm sorry you had to make a trip out."

"What've you figured out, girl?" Woody slapped her shoulder.

"Oddly enough, a fuel line from the right wing tank came loose at the selector." She gestured to the open cabin door. "I think I've tightened it adequately."

Woody looked in and nodded. He took her crow's-foot and

double-checked her work. "I'd say you did fine. Seems you've been watching the mechanics too."

"Charlie's shown me a lot. And she said I should never go anywhere without a small toolkit."

"Good advice. Want help closing it back up?"

"I can get it." She straightened her shoulders.

"Okay." Woody stepped out of the way. "I'll wait until you're done and ready to launch. I'll make a note in the maintenance records when I get back and we'll give it another look-over after you get home. Let me see your logbook."

Woody made an entry and signed off for a landing "near" the Cromley Ranch, State Highway 120, New Mexico, while she wiped down the space under the floor and then closed up the access panel. She wiped the plane's belly and double-checked for traces of fuel dripping or running out of drain holes. Finally, she was happy and tucked the rags in a plastic bag and sealed it, then she put her toolkit back in the baggage compartment.

"You ready?" Woody walked back and handed the logbook to her.

"Yeah. Should be good to go." She smiled as she looked at his entry in her logbook for the unscheduled landing.

"Check for drips at Las Vegas." He clapped her shoulder again. "Do you want me to follow you?"

"Woody! It's supposed to be a solo cross-country," she rebutted sharply, and grinned. "If there's another problem, I'll call and try to take care of it myself. Thanks."

"Good girl. You better get going then."

Woody had *Box Car* idling and waiting as Rosita did a ground run and double-checked for leaks, pulled her chocks, and then pushed the throttle up and took off to continue her cross-country. He was very proud of her and for the other kids that grew up on the ranch. Philip was first, helping Cappie and some up top; Belle was second, helping with the communications and traffic control; and now Rosita was the third, with her dream of flying and learning what the ranch had to offer for a future.

He smiled as Rosita made a left turn and started her climb to get back on course. He heard her call the Ghost Ranch as he pushed the throttle forward and she passed overhead, heading west.

Saturday, May 27

"Ham and cheese," the woman's voice said in West's phone.

West instantly looked around and saw Charlie inspecting an area of *The Lady's* engine installation. He waved for her to come as he stepped into the locker room.

"West here. Encrypting." He selected an app on the phone.

He switched to speaker and lowered the volume as Charlie came in, wiping her hands with a clean but oil-stained rag. She closed the door behind her.

"Good morning, Jess," he greeted.

"Good morning, West. Is Charlie there too?"

"Yes, I'm here. Good morning."

"Sorry to bother the two of you, but I have a couple of coding questions. I know West will understand, but I figured you'd want to hear also, Charlie."

"Thanks. I appreciate that."

Jessie explained the situation she was trying to work around, she and West exchanged a number of options and possibilities, and finally Jessie suggested a course of action and West agreed on the approach.

"Is there something else you need?" West asked.

"One more thing for now," she admitted softy. "I'd like to run my beta versions on an appropriate server. Do you have a server address that I can use?"

West looked at Charlie and raised his eyebrow.

Charlie slowly smiled and gave her an address. "You're sure they won't know you're listening?"

"They won't know. Is something wrong?"

"Yes and no, but nothing for you to be concerned about." She mouthed a silent "I'm sorry" to West for letting her worries slip out. He squeezed her shoulders.

"Last I knew," Charlie continued, getting her voice under control, "there were only four or five users on that server. Might want to see how many are obvious now and look for a couple of 'anonymous' tags. They were using those for private conversations."

"Thanks. I'll give you an update in a day or so."

"Very good." West sighed and looked at Charlie. "Thank you."

In many respects, Memorial Day weekend's Saturday was no different from any other Saturday. Monte got up early and ran his two miles around the Heritage Park foot trails, a little over a block from their home in the Farmington suburb of Detroit. He ate a light breakfast of fruit, juice, and a cup of coffee while the kids got themselves around for their usual morning soccer practice and Cat dressed for a morning of grocery shopping.

He was a little surprised that nearly all of the kids on Michael and Melony's soccer teams were present, especially with it being a holiday weekend. He realized he was expecting more people to be away, visiting family or something. Then he smiled and chuckled to himself, thinking maybe people today were not that invested in family, lived closer to their families than he first supposed, or they just viewed the holiday as another three-day break from work.

After soccer practice was over, he stopped at the intersection of Orchard Lake Road and Ten Mile Road for gas at the convenience store. Michael and Melony went inside for a snack and bottled water while he fueled his car and paid at the pump.

He found Michael standing beside the wire rack of gossip

newspapers with his bottle of water and a small bag of cheese twists, reading a half-sized format, newsprint booklet. Melony was intently looking around his shoulder.

"What did you find?" Monte stopped to look.

"It's about the airshows coming this year," Michael explained eagerly. "Can we go to one?"

"There's going to be one in Ypsilanti in late summer," Melony added with a smile. "That's not very far away."

"Here's one next month." Michael held the booklet up for him to see.

"Those look like they might be fun," he agreed absently. "Do you have everything?"

"Yeah." Melony turned to the counter.

"Can I get this?" Michael asked, and Monte agreed as he took a granola bar from the rack and followed the kids to the counter.

When lunch was finished, Michael and Melony left to spend their afternoon with the neighbor's kids and Monte went off to his weekly racquetball match. Cat put the lunch leftovers away, cleaned up the lunch dishes, and was straightening up the family room when she found Michael's booklet partially wedged between two pillows on the long couch. She picked it up and continued around the room, adjusting pillows and tweaking the furniture until the room was back to her liking.

In the kitchen, she took a moment to look at Michael's booklet, smiling at the front-page pictures of airplanes in all sorts of attitudes, trailing streams of multicolored smoke. Intrigued by the unusual subject, at least unusual in their family, she thumbed through the pages, smiling at the various images and headlines. Near the back of the booklet, she stopped suddenly and stared at a large, four-panel spread.

Each panel was a photo of a person standing up in the cockpit of an airplane. The headline "Rare Ghost Ranch Appearance" made her read the taglines under the panel, but she looked closer, mouth still agape, at the one of the woman pilot. The tagline identified "Mrs. Charlie West," the wife of Mr. Glen West, shown in the last panel, as flying a North American P-51D fighter named *Hell Raiser*.

But how? Cat questioned herself. *How can you look so much like Emli?*

"So you really think she's ready?" West asked, nudging Charlie's shoulder as they walked up the ramp, following Bump as he towed *The Lady* out into the sunny afternoon.

"Of course." Charlie nudged him back. "I wouldn't have signed the maintenance logs if she wasn't."

West stuffed his flying gloves in his suit's leg pocket and slipped his arm around her shoulders. "Did the new electronic maintenance logs work as well as you expected?"

"Yes, and no. Still have some glitches that we uncovered, but the method does keep us from skipping items in the list. We just have to be sure we have everything in the list to start with."

"That's a plus." He stopped and looked at her when Bump swung *The Lady* around and stopped to unhitch. "Ratchet is going to fly Safety in *Lucky*. Only because he's always flown my wing."

"That's okay." She held his eyes, seeing he was not finished.

"But I'd like you to pick a ride and fly escort, to watch what goes on. I know you know all the details of how it's supposed to work, but I want you to be absolutely certain you have it down before I throw the whole burden on your shoulders."

Charlie smiled. "Thanks. I do understand. I'll see which one needs exercise."

He pulled her to him and held her tight. "It isn't about your abilities. But I can't just stop using everyone else and start using you alone for everything we do here. I hope you understand it isn't favoritism or choosing them over you."

Charlie started shaking and he looked down at her. He was startled to see she was laughing.

"You're so funny." She pushed herself up and kissed him. "I know all of that and I would be very upset with you if you did show preferences and favoritism. We, you, have an organization to run, and it needs every one of us. Sometimes we could use more, but it takes us all."

"Thanks for understanding." He squeezed her hands. "Now go find something to fly."

"Yes, sir," she agreed enthusiastically with a huge smile, and turned back to the hangar.

Charlie circled the Kitty Hawk, *Anxious Delivery,* overhead and watched as *The Lady* accelerated with *Lucky* slipping into its four o'clock, one wingspan to his right. She smiled as she remembered how West slipped into her eight o'clock when she flew the Spit Fourteen and the IIIB, close enough to see what was happening, yet far enough away to not interfere or cause undue concerns.

She dropped down and joined the formation in a trailing seven o'clock position, slightly low as *The Lady* and *Lucky* climbed and turned north, toward the test area over the larger half of the mesa. She patiently followed the steps in West's test plan as he executed them and conducted checks on all of the airplane's systems, including those that should not have been affected by the engine work.

Satisfied and with Ratchet reporting a clean run from his perspective, he climbed up to five thousand feet over the mesa for the maneuvering and power checks.

Again, she felt the familiarity of the tests, remembering the Fourteen and the IIIB. *The Lady* was running very well, without any signs of stress, as he put her through her paces. Finally, he announced the engine responses were as they should be, without any burbles or hesitations, and the test plan was complete.

She followed in formation as he descended to the ranch. She flew a higher line and let Ratchet escort *The Lady* down to the field and a smooth, seemingly effortless landing. She started around and entered downwind as Ratchet pulled up and turned crosswind behind her.

"Looks like you can put *The Lady* back on the flight roster," West said as Ratchet walked up and joined them. "We obviously need to do the usual post-test inspections, but she flew out nice."

"Very nice, indeed," Ratchet said, and gave Charlie a high-five.

"Thanks to all of you," West admitted. "When the inspections are done, put the drop tanks back on and fuel her up. We'll take her out on Monday and shake her down with some cross-country work."

"Will do," Ratchet concurred.

West studied the newspaper booklet he had propped open on their wide nine-drawer dresser as he unbuttoned his shirt. Charlie stepped up behind him, slipped it off his toned shoulders and arms, and tossed it on top of the hamper on the other side of the bathroom door.

"It's a bit fuzzy like most newspapers are"—he caught her arms as she slipped them around his waist and squeezed them against himself—"but I'd recognize you."

"That's good to know," she admitted as he bent slightly toward the picture and she fondled the elastic waistband of his briefs. "I'd recognize you as well. Catch the light?"

West noted the tone in her voice, the feel of her arms around him and of her warm flesh tight against his back, and obediently reached for the wall switch. He flipped it off.

"You know," she continued, savoring the feel of holding

him, "this room reminds me of the one where we stayed on our honeymoon."

"It does?"

She nodded with her cheek pressed against his back. "If it just had a fireplace and a bearskin rug, it would be almost the same."

"I think you're right."

She stepped back, pulling him with her until she fell back onto the bed, twisting so he would be beside her. He laughed and rolled to kiss her, gently wrapping her in his arms, completely distracted in the moment.

"Personally"—she sighed and giggled at his nips on her neck—"knowing that booklet and those pictures have been spread all across the country scares me to death, worrying about who might see them and what can happen because of it. But on the other hand I feel safe here, safe here with you. Besides, the half-page article gives you and the ranch very nice publicity without divulging too much."

"Your picture and write-up is what makes it significant," he added, and his nuzzling made her giggle again, "not the number of airplanes. Everything about the ranch has changed for the better since you came to visit, and everything important to me changed when you flew into my life."

Charlie sighed. "You've changed my life too. More than I ever imagined possible. Before you, I hated the mere thought of some man having his arms around me, and you changed that. I can't wait to be in yours."

"Or me in yours." He tickled her side gently and then began kissing her chest.

Their verbal conversation faded quickly, with kisses and loving caresses pushing the worries of the world away. They were together, and that was all that mattered.

Sunday, May 28

Charlie, lying on the left wing, thumbed the overhead hoist

and nudged the fuselage another half an inch to the right.

The TF's wing had passed a thorough inspection after the minor damage was repaired. The fuel tanks and controls and plumbing were installed before it was laid in the support cradles, and now positioned in the back corner of the recently rearranged Hangar Two. With Lenny and Bump's help, Charlie was slowly moving the center and aft fuselage assembly into place to mate with the wing attachment fittings. Once in place, they would place the cutout contour cradles under the aft fuselage to support the overhanging structure and get the plane ready for attaching the tail group.

"How's it looking, Lenny?" She looked down the side of the fuselage to where he was watching the aft fittings.

"Down about a quarter more."

"Bump?"

"About the same on this side."

Charlie thumbed the control box again.

"My drift pin's in," Lenny announced loudly as he slipped his alignment pin into place.

Bump put his shoulder under the aft fuselage and pushed a few times before he declared his pin was in. "How're you looking, Charlie?"

She reached through the structural opening and pinned her first fitting.

"One pin's in. Put your bolts in." She sat up on the wing and stretched, arms high over her head, while they installed their bolts.

Charlie was sitting at a small table nestled under the TF's left wing, studying the Erection and Maintenance Manual and taking notes in her digital notepad when West entered from Hangar One. Lenny and Bump were securing the wing attachment bolts and double-checking the electrical and system connections that had to happen at the same time as the wing-to-fuselage mating.

"Hey." Charlie smiled when West stopped and sat down next to her.

"Looks like you've made some headway."

"Yeah. Probably the easy part," she admitted. "Philip's down in stores collecting the parts we need to rig out the aft fuselage systems, especially tail wheel, elevators, and rudder systems. I'm trying to figure out the priorities we should be following. What've you been up to?"

"Inventorying a couple of planes in stores. Trying to see what might be a good candidate for a new rebuild. But I stopped by because it's getting close to dinnertime. Mom will be calling in a few minutes."

"Okay." Charlie turned and called to Lenny and Bump, "Let's break for lunch. Helen's about to call."

"Okay," Lenny called back as Charlie stood up and went to the people door with West.

"So?" he asked. "Have you thought of a name for your plane?"

"A few." She nodded and slipped her arm through his. "But no serious contenders yet. It's a trainer and not a 'fighter' like '*Hell Raiser*.' I want something 'softer' like '*The Lady*,' unless I am very angry." She chuckled. "It's normal for guys to name their planes after women, but I haven't seen any planes named for a guy."

"I'm sure there are some someplace. Names for women are definitely more popular since there are more men pilots than women pilots. And men pilots do like their women. And I especially like mine."

He lightly swatted her bottom and, laughing, she quickly sprinted ahead. He smiled and gave chase.

Monte and Howard had paused and recorded the Indy 500

race long enough for them to enjoy their Sunday dinner at Cat and Monte's home. Cat and Mary knew they were anxious to get back to the race, and Cat was happy that Monte spent a little of the transition time at the dinner table after they finished eating before he took Howard back to the family room and resumed watching the race. Cat visited with her mother and Melony for a while and then started clearing the table. Mary and Melony lent a helping hand and joined in the small talk about the kids' plans for the summer and whether the family had any vacations planned.

After an hour or so, when the race was interrupted with a caution flag and a couple of commercials, Monte muted the sound and Michael scooted up beside Howard.

"Grandpa? Can I show you what I got yesterday?" Michael asked, and laid the newsprint booklet in his lap. "There're two that're going to be close by and I'm hoping Dad will take us. They should be a lot of fun."

Howard smiled at his grandson and glanced at the front-page pictures.

"Airshows? Sure looks exciting. The planes look fast."

"Yeah," Michael agreed, bouncing enthusiastically. "There are articles talking about most of the shows and about some of the planes and what they can do. Some of them can go faster than three hundred miles an hour."

"That's fast," Howard agreed, and glanced at the television, seeing the race was still running under the yellow. He looked back at the booklet and quickly scanned through the rest of the pages. "There seem to be a lot of shows."

"Some have already happened, but only a couple," Michael explained.

Howard saw the yellow was lifted and the race was resuming. "I'll look at this a little later, Mike. The race is on again."

"Okay, Grandpa." Michael slid back to his previous place on the couch, laid the booklet aside, and started watching the race.

Cat was rinsing dishes and placing them in the dishwasher. She was about to answer a question Mary had asked when she saw Michael slide next to Howard and show him the airshow booklet. Cat inhaled sharply, her heart caught, and she forgot what she was going to say. Later, she wasn't sure if she had taken another breath until Howard laid the booklet aside and Michael slid back to his previous place, afraid Michael would notice and say something about the page missing from his booklet.

"Cat? Cat?" Mary was asking when Cat finally turned and looked at her. "Are you all right? Something the matter?"

"What? Oh, no. I...I just remembered something I promised to do this week." Cat tried to remember what they were talking about. "I...think I better write it down before I forget again." Cat pulled a drawer open at her kitchen desk and scribbled a note on a small note pad. She tore the sheet off, folded it, and slipped it into her pocket. "Beverly will be so upset if I forget, again."

Mary watched her a long moment. "Are you sure you're all right?"

"Yes. I'm fine." Cat forced a smile. "Now, what were we talking about?"

Monday, May 29
Memorial Day

Norman sipped his coffee and looked at Celia sitting beside him at the end of his dining room table. She had bathed when they got up, but had thrown on one of his T-shirts after she had dried, instead of dressing.

"I sure hope your dad and sister aren't too mad at me for stealing you away for the long weekend," he said, and set his cup down.

"I told you, I stole myself away. You were the reason, but you didn't do anything except agree to let me stay."

"And now, I'm the reason you're leaving New York and moving all the way out to Colorado." He leaned forward, forearms on the table. "Are they going to be happy with that? Is this what you really want?"

"What? What are you asking?" She was startled by his questions.

"Colorado? Me?" he asked. "I told you how I want my future to go, at least in general, as far as I can control it—"

"Norman! Quit beating around the proverbial bush." She leaned closer to him. "If you want my answer, just ask. I won't answer a question I'm not sure you're asking. I think I've shown you how I feel and what I want to do with my future. With you. In Colorado. Or wherever."

He nodded, sipped his coffee, set his cup down, and took her hand. "Well then, if you'll marry me, we'll truly start a new chapter in our lives. Will you?"

"Yes, silly." She slapped his arm. "You know I will. Why did you take so long to put it into words?"

"To be sure, I guess. I've always been afraid you wanted something I couldn't give you." He stood up, held her tight, and kissed her.

"Come with me." She took his hand. "There's something else I want to talk to you about before we start the day."

"I think that's my last box"—Norman taped the box closed—"except for the one in the kitchen for the last-minute stuff tomorrow. Do you want to finish packing your things? I can have the movers pick your things up and ship them out with mine."

"That would make sense," she agreed, "but I have to work tomorrow—last day. I'll have to change after work."

"We'll pack our suitcases with clean clothes for the trip," he thought out loud with a shrug. "And I've already got a hotel room at the airport for tomorrow night."

"Looks like you've got it figured out." She set the box in the living room with the others.

"Now"—he glanced around the room—"I think it's lunchtime. Then tomorrow I'll only have to go by my bank to finish up."

"Lunch will be good. Your bank? To close your accounts?"

"I have something in my safe-deposit box that I need to get before we leave. And I need to have them transfer most of my funds to my new bank in Colorado. I'll close them after I get credit cards on the Colorado accounts."

"I don't have a bank or an account in Colorado." She suddenly realized she could not transfer her accounts.

"We'll have you an account on Wednesday, and tomorrow we'll just let your bank know that's going to happen. Ready?"

"She's twenty miles out," Helen's voice said in West's phone.

"She's six or seven minutes southeast of the mesa," he announced, and looked around at the small crowd that had gathered. "Are you coming up?" he asked Helen.

"No. I'll congratulate her at dinner," Helen said. "You better get outside. She's almost to the mesa."

"Thanks. We're going." He disconnected.

He caught Charlie's hand and led the group up the ramp.

Rosita's family—Robert, Madra, and Belle—followed quickly, then Cappie, Celina, Philip, and Peter with Gracie and her family joined with Lenny, Ratchet, and Bump as they hurried up the ramp.

Woody was already standing out in front of the hangar when those gathering formed a line across the ramp at ground level. West watched the southeast lip of the mesa and spotted the 172 as Rosita climbed above the rim and circled to the east and set up a left base. She rolled onto final and settled a quarter mile from the hangar.

When Rosita reached the hangar, swung the 172 around, and shut down, Woody stepped forward and stopped at the left wingtip. He waited for her to secure the cockpit and get out.

"What's everyone doing here?" Rosita asked as she stopped and handed him her logbook.

"They just wanted to congratulate you." Woody flipped to the last entry, checked each from the airports on her flight plan, and then added his own notations. "I sent your last ground school tests in, and now I think you only have one more cross-country left."

"Thank you. When will that be?"

Woody looked at her. "In a hurry?"

"No, sir. I didn't mean it to sound like that. I was just wondering. Since there's weather coming in late in the week, I was just wondering if you thought it would be this week or after the weather clears."

"I figured." Woody patted her shoulder. "You've always been a very patient and good student and I think you're going to do very well. I'll let you know when."

"Thanks." She grinned and nodded to the crowd. "I was very surprised when West gave me a Ghost Pilot number. I want him and Charlie to be proud of me."

"They are, Rosita. They most certainly are." Woody handed her the logbook. "We all are. Now, go and say hello to your waiting fans."

"Have you heard anything?" Elrich Voster asked as he looked up from his desk when the Deputy Minister of Rural Development entered his large office. A large portrait of the South African president hung in a massive, ornately carved frame above a credenza along one wall. The portrait of the Minister of State Security hung similarly on the opposite wall.

"No," Deputy Minister deVon said as he crossed the room,

stopping in front of Deputy Minister Voster. He laid a short stack of manila folders on the front edge of the desk. "I am surprised you keep waiting and have not acted."

Elrich looked up. "I will honor the contract, at least in the terms of time."

"Does Collingsworth's silence mean he thinks he can ignore the terms?"

"Possibly," Elrich conceded. "Howard has a problem and I think he is actually trying to find a solution."

Deputy Minister deVon chuckled. "I'm certain he is. If he does not, his future is not very pleasant."

"You do remember that he has two daughters?" Elrich asked, but it was not actually a question. "And one was married off to solve a problem he had with financing a Spanish contract years ago."

"Yes. I remember."

Elrich opened a desk drawer, fingered the files arrayed within it, and pulled a folder out. He laid the folder squarely in front of himself and opened it. "That was his oldest daughter Catherine, a quiet woman that did not question him and allowed him to direct the events of her life. That left him with his younger daughter, noted for questioning everything."

"Difficult to handle?"

"Most likely." Elrich placed his finger on the document in front of him as he looked back at deVon. "She is the one he promised so many years ago, but her attitude and independent nature is not the problem."

"How so?"

Elrich smiled and shook his head. "A few years ago, when he asked for his first contract extension, I had heard Howard was unable to locate her."

"She ran away?" DeVon took the chair to which Elrich gestured.

"Likely, but the problem is that there is no trace of her," Elrich continued. "No trace anywhere."

"So you do not think he will succeed in producing her."

"No. I don't." Elrich glanced down at the document in the folder. "We exhausted every avenue we could think of to verify her disappearance and did not find any traces ourselves. So we started watching Howard's activities to see if he was hiding her. Maybe he found her and wants to use her somewhere else. Or maybe he had a change of heart and wants to spare her. Or maybe she is actually unavailable. There are many possibilities." He closed the folder, put it back in the desk drawer, and reached for the folders deVon had brought. "Keep listening and watching for a response from him."

"Certainly," deVon said. He stood and turned to leave, but stopped and asked, "I know you said you have exhausted everything you can think of to see if she has actually disappeared, but I would think having a man watch what he does might give a clue as to what he's thinking, planning."

"Yes," Voster agreed. "And for that reason I have two men assigned that very task."

Sixteen
Tuesday, May 30

Norman followed the movers out of his apartment and locked his door. He followed them to street level and gave them the address of Celia's apartment.

"It'll take me about twenty minutes to get there," he said to the driver. "If you get there before I do, just wait on me so I can let you in."

"Hey buddy. Why don't you just come with us? We're only supposed to transport furniture and boxes"—the driver said with a smile—"and it may still take twenty minutes, but we won't beat you there and won't have to wait."

"Sounds good to me."

He guided the men through Celia's apartment, and when they pushed the last hand truck of boxes out, he took one last look around her small studio apartment, satisfying himself that everything was loaded except her suitcase.

"Very good," he addressed the mover. "I guess we've got it all."

He stopped at the kitchen counter and signed the papers.

"Thank you, Mr. Kent." The driver took the papers and separated the copies from the originals. "When's the happy day?"

"No date set yet, but I hope it's only a few months. How long did you say it'll take for everything to get to Colorado?"

"If all goes well, Friday." The driver gestured for his helpers to leave.

"We'll be looking for you." He shook the driver's hand. "Well, our things."

"Norman?" Celia was surprised when she answered her phone. "Is everything all right?"

"Certainly. I know you're going to have lunch with everyone in your office for your big send-off, last day and all, but I'm wondering if I can see you for just a couple of minutes."

"When?"

"Can you come to the lobby now? I'll only take a minute or two."

"Okay. I'll be right out."

Celia set her stack of folders on her desk and turned to the lobby doors. Norman was waiting, slowly pacing in front of the empty reception area chairs when she stepped into the lobby.

"What's up?" she asked when he stole a quick kiss.

"I just thought you should have something before you bid *adieu* to all of your colleagues" He took a small box out of his pocket. "I know there've been a number of questions about your decision to leave, but maybe this will help everyone understand."

She was all smiles as she opened the box and saw the rings, diamonds and turquoise.

"I cheated and got your ring size from the ones in your jewelry box."

"This is the ring set we saw in Denver." She stared at him in disbelief.

"Yes, it is. When I saw your eyes light up when you saw it, I knew I had to get them for you. They're so unique, so beautiful, so much like you, there wasn't another choice."

Norman took the engagement ring out of the box and slipped it onto her finger.

"I want everyone to be envious and happy for you. One more kiss and then you have to go back." He stole the kiss but she caught his neck and prolonged the moment.

"Meet me when I'm off?" she whispered. "So you and I can

go celebrate?"

"You bet. Call me when you're ready."

Howard's thoughts were still locked in his debate over the morning's trials as he closed his office and locked the front door. With no meetings scheduled for the afternoon, he had decided to work from home through the rest of the day, maybe relax a little to regain his balance. No one had answered any of his morning emails, and that bothered him. He only wanted to remind his partners and investors of their obligations, per their agreements, that they would step up to any arranged pairings for their children, daughters mostly, if the business ran into any nonnegotiable roadblocks and required their help. And they were facing just such a roadblock. Of course, he did not mention that the roadblock was nonnegotiable because the alternative would cost him more money than he was willing to spend.

He stopped at a deli a couple of blocks from his office, ate a small specialty sub and a soda, and then drove to a grocery store on his way home to pick up the few things Mary needed for dinner. There, he walked the aisles, absently checking his list and placing the items in his cart as he pondered the morning's fruitlessness. At the checkout counter, he saw a stack of the newsprint airshow booklets Mike had shown him and he dropped a copy on the conveyor, thinking it might be good to see what had his grandson so excited.

Home, Howard sat the sack on the kitchen counter and put the cold items in the refrigerator. He took the booklet and dropped it on the pile of papers occupying the corner of his large desk and then went to the family room and sat down in front of an afternoon network news show.

He figured he'd make a few calls that afternoon and see if Monte had heard anything on the negotiations or on his hunt. He closed his eyes and decided it could wait, at least for a little while.

Wednesday, May 31

Howard's morning was only marginally better than his yesterday. He made the necessary calls and reemphasized he was only making sure everyone remembered their obligation "if" the need arose, which he admitted looked likely. Grudgingly, they each conceded they remembered and knew what he was saying. He checked on the progress of his active projects but was not appeased by their mildly encouraging performance.

Finished, he leaned back in his high-backed chair and sighed. None of this would be necessary if he could find Emli. He needed to use her and he figured she owed him big time.

Howard went into the kitchen and microwaved a cup of water and then added a teabag and a spoonful of sugar. He absently wondered where Mary was, but stirred his cup, went back to his office, and set the cup on the coaster by the desk pad. He picked up the airshow booklet and scanned the front page as he sipped the tea.

Slowly relaxing with the change in pace, Howard read the articles accompanying the flashy pictures, and he admitted he could see why his grandson would be attracted to the action and the excitement captured in the photos. The articles further depicted the preparation, the details of the planes flown, and the backgrounds of the pilots flying them.

Howard fixed himself a second cup of tea and returned to his office, the booklet, and the articles. He settled again in his high-backed chair, took another sip of tea, and finished reading the article on the right-hand page near the back of the booklet. He flipped to the next page and read the two articles on the aerobatic teams that had performed at a small-venue regional fly-in in Alamosa, Colorado. One team was considered a serious contender in the National Aerobatic Championships and the article described the airplanes used in significant detail, highlighting their strengths and power.

The second article covered a local Colorado pilot in a Pitts biplane and gave similar details. The pilot planned to compete in a different category at the Nationals and flew an entirely different routine, compared to the first.

Howard glanced at the half-page article on the right-hand page with a full-width four-panel picture of four people standing in their planes. He glanced at the headlines and wondered about the name "Ghost Ranch" before he dove into the article and began reading about the four pilots. He chuckled at John Powers' nickname "Ratchet" and thought Lester James' "Lenny" was more normal.

But when he read about the other two pilots, the husband and wife team, Glen West and his wife Charlie, he had to look up and study the pictures. Howard's mouth dropped open and he stared at the woman standing up in the cockpit of an airplane.

"Emli? That's Emli!" he half shouted.

He reread the captions and looked at the picture, but his mind would not accept that her name was Charlie West.

He turned to his computer and ran a simple search for Charlie West, and only minimal information popped up on the screen. An experienced mechanic and pilot with many ratings and significant flying hours, Charlie Bassett, originally of Jackson, Wyoming, married to Glen West of West's Ghost Ranch.

He searched for "West's Ghost Ranch" and scanned the webpage, surprised there was no contact information given besides a web address. The only location information was "in the Colorado mountains."

His hand instantly picked up the phone's handset and a finger punched a speed dial button.

"Monte?" he asked when the connection was made. "Did you look at your son's airshow booklet closely? There's a picture of Emli in it. Says she's a pilot flying for some place called the Ghost Ranch. Find out where that is and get someone to go and get her."

Norman stopped the rental car in the curved drive beside a house situated slightly up from the Gold Camp Road in southwest Colorado Springs. It was one among six houses that formed a small neighborhood cluster at about seven thousand feet along the foot of the Rockies' front range, with an expansive view across the city and out into the grasslands farther to the east. To their north, the foothills curved west and embraced Manitou Springs and the highway climbing up into the mountains toward Woodland Park and beyond.

He got out and helped Celia out of the car.

"Is this the place you rented?" she asked as she stood beside the car and looked at the house and then at the view.

"Yes. It has nearly a half an acre of land within the privacy fences and an oversized two-car closed garage."

He led her up the steps to the wide front veranda, where he stopped and turned her to again take in the view.

"I admit it is a grand view," she said, and followed him inside.

He gestured to the left of a central staircase. "It has a nice size living room, and to the right, a formal dining room with the kitchen behind it. Two bedrooms across the back." He led the way to their left, past the open stairs, past the bath in the hall, and then peeked into the two bedrooms.

Then he led her to the entry and up the stairs. She stopped and admired the size of the master suite stretching across the entire house and over the back half of the structure. He opened a pair of wide French-style doors and stepped out onto a large terrace extending from the bedroom to the front of the house.

"I know it isn't a large house," he admitted, "but I think it has some very nice appointments. It's only ten years old and was updated last year—new windows and kitchen appliances and so on. But there is one more thing I must show you."

He turned and led her to the back of the bedroom and another set of French-style doors that opened onto a small, private deck.

"A hot tub?" She stared at him with an ear-to-ear grin. "Really?"

"I thought you might like that feature."

She hugged him enthusiastically. "I think I know where we'll be spending a lot of our time."

"So? Can you tolerate the house for a while?" he asked as they drove back into the nearest part of town in search of a big-box general store and a grocery store.

"Yes," Celia replied. "I think I can. You did a wonderful job of selecting it. We'll have fun making it ours."

"Well, I do have to admit that my new business client suggested it. Aah, there's one of the stores we need. We'll get some new bed and bath linens and pick up some necessities and food, and we can stay in the house tonight like you asked."

"That'll be wonderful."

"Do you want to set up a bank account today or wait until tomorrow?" he asked as he parked the car.

"Is your bank very far away?"

"Near the center of town. Ten or fifteen minutes away."

"Okay. After we get the shopping done, we can do that." She smiled again. "Then maybe I'll feel like this is really happening."

Monte arrived home for lunch and dropped his briefcase in his office.

"Everything all right?" Cat asked. "You sounded strange when you called and said you were going to work from home this afternoon."

"Very strange morning." He met her in the kitchen and kissed her cheek. "What're you fixing?"

"Sandwiches, unless you want something more substantial."

"No. Sandwiches are fine."

She set three different meats and a couple of selections of sliced cheeses on the island, then sliced their favorite bread. He set out the condiments and plates.

"So what made your morning strange?" She placed the bread on their plates. "Something to drink? Iced tea? Soda?"

"Tea is good." He got two glasses from the cabinet and filled them with ice.

Cat got the pitcher from the refrigerator, filled the glasses, and set them on the eating side of the island. She plated the meats and cheeses and set them between their plates as Monte walked into the family room and then returned.

"Your father was my problem." Monte sighed as he took the right stool and sat down, laying Michael's airshow booklet on the counter beside him.

They fixed their sandwiches and Cat got up and retrieved a bag of chips.

"I hope it wasn't something bad." Her eyes flicked to the booklet.

They ate for a few minutes before Monte spoke again.

"Cat. Your father picked up a copy of this booklet and called me to say Emli's picture is in it." He flipped through the pages.

"The picture he saw isn't there," she offered softly. "Page seventeen. I cut it out so he wouldn't see it."

"What? Why?" Monte stared at her as if he hadn't heard her correctly. "If it's Emli...? Don't you want to find her?"

She shook her head. "No. And I think this Charlie is just a lookalike. I did some checking—I'll show you—but Father's convinced it's her, isn't he?"

He nodded. "He wants me to send someone to bring her

back."

"Oh, Monte. You can't," she pleaded, holding his eyes. "Everything I've found out says she was Charlotte 'Charlie' Bassett, from Jackson, Wyoming. Her permanent address was there until she married Glen West."

"I have to send someone," Monte said emphatically. "It's out of my hands, and if I don't he will."

"No. You just can't."

"Your father does not see this woman as a lookalike. He's convinced it's your sister."

"Of course he is! He'll never be convinced otherwise!" Cat stared at her plate, trying to keep her anger under control. "He knows nothing about this woman and yet he has decided she is Emli! He doesn't need any proof! He wants her like he wanted me—only to further his business. I'll bet he has lists of partners or investors that have single daughters he can somehow drop into arranged marriages for his benefit."

Monte went pale, but Cat did not notice and continued.

"I think the only reason he wants to find her is for revenge. He won't be kind if he does find her. And he won't be kind to this woman if he's decided she's really Emli in hiding. It won't be pretty, and she'll simply disappear when he's finished with her. And I mean she'll really disappear—no one the wiser." She was breathing heavily, watching him staring at her. "And if he thinks this woman is Emli, she's in very serious danger."

"He wouldn't do anything to—"

"You don't know him," Cat stated sharply, tears coming to her eyes. "He was abusive to mother, to me, and to Emli. He wants what he wants, and will settle for nothing less. I'm surprised he hasn't threatened you for something at one time or another."

Monte inhaled sharply again at Cat's instinctive accuracy. He let his breath out slowly, remembering Howard's demands. "But why would he want to hurt her?"

"First, she knows too much. She knows him and what he has done, privately, personally and in his business. She told me about some of the things he's done, but she knows a lot more than I do." She shook her head. "Second, she got away, and he doesn't like losing anything he thinks he owns or controls. He certainly doesn't want her talking to anyone about what she knows. She'll pay for making him lose money on some deal he was planning to use her in and she would not consider an arranged marriage in any way.

"She talked Father into letting her go to college to get out of an arrangement he was planning, but the last time she was home, I'm sure she overheard Mother and me talking about how Father considered her college education as something to make her more valuable in a different arranged marriage he had in mind. The next morning she got on a plane back to school and that was the last we ever saw of her. Mother got the usual school reports and she stayed back East through the summer but didn't reenroll in the fall. She was gone. Sometime in the summer, she disappeared."

"She didn't leave many tracks," Monte admitted softly.

"From your searching, you said you found some information about her, and then about her twenty-second birthday everything stopped, vanished."

"Yeah. Your father had me check her out as far as I could. Her pilot's license was inactivated, suddenly no longer in use."

"I think she's dead. If she was alive, I don't think she'd just turn her back on something she liked so much. If she isn't and Father finds her, she'd be better off if she was dead."

"But you get a yearly card from her. How can you say you think she's dead?"

"I've been looking at those old cards," she admitted softly, "and they're all identical. Her note inside and signature came off a printer. Every card is the same. I think she arranged to have them automatically sent every year, maybe just to stir Father up. There's nothing personal written in any of them."

Monte stopped pacing and sat down on a stool beside her at the kitchen counter.

"Cat, I know when we got married you were unbelievably scared and were a real trooper, making everyone at the reception feel like this was what you wanted. But why did you go along with it?"

"I had no choice." Her eyes began to water again.

"Sure you had a choice."

Cat shook her head. "He would've killed me if I didn't. Literally. One day while I was in high school, he hit me so hard it knocked me unconscious, just for letting a boy walk me partway home." She caught the edge of the counter to keep from falling off her stool. "When I came to, he jerked me up off the floor, shook me until I couldn't speak, then he threw me down on the dining room table. He jerked my blouse and bra down and stripped them off with my skirt and panties. Then he raped me to show me what boys were really after and how little my worth really was as a woman."

She was breathing hard, deep, raspy breaths that kept her from continuing. Finally, after a long moment with Monte watching her in quiet surprise, she continued softly.

"Mother just sat to one side and didn't move, and when he was finished, he left me laying there, naked, dazed, and stunned, and ushered her out of the room."

"Your mother just sat by and watched? She didn't try to stop him?" Monte was still staring at her, transfixed, as if he were unable to move, unable to believe...

Cat slowly shook her head. "Later, after I crawled and limped back to my room, she helped me clean up and assured me I wouldn't get pregnant. Every time I remember her going up against Father, he beat her. For all of our childhood, Emli and I were scared of him. I still am. I can't let him be around me or the children without you being here, I can't leave the children with Mother, for fear she'd let him be around them alone. I can't trust him and I don't trust him now."

Slowly Monte stepped forward, put his arms around her shoulders, and held her close. He shook his head slowly, still trying to grasp what she had told him.

"I was never like Emli. I was her big sister, supposed to

protect her, but I didn't. She had a strength I don't have. I never did. Sometime during my last month of high school, Emli told me he'd done the same to her, but instead of cowering like I did, she told me she went to the attic and rummaged around in our grandfather's belongings. That was Mother's father's stuff. She found his old army pistol and two clips of ammunition and another pistol. She told me she kept the army pistol under her pillow at night and under her mattress during the day. She said if he stepped into her room at night, she'd simply kill him for what he was. When she left, she had put the army pistol back in Grandfather's things, but the other one isn't there."

"I can see why you were scared of me," Monte whispered. "I'm so sorry that I pressured you so much in the beginning. I really am. I had no way of knowing what you had gone through."

"Why did you go along with our marriage? Was it just the money you and your father would make?"

He smiled for the first time since he got home. "No, it wasn't the money. I wasn't going to go along with it until I saw you. Then I decided I had to try to make it work."

Cat smiled, but it quickly faded. "I wanted to feel that way. And I know it took me a long time to be comfortable with you. Too long maybe, but I really do love the children. More than I can say." Her expression turned somber. "And I've gotten to love you some, but it's very hard for me when you are mindlessly, blindly obedient to Father and his wishes and demands. I've heard you two talking and I see how you do anything he asks. I feel like you're becoming more and more like him, and I cannot love that.

"And you have a responsibility, to me, the children, and to this woman. If you cannot prove this Charlie West is really Emli, beyond all doubt, then you have to leave her alone. You have to try to make Father leave her alone. She is a grown woman and has a life and a right to have her own happiness. You have to stop Father from pursuing her."

"I don't know how," he admitted feebly. "He doesn't need me if he wants to. Like I said, if I don't help him, he'll just send someone else."

Cat pushed herself up and straightened her shoulders. She held his eyes in a steely stare.

"He's no more than an abuser, a rapist, a kidnapper, and a slave-trader! If you don't try to stop him"—her voice turned cold—"and I mean really try, then you're no better than he is. And the children and I cannot live with that."

Thursday, June 1

West stood at the head of the breakfast table, like he always did, and waited for everyone to take their places. Helen and Charlie were in their chairs on each side of him, Lenny and Ratchet filled out Helen's side of the table, Bump and Woody filled out Charlie's side of the table, and Rosita took the chair at the foot of the table.

As he sat down, Celina's cousin Gracie and her daughter, fourteen-year-old Camilla, began serving. Camilla was shorter, just over five foot, and wore her dark brown hair in a braid similar to Rosita and Belle. She wore a simple long skirt and a pretty blouse that only attempted to hide her maturing figure.

"Good morning, Gracie, Camilla," Charlie greeted. "Are you settling in okay?"

"Fine. Fine," Gracie admitted happily. "Everything is very nice. Thank you. Robert says the new house should be ready in about three or four weeks."

Charlie smiled. "Be sure he puts everything you want in it."

"Yes, ma'am, er, sorry, Charlie," Gracie corrected herself, nodded, and smiled.

As Gracie and Camilla stepped back into the kitchen, West gestured for the table to start filling their plates and asked everyone for a project status.

Bump explained that he and Lenny had all of the logged squawks worked on the flyable planes and that they had been helping Charlie on her TF. Ratchet summarized the final checkouts on the new hangars and the relocation of the planes to make more room in the second and third hangars for "rebuild" projects.

When Ratchet finished, West looked at Woody and then at Rosita.

Woody cleared his throat. "I would like to announce that Rosita, Ghost Seven, has completed all of the requirements established for a private pilot's license and is ready for her check ride."

Everyone clapped, and Rosita forced herself to face them with a smile. She glanced around and saw her mother, father, and sister standing behind West. Gracie, Camilla, and Becky stood in the kitchen doorway clapping with everyone else.

Woody grinned happily and continued when the clapping subsided. "I have contacted a good friend of mine, a flight examiner, and asked him if he would be available to give a check ride and when he could. " Woody looked at Rosita. "I should hear back from him today or tomorrow, and then I'll let you know when and where."

"Thanks."

West raised his juice glass to Rosita. "To our newest pilot. One more flight and then the fun begins."

Everyone raised their juice glasses to Rosita.

"I was thinking about leasing a couple of cars," Norman said, "and letting the rental go."

"Jeeps," Celia announced softly. "We should lease jeeps, since we are in Colorado and are about to become embedded in the culture here."

"Jeeps? You wouldn't like one jeep and maybe a nicer car for the other?" He sat down beside her on the veranda loveseat and slipped his arm around her shoulders.

"If we're going to help families in need"—she grinned and

snuggled into him—"I think we should be careful to not look too stuffy."

He nodded. "The more I'm with you, the more I like the way you think. We'll drive into town and see what we can do about a lease package for two jeeps."

"Good. Want something for lunch before we go?"

"Sure. And then I guess I should call our client and let them know we've arrived and have moved in."

"I guess you should. Can you tell me who our benefactor is yet?"

Norman chuckled. "I'm glad you're sitting down."

"Why is that? Who is it?"

"Have you heard of Glen West's Restorations?"

"No!" Her mouth dropped open. "You're kidding me. *The* Glen West? The same one—"

"Yes. I was just as surprised—actually, a lot more. They called for an interview out of the blue, and I talked with a board member—his name is Bill Strong—and their investment manager, Thomas Grant."

"Why? Why did they call you?"

"They never said why, other than they recently removed their previous counsel and they liked my credentials, but I've wondered if it had anything to do with my email to Glen."

"Well, even if it doesn't, I'm still glad you let them know what we feared."

"Me too."

"Call them while I fix something for lunch." She got up and went into the house.

"That didn't take long," she remarked when he came into the kitchen.

"Actually, Bill said they were expecting my call. He said they'd send the documents we'll need to review and understand to start supporting them. We should have them by Monday,

Tuesday at the latest."

"That's good." She slid their plates to him. "Iced tea?"

"Sure." He took their plates to the dining room table. "Bill also told me to take you to a new restaurant near someplace called the Depot Square. He gave me the name and said to dress nice, our reservations are for seven this evening. He said it's to welcome you to the Springs and to your new life. He hopes it will be a good one."

"What did you say?" Howard asked, startled by Monte's tone.

"Just what you heard," Monte replied. "Until you can prove this Charlie West isn't who she says she is, I will not help you find her. If you go through with what you've said you're going to do, that's outright kidnapping, and I did not sign up for anything like that."

Howard's face turned red. "You'll do what I tell you to do, or—"

"Or what?" Monte stared at him, his tone abruptly turning hard. "I agreed to an arranged marriage with your daughter. I promised to take care of her and our children and that is what I'm doing. I'm doing my job for Dad's company and its interests, but I did not agree to extorting people for your gain in your investments, or to kidnapping and seizing people so you can arbitrarily sell them off to increase your business opportunities, or—"

"I'm not selling—"

"You are! For favors in return and sometimes money." He held his stern composure, unsure of how long he could keep it up. "If this is truly about Emli, then you have to prove you've found her. For all we know, she's long dead. Maybe killed in a car wreck or worse. Or maybe you found her years ago and this is a ruse you—"

"What?" Howard's ruddiness deepened.

"Don't burst an artery. I know how you persuaded the sellers in three of your last four deals. I didn't sign up for eliminating obstacles that way either, or being implicated because I know." He shook his head. "I know how you work. And if you try to make your threats good toward me, Cat, or the children, I will personally return the favor."

Howard was quiet, and Monte knew he was thinking of what he was going to do next.

"Before you decide on what you want to do to me next, and you let your temper get in the way of your reason"—he slid a thin folder across Howard's desk—"this is what we've found out about Emli's lookalike. Yes, she is obviously independent, but her childhood would make her so. Records show she was born Charlotte Angelina Bassett in Jackson, Wyoming, and her parents died when she was very young. There's a birth certificate you can look at online. An aunt raised her until the aunt died when Charlie, as she likes to be called, was about sixteen. That cast her out on her own. She worked her way into a career against all odds and became an airplane mechanic and pilot. I'm still gathering information on her work history. Some of it I have confirmed and some of it will likely require verification by talking directly with the people she worked for.

"Now she has a bigger life, married to a man of means, and seems to be happy. If you think Charlie is not who she says she is, you will have to prove that before you try to claim she's your daughter. And even then, if she is or isn't, if you find Emli, she is an adult and you cannot legally make her come back. She has been gone for nine or ten years and if she's alive, which I doubt, she doesn't seem to want to come back. Possibly because of how she was treated growing up."

"She was treated as she should," Howard argued loudly. "There was nothing wrong with her childhood."

"Just you and your tyranny, for one," Monte continued flatly. "Where should I start? Cat has told me many things they endured during their growing up that I would consider improper, even criminal. Mary had to endure your heavy-handedness for years, and maybe even after Cat and Emli left your household."

He watched Howard carefully for another long moment, hoping he was thinking about what he had said. If not, he tried to steel himself for whatever Howard might do next.

"We know she's alive," Howard said softly, and Monte knew he was still not saying what he was thinking. "Cat gets those cards—"

"Cat says they're all the same. The message and signature are printed, identical. She's certain they're not real. She thinks Emli is dead and has been since about the time her history stopped, and the delivery of the cards was an arrangement."

Howard stared at him, blinked, and his shoulders sagged.

"Then send someone to confirm this woman's who she says she is!"

Friday, June 2

"What's the lineup for today?" West asked Ratchet as they finished breakfast.

"Well with the weather, all work will have to be inside. The rains will continue through the night tonight. Philip and I will continue taking inventory. Buck said he has a lead on a fair- to poor-condition Junkers Jumo 213 engine for the Fw. 190D-9 and asked for you to call him. We've worked all of the squawks we know of, so I'm thinking we can descend on Charlie's TF 'en masse' with Lenny, Bump, Woody, and Rosita. And I need a little of your time this morning. We can stop off in stores on our way out."

"Very well," West agreed. "Let's get to it."

West stood up and took Charlie's hand and led the way to the stairs to the basement. They took the tunnel from the main house to the horse barn, nestled up against the rising foot of the mesa.

Woody went to the four-bench tram and took the driver's seat as everyone settled in for the mile-and-a-half ride to the stores.

"We're loaded," Charlie announced when everyone was seated.

Woody nodded and started down the wide, illuminated service tunnel into the mesa.

"Have you thought about a name for your TF?" West asked Charlie.

"Nothing yet," she admitted. "I keep trying to think of a masculine name, but haven't come up with anything I like, or that works."

"Masculine, huh?" West smiled. "Why not something simple that says it's yours? 'Charlie's Horse,' pun intended, or 'Charlie's Other Love' or 'Second Love.' Something like that."

"Yeah." She smiled. "'Charlie's Second Love' might work. Of course 'Charlie's Horse' is cute."

"You have time." He squeezed her shoulders.

"But not a lot. I'm hoping I can have it ready and maybe take it to Reno."

"That's three months? We should be able to make that."

They had just sat down at Charlie's desk under the wing of her TF when West's phone rang.

"Ham and cheese."

West caught Charlie's arm as he stood up.

"West here. Encrypt," he answered, and the phone responded to his voice command. "Morning, Jess. Give us a minute."

West led Charlie to the locker room and closed the door.

"We're on speaker. What do you have?"

"Again I apologize for calling out of the blue, but I've intercepted some unsettling emails from that server you asked me to use to check out your eavesdropping software."

"Like what?" He looked at Charlie.

"I started 'listening' on Monday and saw eight or nine emails from a Howard to various recipients, each asking them to remember some contract clause and their responsibility to provide assets as necessary to offset delays in project negotiations. The reference to assets seemed to vary, but in one, instead of mentioning assets, the email asked how the recipient's two daughters were doing."

Charlie inhaled sharply and stared at the phone.

"Each recipient replied," Jessie continued, "but the tone of the emails was somber and terse. Then last night, an 'anonymous' email was sent from this Howard's computer to four new recipients."

"New ones?" he asked absently.

"Yes. I don't know where they are physically, but this Howard asked each of the four to work in pairs and to find out any and all that they could about you, Charlie, and the Ghost Ranch. He wants to know specifically where you are."

He looked at his mate, worried about what might be going on in her mind when she did not answer immediately.

"Was this something you were expecting?" Jessie asked.

"Yes," West answered softly. "Did you happen to save the messages you intercepted?"

"Yes, I did." Jessie's voice sounding brighter. "I'll send copies to the email URL you gave me."

"Thanks. Keep listening." West was still watching Charlie.

"Jess?" Charlie finally asked. "Also keep a look out for anything about a Monte or a Cat, Cathy, or Catherine."

"I will. And the Ghost Ranch? I suppose you know what that is."

"It's our home," West said. "Very few people know where it is."

"Aah. I see," Jessie said. "And after what you said when we met, you don't want that to be public knowledge."

"Too many valuable airplanes," Charlie added, "and too many people would be at risk if the ranch was available to the public."

"Not to mention fortune hunters, extortionists, and basic criminals and thieves," Jessie finished. "I understand. I'll let you know if I hear anything more."

"Thanks," Charlie acknowledged.

West broke the connection and she started to pace slowly.

He sighed. "Well, we knew his would come sooner or later."

"I just wish it had come later. A lot later."

"I know." He turned her to him and held her tight. "I know."

Seventeen

When the movers arrived, Norman had them stack all of the boxes in one side of the two-car garage. He confirmed the correct number of boxes from each of their apartments and signed the contracts as completed when they were finished.

Celia quickly looked through those from her apartment and found three she wanted taken up to the master bath, and he obliged and carried them up for her. They ate deli cold cut sandwiches for a light lunch and spent most of the afternoon emptying boxes. When they took a break midafternoon, they sat out in the loveseat on the front veranda, even though rain clouds covered most of the city and plains beyond.

"When I saw this view," he noted softly, "I couldn't wait for you to see it."

"It is impressive. And last night, as clear as it was, it was unbelievable."

"I'm so very glad you like it. Have you called your dad and sister yet? To let them know you've arrived safe and sound?"

"A quick call on Wednesday, while we were shopping for bed linens, before we went to the bank. And you?"

"Same. I called Wednesday evening after we got back from town. They were happy we made it and were happy you liked the place. I was really out on a limb if you didn't like it." He winked at her. "Have you thought about when you'd like to make it official?"

"Some. After I take the bar exams, but probably before I get accepted."

"August sometime?" He cocked his head. "We might want to go to Reno this year for a couple of days."

"Maybe. A couple of days could be fun," she admitted, and

squeezed his arm. "Can I gamble a little?"

Saturday, June 3

"Ratchet?" West asked when his phone connected.

"Yeah, West," Ratchet answered. "What's up?"

"Can you come down to the stores office for a few minutes?"

"Sure. I can break away. Charlie, Rosita, and Lenny have things covered here. See you in a minute."

He turned back to the long crates in front of him, ran his hand along the edge of the top one, and waited. Philip was down on the lower stores floor inventorying parts for the Mosquito, but they all knew they didn't have enough pieces to start a rebuild and West was pleased he would not have to make excuses or make up a task for him to go and do.

Ratchet stopped at the office door, and when he did not see West, he tapped the speed dial icon on his phone.

"I'm at the office."

"Aisle M, north end," West commented, and disconnected.

Ratchet's eyebrows raised as he put his phone back in his pocket and turned toward aisle M. He knew all too well what was stored in the secure area there.

He reached the heavy steel door halfway up the aisle and punched in the seven-digit code. He pushed the door open, not surprised to see the lights on and West standing at the far end of the room. He closed and locked the door and walked to meet him.

"This looks serious," Ratchet noted when he stopped and looked back down the long row. The multiple rows of crates were stacked chest high, and in some places higher, extending the length and width of the long room.

"It may get very serious." West explained a little of Jessie's message. "It looks like Collingsworth is sending people out to find Charlie. Everything we know indicates he saw our newspaper pictures from the Alamosa fly-in and our guess is he thinks Charlie is his missing daughter. As you know, he has been trying to find his daughter and take her home, no matter what."

"And he really thinks Charlie is his daughter?"

"Yeah. Like we've talked, this Collingsworth used his first daughter to advance his business by pairing her off advantageously in an arranged marriage. His second daughter disappeared when he wanted to marry her off and he's been searching for her ever since. I doubt he wants her for a marriage now. We think it's revenge for her running away, and now he's seen how much Charlie looks like her and has apparently decided they are one and the same."

"What are you going to do?"

"I want to try to be better prepared." He caressed the crate in front of him.

Ratchet followed his gesture.

"If I remember correctly, we have eight fifty-caliber Brownings modified to keep the spent casings onboard."

"Yes," Ratchet agreed. "We have over five hundred operational Brownings of varying model numbers in stock, and the eight you mentioned that don't discharge the casing overboard. What are you thinking?"

"Clean up four of those modified guns and have them ready for quick installs in *The Lady* and *Hell Raiser*, outboard positions. When we do install them, we'll leave the dummy barrels in the center and inboard positions and let the spent casings bag collect them in the inner gun bays."

Ratchet stared at him but nodded. "Ammo? We certainly have more than you need."

"Belt up two hundred rounds for each one, and a couple of extra belts," he ordered. "I really hope this doesn't become necessary, but I can't let anything happen to Charlie. Not if I can help it."

73

"Got it, boss," Ratchet said. "We hope it won't be necessary either, but we'll be ready if you need it."

Sunday, June 4

"This is sooo not Big City," Celia said as she drove her new red jeep northeast up Highway 24 and out of Colorado Springs.

"The jeep, or the open spaces without the tall buildings?" he asked, chuckling at her exuberance.

"Both, I guess," she admitted, and smiled. "But I really like not riding a subway everywhere we go, being outdoors where you can see for miles and miles. It's a little like going to my dad's place in New Hampshire. Bigger city than at Dad's, but more of a small-town feel—not like New York."

"I know what you mean," he agreed as they passed through a major intersection. "That's Woodland. A little over a mile and a half farther to a right turn on Judge Orr."

"I can't believe you're thinking about flying again," she remarked.

"Well, this is just to visit with a couple of operators and get a feel for what it'll cost to get current again."

"So you said. This looks like it." She slowed and turned onto Judge Orr and headed east, the Meadow Lake Airport visible on the south side ahead. "Where to?"

"Let's stop at High Plains first, the Cessna dealer just before the main road called Cessna Drive."

Norman pointed to the Cessna Aircraft sign sticking up out of the trees and she turned in and parked beside some other cars next to the hangar.

"Not a lot of activity," she noted as they got out and started walking to the hangar.

"Kind of how I remember rural airports." He opened the door to the office for her.

They visited with the owner and discussed what Norman was hoping to do and what kind of equipment was available for rent, and the associated costs for each area they discussed. After a pleasant twenty minutes, he led Celia back to the Jeep and they drove to Cessna Drive and turned south. At the second right, the first turn that was obviously a road and not a taxiway, she turned and drove to the end. She parked with the other cars against a bumper log between two hangars with the runway just beyond.

"This one, on the left, should be Central Colorado Aviation," he decided, and took her hand.

They walked to the hangar.

"Good afternoon," a middle-aged man greeted, walking toward them and wiping his hands on a rag. "What can I do for you?" he asked, and stuffed a corner of the rag into his back pocket.

"Good afternoon," Norman greeted in return, and introduced himself and Celia.

Norman explained what he was considering and what he was thinking concerning his getting back into flying.

"We can help with all of that, son," the man said. "I'm Will Little and we can certainly get you back in the air when you're ready. Ever flown around mountains?"

"No," he admitted. "All my flying was before I went to college and all back East in New England. We had hills, but no significant mountains."

"Then I'd recommend we add some mountain flying in your refresher," Will explained. "It's generally common sense stuff, but it's easy to overlook what's needed if you haven't done it before."

Will stepped into his small office in the corner of the hangar and returned with a trifold brochure.

"These are hourly rates for dual instruction and airplane rentals," Will continued. "I'd suggest starting out in the 172. The newer ones fly well at these altitudes and give you a good respect for moderately powered airplanes in this environment. Then, between myself and Curt Kullet up at High Plains, we can get you into higher-powered and turbocharged airplanes when you're ready."

"We met Mr. Kullet on our way in," Norman admitted. "He showed me what he has, and you two seem to have the normal needs pretty well covered."

Will looked up as two men in wrinkled summer business suits, sans ties, stepped in. He waved and said he'd be with them in a minute.

"Will?" He glanced at the men, thinking they looked more like disheveled Mormon missionaries than customers wanting information on airplane rentals, but their bearing and manner suggested they did not have religion on their minds. "Can we just look around at your equipment and let you get to your other customers?"

"Sure, sure." Will nodded and gestured for them to look around. "I doubt they're customers," he added in a lowered voice. "Go ahead. I'll get back to you in a minute or two."

Norman guided Celia to the nearest 172 and set her up on the right front seat. He went around and stepped up and settled onto the left seat and began explaining what she was looking at. He glanced at Will and the two men and had to agree: they certainly did not look like customers. They were showing him photographs and a newspaper, and between Celia's soft questions he heard Will mention the Wests.

He held his hand up for Celia and listened. She turned and listened with him, and they slowly realized the newspaper had to be the Alamosa fly-in paper and he could guess who the pictures were of.

Then he heard one of the men ask about someplace named the Ghost Ranch, and Will turned to the west and nodded.

"Out in the mountains somewhere."

"Where in the mountains?" the man asked, irritated.

"No one seems to know where exactly," Will continued. "But I have a Colorado Airport Guide you can use to look for it. Only twenty-four ninety-five, tax included. There are four hundred and forty-six airports registered in Colorado, and maybe a few that aren't."

The second man made a disgusted noise and tugged on the first man's arm, suggesting it was time to leave.

As Will ended his conversation with the two men and stepped into his office, Norman returned to answering Celia's questions about the plane. He almost jumped when Will was suddenly beside Celia, asking if they were doing all right.

"I don't mean to be nosy," he said, "but those men, they were asking questions about someone and I thought I heard the Wests mentioned. Would that be Glen and Charlie?"

"Yes, they were." Will nodded. "Do you know them?"

"Only briefly," he admitted without going into the embarrassing details, "last September, and then we saw them and their show in Alamosa last month."

Will nodded and smiled. "A wonderful lady, that Charlie. I've known Glen for eight or nine years now and I was so happy when he found someone that fits him so well. Straight shooters, those two. Actually all of the Ghost Ranch people are."

"What were they looking for?" Celia asked casually, nodding to the door.

"Where to find them," Will replied, and then scowled, "but they seemed to be more interested in finding Charlie than they did finding both of them. Made them real upset when I wouldn't give them an address to the ranch."

"I've heard going to the ranch is by invitation only," Norman added.

"Sometimes an invitation isn't enough to get you in." Will smiled as if he knew personally. "Anyway, unless you're taken there, you don't go. I heard Glen is smart with electronics and stuff, and someone told me once he can see company coming long before they get close enough to find the place." Will laughed. "At least that's what I was told."

They laughed with him, but they were beginning to see how serious Glen really was about their secrecy and safety.

"What do you think those two will do next?" he pressed a little more, suddenly feeling like he might be going too far. "There are a lot of airports in Colorado and I doubt the Ghost

Ranch is listed in any publication."

"It isn't," Will acknowledged, and grinned again. "But those two will have their hands full looking."

"Sorry to be so nosy. After seeing the Wests together in Alamosa and how happy they are, it makes me feel uncomfortable when strangers start asking a lot of questions about them."

"Well, I think West will take real good care of Charlie," Will chuckled. "One of his pilots was in here a few weeks back picking up a plane, and he told me about some guy at Reno that grabbed her arm and was suddenly face to face with West himself and two or three of his mechanics and pilots ready to defend her."

He swallowed hard, knowing he went instantly pale but somehow managing to keep his groan from being too loud.

"No," Will added, still chuckling. "I don't think West will let anyone get too close to his lady. But I will admit, she sure is pretty enough to understand why someone might try and grab her. Not a good idea, but understandable."

Norman glanced at Celia's brightly laughing eyes and slowly got his voice back.

"I think I have enough for now," Norman continued. "We'll look our finances over and I will certainly get back with you on getting current again. Thank you for your time. It has been a pleasure to talk with you."

As they walked back to Celia's Jeep, she was still giggling and finally broke their silence. "Is there any way you can let them know?"

"I'm not supposed to contact them directly," he said softly as he opened her door for her, "or talk about their personal lives, but this is too serious, and it's very personal. I'll call Bill Strong and ask to talk to Glen. Otherwise I'll have to disclose the details to someone on Glen's board, and I certainly don't want to do that."

He looked around and gestured to the black sedan slowly driving down the adjacent row of leased hangars. "At least it's good to know they don't know where to look and at that they could be looking for a long time."

He got in and she started driving back toward the city. He took out his phone and dialed a number. It rang more than once before the connection made.

"Hello? Bill?" he asked. "Norman Kent here, Bill. I'm caught in a bit of a dilemma and thought I'd ask you what I should do." Norman listened a moment, then continued. "It's a personal message for West and Charlie. And you know I'm not supposed to contact them directly. I understand why they want to keep their personal and business lives separated as much as they can, but this is private and affects their personal lives. I think it's serious and they'll want to know what I have to tell them." He listened again. "Thanks, Bill. I'll not abuse the opportunity. Thanks again."

He slipped his phone back into his shirt pocket, sat back, and smiled.

"So? What'd he say?"

"He's going to let West know I'm going to send them a private email." He glanced at the time on his phone. "I think it'll be best if I send it from my computer at home and not by my phone. Let's go home so we can take care of this, and then I'll take you out for a big steak dinner."

"Make that a 'small' steak dinner." She patted her stomach. "I swear you're trying to make me fat."

He quickly caught her hand and kissed it. "I certainly don't want to do that. A small steak dinner it is."

Monday, June 5

"Only one more thing to mention, West," Woody remarked casually, and glanced at Rosita at the foot of the breakfast table. "It seems that our student has to be in Trinidad, to meet Mr. Paul Clark, promptly at ten this morning."

Rosita's eyes lit up and a wide smile spread across her face.

Woody slid a sheet of paper to her.

"This is your itinerary for the day," Woody explained as she picked the sheet up. "When you're finished with Paul, you'll let Helen or Belle know, and Charlie will fly out and pick you up."

Rosita looked closer at the sheet.

"Meadow Lake? I'm to take the 172 from Trinidad to Meadow Lake and Charlie's going to pick me up?" Rosita, her expression suddenly full of concern, looked back at Woody and then at Charlie.

"Yes, that's the plan. You won't be needing the 172 any longer, so you'll take it back to Will and Charlie will bring you back to the ranch."

Rosita looked crestfallen. "But...? What will I...?"

"You'll be flying the T206 and the Beaver for the weekend family flights," Woody said, and chuckled. "And using the T206 for furthering your training. If you want to keep flying, you'll need your commercial and instrument."

"Yes. Yes, please." She stifled a childish urge to bounce in her chair.

"Well then." West glanced at Charlie with a wide smile himself. "Don't forget to call the ranch when Paul is finished with you."

"Yes, sir," Rosita confirmed. She swallowed at West's stern expression. "Sorry, West."

"Then you'd better get ready and get your plane checked out. Probably ought to wear your Ghost Ranch flight suit today," West added. "Ratchet, we'll need to get *The Lady* and *Hell Raiser* ready this morning also."

Rosita chocked the 172's left main tire and then closed the pilot side door. It was ten till ten by her watch as she turned and walked to the Perry Stokes Airport terminal building. The airport laid northeast to southwest, situated east of Trinidad along Highway 350, just across the agricultural expanse between it and the farming community of Hoehne to the northwest. A middle-aged man met her at the terminal door and opened it for her.

"Miss Rosita Ventura?" the man asked.

"Yes. Mr. Clark?"

"Yes. Good flight this morning?" He led them into a conference room.

"Typical summer day," Rosita answered. "A few bumps with building scattered cumulus."

"To start, I want you to plan a cross-country from here to Pueblo and then to Grand Junction. Use your pilot's manual and figure fuel for the weight with you and me on board. I'm two hundred and five pounds. Get your weather forecast and winds aloft. Call me when you're ready to go."

Rosita collected the necessary manuals and information, calculated their empty and full weight and balance, fuel required for the 296-mile trip and the maximum fuel she could put onboard. She plotted the trip on her Denver Sectional, seventy and a half miles to Pueblo and then the direct two hundred and twenty-five miles to Grand Junction Regional. She looked at the route and plotted a second one, bypassing Pueblo.

Finally, with her calculations in hand, she stepped out of the conference room and found Paul reading a paper and drinking a cup of coffee. He looked up when she approached.

"Ready?"

"Yes. But I have some concerns," she confessed, and led him back to the conference table. She sat down and tapped the map. "A direct flight from Pueblo to Grand Junction puts us up over ten thousand feet for a long period of time with some terrain over eleven thousand. It's a bit of a struggle for the 172 and will require a lot of oxygen. Second, the winds aloft at twelve thousand feet are forty knots out of the west and that would stretch that leg to over three hours." She paused and shook her head. "If you want us to go to Pueblo, then I suggest we drop

81

back south and cross at the La Veta Pass, west of Walsenburg, around Blanca Peak, then northwest over Saguache, cross the ridge on a straight course to Gunnison. It's just below ten thousand so we could minimize the time above ten. Then we basically follow the river and falling terrain up to Grand Junction."

Paul looked over her calculations and the trip planning and nodded.

"Okay, let's go to Pueblo." He stepped to the conference room door as she gathered up her charts, papers, and notes.

Rosita led Paul to the airplane, did a quick walk around and an oil check, and then got in. Paul belted himself in the right seat. She clipped her folded chart to the map holder and strapped it to her right thigh, conducted a cockpit check, verified the passenger door was latched and locked, set the throttle and mixture, called "Clear!" to the empty ramp, and started the engine.

At the boundary lines on the main taxiway, Rosita turned the 172 to visually check for traffic and announced in the blind on Unicom that she was taxiing back on the active for a takeoff on Runway Two One.

In the run-up area, Rosita made her preflight engine and magneto checks and again turned to visually scan the pattern for traffic. She called Unicom and declared she was taking the active and taking off. She made her left turn to crosswind and then made a departure turn away from the airport, climbing to her VFR altitude and turning to her heading to Pueblo.

"You've flown this route before?" Paul asked conversationally.

"Yes, many times," Rosita said. "If you look north immediately after takeoff, you can see the 'gun sight,' the two Rattlesnake bluffs up on either side of Highway Ten from La Junta to Walsenburg. Fly straight through the 'sight' and you'll end up between five to eight miles west of the Pueblo Airport, assuming the winds don't change on you."

Paul chuckled softly. "Woody taught you low-level navigation as well, did he?"

"Yes. Helps make you aware of the changes in terrain."

They flew on in silence until they had passed over the Rattlesnake Buttes.

"Okay," Paul commented, "let's go back toward Trinidad and do some maneuvers on the way. Give me a right and then a left climbing power on stall."

For the next three quarters of an hour, Paul tested her on all of her basic maneuvers and some unusual attitude recovery maneuvers. They let down to a lower altitude and Paul had her fly out west of Trinidad, into the rising foothills, and gave her an "engine out" emergency. She calmly picked a suitable section of a dry riverbed and glided the 172 down for the approach. At approximately two hundred feet above the ground, he gave her the engine back and she climbed up to her previous altitude. On the way back to Perry Stokes, Paul had her demonstrate how she would handle various equipment failures, caused by him switching radio equipment off or covering an instrument and making her perform various normal maneuvers.

On downwind to Parry Stokes, he covered her airspeed indicator and told her to continue.

Rosita smiled, remembering the many times Woody had done the same thing to her, and she settled into the task. To her, the flying was the same and the airspeed indication she needed came in the gentle changes in the sound of the air moving around the airplane and the feel of the controls. As she got closer to the ground, she listened more and paid less attention to the sensation of what she saw, knowing her ground perception would be biased by the wind, while the sound of the air moving around them and the feel of the controls would not be.

The landing was uneventful and Rosita taxied off at the first taxiway to the terminal ramp. She stopped and shut down like she always did, and chocked the left main wheel when she got out.

"Bring your logbook and come inside." Paul hurried to the terminal building ahead of her.

Rosita followed and waited in the conference room until

Paul joined her.

He sat down at the table across from her and looked through her logbook. Then he made an entry, signed it, and closed the cover. He took two cards from his document case and filled them out in silence.

Finally, he looked up to face a squirming Rosita, watching him.

"Congratulations, young lady. You are now a private pilot," he said, and smiled as he slid her logbook back to her and handed her one of the cards he filled out. "Your official, permanent card will come in about a month in the mail. I'll call Woody and let him know he still does a very good job of teaching. I saw you had a successful, actual off-field landing on one of your cross-countries."

"Yes. Leaking fuel line connection at the selector valve," she said, and smiled. "I had it fixed by the time Woody got there."

Paul smiled. "Well, congratulations again, Rosita."

"Thank you, Paul." Rosita stood as he did.

Paul extended his hand and shook hers. "I wish more of my check rides were as prepared as you were. Thank you."

Paul smiled and then turned and walked out of the conference room and out onto the ramp. She watched him as he turned left and strode off toward a Turbo 210 parked near the closest Thangar.

Smiling with a grin that almost would not fit on her face, Rosita gathered up her logbook and walked back to her 172. She wanted to jump and shout for joy, but she controlled herself. Right then, she needed to keep her head. The jumping and shouting and celebrating would come when she was back home.

"She's airborne, Glen," Helen's voice said from West's phone.

"Paul passed her."

"Of course he did. Better get the party ready," he chuckled, and smiled at Charlie. "The pilots are going to be whooping it up tonight. Thanks, Mom. We're off."

He caught Charlie's hand and started up the ramp.

"Ratchet!" Charlie shouted in his direction. "She passed and is on her way to Meadow Lake."

"Great!" Ratchet shouted back. "See you all when you get back."

Charlie nodded and followed West to the waiting planes. She climbed up on *The Lady* and West mounted *Hell Raiser* and waved back at her.

Buckled in and engines started, West gestured for her to lead off and she swung *The Lady* into the wind and pushed the throttle forward.

"Ghost One and Two, *The Lady*, and *Hell Raiser* are off as a flight of two," Charlie called on the radio, glancing over her left shoulder to see *Hell Raiser* just behind her wing.

When they flashed over the rim of the mesa, she corrected their heading to take them to Trinidad.

"I'm going to overfly Trinidad," she commented on the ranch's frequency, "and go up the valley behind Walsenburg, over Westcliffe, then up the valley past Cripple Creek to Florissant and then east and down into the plains to Meadow Lake."

"I'm with you," West replied.

"Good flight, Ghost Two," Helen added.

Thanks, Mom," Charlie said, and then settled to enjoy the beautifully serene, empty country slipping quickly beneath them.

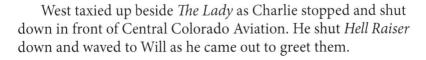

West taxied up beside *The Lady* as Charlie stopped and shut down in front of Central Colorado Aviation. He shut *Hell Raiser* down and waved to Will as he came out to greet them.

"Good morning, Will," she greeted cheerfully as she slid down *The Lady's* left strut.

"Hello, Charlie." Will returned her greeting with a wide smile as he reached her and shook her hand. He greeted West as he walked up. "What brings you two out on such a beautiful day?"

"Rosita is bringing your 172 back," West announced. "She passed her check ride this morning and we came to pick her up and take her home in style."

"In style is right." Will nodded and turned to admire the two planes. Then he turned back to West. "While we have a minute alone, I need to tell you something. Yesterday, two men in semi-casual summer suits, very unusual dress for these parts, came in and started flashing pictures and that Alamosa fly-in newspaper around. They wanted to know if I knew the woman in the pictures, and I told them they were of you, Charlie. But they kept trying to call the woman in their pictures by a different name, and Em...Emma, or something like that." He paused and sighed deeply. "I told them they were mistaken."

"Did they say why they were looking at my pictures?"

"Not really. Just said they wanted to talk to this Emma...somebody, but not why. Then they asked about the Ghost Ranch and I explained that very few people actually knew where it was, and I was not one of them."

"Thanks," West said. "We'll keep our eyes open for strangers lurking around."

"You're welcome. Now, I need to get back inside and take care of a few things. Let me know when Rosita gets here. I'll have the paperwork ready."

"Oh, Will. Just so you know, I have a feeling we'll be needing to rent another 172 before too long."

Will nodded and hurried inside.

"Thanks," Charlie hollered after him, just as he disappeared through the people door.

"Well, that confirms Norman's message," Charlie acknowledged softly as she watched Will go back inside. "I don't feel any better about the situation. It's still very upsetting."

"I know, but at least we're getting some feedback, and what we're being told fits with what Jess is seeing and passing along." West took Charlie's hand. "Maybe we can keep them at a distance."

They stood beside *The Lady* and watched Rosita taxi the 172 up to Will's hangar and shut down. Rosita immediately got out and chocked the left main tire. When she stood up and turned, Charlie was there and caught her in an enthusiastic hug. West grabbed them both in a bear hug and spun them around best he could.

"Congratulations, Rosita." West thumped her back. "You've made the first step. I'm so proud of you."

"Me too," Charlie added. "Now let's go and officially return the 172."

"Okay, Rosita," Charlie started to explain as they walked up to *The Lady*. "Step up on the strut like I do."

Charlie climbed up on *The Lady's* wing and turned to help Rosita up. "There are also steps in the side of the fuselage so you can mount from the back, but this is our usual way up. So long as you don't have stuff stuck to your shoes."

"Thanks." Rosita stood and looked around at the airport, suddenly looking different from her new position on *The Lady's* wing.

"You're going to ride in the back today," Charlie continued. "Have you been up in a Fifty-One before?"

Rosita shook her head and followed Charlie to the cockpit.

"Climb in and sit down and I'll get you strapped in." Charlie showed her how to hook up the various straps.

Once Rosita was securely in place and her helmet on and hooked up, Charlie smiled, patted the top of the helmet, swung her legs over the canopy rail, and settled into the front seat.

"You ready back there?" she asked through the hot mike.

"Yes, I think so."

Charlie ran through the prestart checklist and engaged the starter. *The Lady's* propeller started to turn and the Merlin popped, spit out a small wispy cloud of smoke, and spun up, settling into its customary purr. Charlie glanced back and saw *Hell Raiser* up and running, waiting for her to taxi out.

At the north end of Runway One Five, she made her engine and control checks and glanced back at West.

"Meadow Lake Unicom, Zero Seven George Whiskey is a flight of two, departing one five. Left-hand pattern and two-seventy overhead turn to the west." Then she asked Rosita, "Are you ready?"

"Ready," Rosita answered in an expectant voice.

"Ready. I've got your six."

Charlie smiled at West's reply as she pushed her throttle forward.

"Is my airspeed indicator correct?" Rosita asked through the hot mike.

"Yes, within one or two miles per hour," Charlie answered with a chuckle. "It's a little faster than the 172."

"I'll say." Rosita was studying the needle, wavering very slightly as it hovered just above three hundred miles per hour. "That's...five miles every minute."

"Actually, use your air navigation computer," Charlie advised, referring to the circular slide rule computer they used. "Our true airspeed is just a hair over three hundred and fifty miles per hour, nearly six miles a minute."

Rosita absently looked back on her left side, watching *Hell Raiser* beside and behind them. Then she unfolded her sectional and checked their course and heading.

"We should be coming over Woodland Park," Rosita commented softly.

"Just passed it," Charlie corrected. "If we didn't have drop tanks, I'd roll over and let you see."

"I take it drop tanks mean no aerobatic maneuvers?" Rosita inquired, half a question and half not.

"That's right. At least only very limited aerobatics. We're less than two minutes from our turn at Florissant. We'll head south from there."

"We're disguising our route home, aren't we?" Rosita asked, understanding the why behind the route. "Like I had to do in the 172, but I couldn't cover this much extra ground and not run out of fuel."

Charlie chuckled.

A moment passed and Rosita heard Charlie talking to West, and then the two mustangs made a standard turn to the left. She watched as *Hell Raiser* stayed in position through the turn, just as if they had kept flying straight.

"Take the stick," Charlie interrupted her thoughts. "Be very gentle. West, Rosita is going to be flying."

Rosita placed her fingers around the grip as gently as she could and then her feet on the rudder pedals. She felt Charlie's inputs.

"Rosita, I'm going to let go, but I'll be close if you have any trouble. *The Lady* is sensitive and responds quickly. She's trimmed slightly nose up. Watch your heading and altitude but make all corrections slowly and firmly. She's yours."

Suddenly Rosita could feel *The Lady* push against her hold on the stick.

"Watch your rudder input. She's trimmed, so she'll fly straight," Charlie added softly.

Rosita was suddenly consumed with remembering the basics all over again, feeling as if she'd never flown before. *Ease forward on the stick*: they were already two hundred feet too high. *A little more right aileron*: they were five degrees too far left. *A little rudder, get that damned ball back in the bracket.*

She was perspiring when she felt the stick and the rudder pedals stiffen and knew Charlie was back on the controls.

"I've got her," Charlie announced, and she watched as the altimeter needle drifted back down to its rightful place and the compass settled down and stopped wobbling with the correct number behind the lubber line.

"That was awesome," Rosita admitted. "*The Lady* is graceful, but definitely needs a trained hand."

"When I started flying her," Charlie explained, "I realized she was called a Mustang for a reason. She needs a firm hand, and that hand has to convince her it means well. I had to learn how to use her abilities to get her to do what I wanted. I can't force her like a lighter, more timid airplane. She has spirit, and that makes her a great extension of my abilities. To fly her, you have to learn how to be a team."

"I can see that," Rosita agreed softly.

"It's just like learning to fly the 172," Charlie continued. "Only she can be more demanding if you're not listening. You can't sleep on the job or she'll buck and try to throw you off, or she'll lull you into a place you can't get out of."

Rosita looked around them and realized they were descending and checked the altimeter, winding down through eighty-five hundred feet.

"We're due west of Spanish Peaks airport," Charlie informed West. "I'm looking for seventy-five hundred feet over Trinidad, and then a straight in at a thousand above the terrain." Then through the hot mike, she added, "Rosita, use the third transceiver and call the ranch. Give them our intentions and ETA."

"Okay." She selected the right frequency and switched her mike and headphones to the transceiver. She quickly looked at her chart and confirmed their position.

"Ghost Ranch. Ghost Seven. Ghost One and Two inbound," Rosita called. "*The Lady* as a flight of two are descending. Fifteen minutes out. Will be turning inbound in six minutes."

"Ghost Ranch understands, Ghost Seven. Fifteen minutes out, inbound in six."

Rosita looked at her airspeed indicator and then at the back of Charlie's helmet. "Are we really going that fast?" she asked, almost in a whisper.

"We are," Charlie confirmed just as softly. "Four minutes out we'll start slowing down. Two hundred over the rim and one seventy over the hangars, and in the turn to base we'll get the gear and flaps down and settle on one thirty at the start of final.

"Ghost One? Formation downwind and landing?" Charlie asked.

"Formation downwind and landing, Ghost Two. I'm on your eight and I'm with you. Call the numbers."

At four minutes out, like she said she would, Charlie slowly pulled the power back and Rosita watched the airspeed bleed off. When they passed over the main house, she saw people in the front yard and the front drive, and then they were over the rim. When they passed over the hangars, she saw the airspeed was 170 and Charlie rolled *The Lady* up into a tight right turn.

"Gear coming down," Charlie announced, and Rosita saw West was still in the same spot he'd been for the whole flight and *Hell Raiser's* gear was also coming down.

"Rolling out on final." *The Lady* rolled wings level.

Rosita strained to see, but could not see around Charlie. She visualized the approach, knowing it was the same as she had flown so many times in the 172, just a little wider, a little faster. At ninety miles per hour the mains touched down, and she glanced back to see *Hell Raiser* rolling, tail up in its usual spot beside them.

The Lady's tail finally settled and Rosita saw the small crowd as Charlie taxied to the open hangar and stopped, nose still into the wind. West stopped just off their left wingtip, and together they cleared their engines and cut the ignition and fuel.

Charlie secured the cockpit and Rosita unfastened her straps. Charlie cranked the canopy open, stood up and stepped out onto the wing, then turned and helped her out of the aft cockpit.

Rosita hurried down the left strut with her document case in hand and West greeted her with a gentle hug and slapped her back. Charlie climbed down behind her as Woody, Bump, Lenny, and Ratchet clustered around, slapping her back and giving her hugs all around.

Charlie gently pushed Rosita ahead of her as they entered the side door to the main house. Helen greeted her with a hug when she entered the living room. Behind her was everyone from hers, Cappie's, and Gracie's families, cheering as Helen handed her a flute of champagne.

Becky passed a tray to the rest of the arrivals and each took a flute.

Woody stepped forward and raised a toast to Rosita for her accomplishments and for being an exceptional student. Glasses were clinked and champagne sipped, and then West stepped forward with Charlie at his side. He raised his glass to Rosita.

"To Ghost Seven—officially the newest Ghost Ranch pilot. I know everyone here will agree with me when I say how very proud we are of you and how very pleased we are that you chose to learn to fly and become a part of our airborne family. Thank you for wanting to remain a part of our ranch family.

"Mom and I have had the wonderful pleasure of watching you, and all the rest of you kids, grow up here on the ranch, and watching you make your choices as you grew. And now, because of those choices, Rosita, it is time for you to officially become part of the ranch's aircraft support group. But we have a problem. Helen, Charlie, Woody, Ratchet, and I have conferred, but we cannot come up with a suitable nickname for you. We thought of 'Ace' because you passed every demonstrated skill test and each written exam without any mistakes, including your check ride this morning. But 'Ace' would imply more arrogance than is intended. We had other, also less suitable choices, but I think I would like to know if you have a choice you would like for your 'family' nickname."

Rosita smiled and sipped her champagne.

"West, Charlie, everyone," she responded with a huge smile. "I'm not yet a mechanic, so a tool name like Ratchet's doesn't fit me. Maybe someday. I also don't have a scar hidden under my hair for arguing with a heavy Skyraider propeller like Bump. Again, maybe someday." Someone chuckled. "I didn't grow up with resorcinol stuck to my fingers and under my fingernails and nitrate dope dribbled on my jeans like Woody. Again, maybe someday.

"I've thought about this a lot, knowing each of you supporting our airplanes have a nickname, but I am a pilot today and calling myself 'Pilot' or '*Piloto*' seems rather presumptuous. Charlie came to us, a knowledgeable pilot with a male-sounding name, and now I find myself the second woman pilot. So, I choose to be 'Dani' because I am the second and I want my nickname to be the second in line in a new tradition of female pilots."

Charlie stepped forward and hugged Rosita tightly.

"Thank you, Charlie, for the encouragement and the inspiration," she continued. "And thank you, West, for the opportunity, not to mention the cost involved." She sipped from her flute again. "Not too long ago, when everyone was still calling me Rosie, Charlie asked me what I preferred to be called. I said Rosita because that's my Christened name, but after living and experiencing the wonderful things in this part of my new life, I think I was wrong. I have grown a little, and in private, among my family and friends when I'm not flying, I think I prefer simply to be called Rose."

Everyone raised a toast to Rose, and Charlie noticed Rose glanced at Bump with a smile.

"Robert, Madra," West said, "even though Rose and Belle are the closest Charlie and I have to daughters, I leave the parental guidance for tonight to you." Then he turned to everyone and smiled at Rose. "This celebration is for 'Dani,' our newest pilot and support person, our second woman in the cockpit, and is now officially called to order. Let the party begin."

Eighteen

"Mr. Collingsworth. Tony here," Tony Bellini, Howard's hired man, said into his phone. "We're in Colorado Springs. Arrived Saturday and started investigating local airports yesterday. A lot of people and business owners around here know Mrs. West and her husband, but no one seems to have heard of an Emli or know of the Collingsworth name."

Tony listened for a moment.

"Yes. We talked to the two aviation services owners on a busy local airport. They said they've known Glen West for many years and are very happy that he's married. They speak very highly of Mrs. West. We went back today to see if we could find people that weren't there on Sunday to talk to, and had a bit of luck. Two beautifully restored World War Two fighters landed while we were there. One was piloted by Mrs. West and the other by Mr. West. Someone at the air service we were at said they were P-51s with drop tanks and in military colors. They waited for another airplane to land and the pilot of the third got into Mrs. West's plane and they left."

Howard spoke again.

"No. There wasn't time for us to reach her and talk to her before they left. When I asked about the Ghost Ranch, everyone just says it's out in the Colorado mountains somewhere. And when Mr. and Mrs. West flew in, they came from the west, and when they left, they went west, into the 'Colorado mountains.'"

He listened again.

"Yes, we will try to find someone that knows where the ranch is. I'll let you know when we know more. I understand there are a couple of fly-ins, as they're called, coming up late in the month and around the Fourth of July. We'll also check them out and see if they show up."

Tony listened and then disconnected.

"I guess we start looking in the mountains west of here."

Howard hung up and studied the phone console for a long moment. Then he dialed Monte's home number.

"They saw her in Colorado Springs today," Howard said when Monte answered. He waited until Monte closed his office door and got back on the phone. Howard repeated what Tony had told him.

"You said they flew into an airport where they were seen. Flying P-51s?" Monte asked.

"Yeah," Howard confirmed. "Tony said they came from the mountains to the west and left going back the same way. So they're going to look at likely airports farther up in the higher country."

"Problem is," Monte explained, "they were P-51s, like the bomber escort fighters used in Europe in the Second World War. The specifications I just pulled up on the internet say they have a range of up to two thousand miles with drop tanks. You said they had drop tanks?"

"Yes. Tony said they did."

"Well, Howard, that means they can go a thousand miles one way and return or they can go two thousand and refuel. That means from Colorado Springs to Indianapolis and back, or from Colorado Springs to anywhere on the West Coast and back, or anywhere in the country and refuel."

"So they're no better off than they were before," Howard remarked, his displeasure obvious in his voice. "Have you heard anything from the guys you sent to Jackson Hole?"

"Not yet."

Tuesday, June 6

West was standing at the lunch table in the dining room

of the main house as everyone slowly came in and took their places. Becky and Camilla were placing steaming platters and covered bowls on the table as he smiled and watched everyone settle into their normal seats. Bump and Lenny were exceptionally slow and Charlie chuckled; they had been the last to leave the party.

West glanced aside as Rose came in and stopped to talk to Charlie.

"Charlie? Did you leave the P-51 pilot's manual in my room last night?"

"I gave it to your mom and she slipped it in after she got home," Charlie admitted with a smile. "It's a loan, but read every word until you can recite them and be ready to demonstrate all of the ground operation parts."

West saw Charlie smile when Rose clapped her shoulder and said a soft "Yes ma'am."

When she had taken her seat, West sat down and the platters and bowls began to make their way around the table.

"Ratchet," West began after everyone had settled into their meal, "I think we should have one airplane represent us at the Durango June Days Fly-In. That's Friday and start back on Sunday."

Ratchet looked up, and West noted everyone else had stopped eating and was looking at him and Ratchet.

"I can send Bump and Lenny with the Spit Fourteen or the Hellcat," Ratchet said, and looked at their bleary eyes. "The fourteen hasn't been out since Charlie had it out last, and *Steppin' Out* is ready to go."

West thought a minute and looked at Charlie with a cock of his head.

"The Fourteen's in top shape," she agreed. "So's the Hellcat."

"Okay, Ratchet," West agreed with a smile. "One of them can drive the small van for support. Load the spare engine and whatever you think you might need. If you need something more, call and we'll get it to the guys."

"Sounds good," Ratchet agreed. "Have you given any

thought to the Heritage Days Fly-in in Broomfield on the fourth?"

"Some, but I haven't decided which one or if I want a second there," West admitted.

"I thought maybe we could have the small van and one plane on display," Charlie said, "and maybe a second for flyovers and running back and forth at night."

"Good thought." West smiled. "But it would be simpler if we weren't flying back and forth each night. We'll kick it around a little more."

"Okay," Ratchet agreed.

"What's on the schedule for today?" Woody asked, and glanced at Ratchet and then at West.

"Anyone that wants can help Charlie on her TF. I think she would like that," Ratchet added. "We are still inventorying parts for our next rebuild, so Philip and I can use someone in the stores."

"I can help later." Woody glanced at Dani. "But first thing after lunch, Dani here is going to get some taildragger time. Maybe I can teach her how tenacious a backward tricycle can be before the weekend charter work. I think it's Gracie and Henry's weekend in town."

"Very good," Ratchet added enthusiastically. "Thanks for the warning. I'll keep everyone else inside so they won't get run over."

Dani slapped Ratchet's arm. "I don't run people over!"

"But today you might," Ratchet retorted, laughing as he pulled his arm away.

Charlie's TF looked more and more like an airplane each day, and today, with the tail feathers on and the fabric covered rudder and elevators installed, the engine mount hung and landing gear extended and nearly reaching the ground, it almost looked like any other TF in for a simple engine change. Charlie was in the cockpit working on the mechanical controls before they mounted the instrument panel and West was checking the electrical connectors at the firewall into the engine compartment.

"Have you made any progress on rejuvenating the rear warning system?" she asked as she secured the control rods to the throttle quadrant. "What was it called?"

"Yes, an APS-13." He grunted when his handheld tester gave him an incorrect indication. "It's a short-range radar system. I actually rebuilt the power circuits and got rid of the vacuum tube stuff. Completely solid-state now and with a little extra power."

"Think your changes will work?"

"Work? What are you saying?" He feigned a wounded tone. "You don't think my fixes will work?"

She chuckled at his fakery.

"Should tell if anyone is ten miles or closer and following. Thirty degrees up and down from the flight path and the same side to side," he explained as he rechecked a wire that should not have been showing as grounded. "I replaced the indicator light with a small mechanical dial indicator to display range."

"Have you thought about the type of airplane that might be following?" she inquired further. "I mean, now we have small jets out there and I think they might have a smaller, weaker signature than these big propellers."

"That's a very good point." He stopped to think about that. "Yes, I can add a sensitivity switch to the software so we can enhance a weak signal. But better than that, I'll need to flight check the properties of a propeller's return signal against a clean airplane. I can use the difference to automatically tell which is following."

"Good. When do you want to do that?"

"Probably tomorrow. I'll put my test equipment in the back of *The Lady* and get Ratchet to fly as our target. You can fly and

I'll collect the data."

"Sounds like a plan." She chuckled again.

Wednesday, June 7

Jackson, Wyoming

"We've been to the four city and town cemeteries that we were told about," Sam Peuler, dressed in white shirt and tan slacks that looked like they had been worn for days, said to the young clerk behind the town hall records counter. The clerk looked to the man like he was barely in his twenties. "Are there any small, family cemeteries that you know of?"

"A few," the clerk said. "They aren't normally listed in the city records. Is there a family name you're looking for?"

"Yes. Bassett," he replied, and looked at the man with him. "Lloyd? Do you have the lists?"

"Yes." He handed him the folded paper. "Here it is."

Sam and Lloyd Smithson were private investigators.

He unfolded the sheet and laid it on the counter. "The family of Arthur Bassett and his wife Sarah."

The clerk turned to his computer console and entered the names. "Hmm. Looks like Arthur and Sarah lived southeast of town," the clerk commented softly, "about six miles out Cache Creek Road. Almost to the end on the south side."

"Where did Arthur work?" Lloyd asked absently.

"He worked for the city parks department," the clerk offered. "Senior groundskeeper and head of the maintenance garage. My folks knew them."

"Do you think there's a family cemetery out at their place?" Sam took the paper back, folded it, and slipped it into his shirt pocket. His optimism was fading fast. Monte Williamson had hired him and Lloyd, both private investigators from Detroit, to verify everything they could about the woman Charlie Bassett, from her birth certificate data to where she had lived as a child and lived and worked while she was growing up. Did

100

her parents die as reported, and was there an aunt that took her in and raised her? So far, all they had confirmed was an Arthur and Sarah Bassett had lived in the Jackson Hole area and had died as reported. All of the dates agreed. Now they just had to prove Charlie and the aunt were really part of the story.

"Maybe," the clerk admitted. "You can go and look. If there is one, it will likely be near the foundation of the old cabin. Their daughter had the place leveled after her aunt died."

"Thank you," Sam said, and turned to the door, realizing the clerk had just answered the most important of their questions.

Five miles out on Cache Creek Road, Sam and Lloyd were deeply concentrating on anything that looked like a road or a driveway off the main road.

"Why would anyone live out in the wild like this?" Lloyd asked, and looked at a set of ruts that left the road, but he quickly realized they were just the remnants of someone turning around.

"I guess they liked nature," Sam said, and squeezed the steering wheel, frustrated from a day of chasing empty clues. "The clerk did say Arthur was the head groundskeeper for the city parks."

"There's a drive," Lloyd said, pointing to the overgrown trace that doubled back as it disappeared up the hillside into the trees and brush. A sign at the road said "Private Property. Owner C. Basset."

Sam stopped and surveyed the entrance to the drive and finally decided to follow it.

A stone foundation peered out of thick underbrush a quarter mile up; the house was missing. Sam stopped the car in front of the crumbling stone steps that once marked the front entrance to the house. They got out and Lloyd started walking around the empty foundation, sidestepping around crumbling flower bed and planter edgings. Sam scanned the yard and trees around them, looking for any indication of a family burial site.

A half an hour later, Sam spotted an odd accumulation of tree limbs piled among bushes growing to the south of the house.

"Over here, Lloyd," Sam announced.

Lloyd reached Sam as he tossed the first limbs away and began stripping the brush and vines off the stones hidden beneath.

"Looks like you found something." He smiled as Sam pulled the last limb away.

Sam knelt down and read the headstones.

"Looks like we found Arthur and Sarah Bassett." Sam nodded absently and pulled the list from his pocket. "The dates match. Get me some of that butcher paper from the car."

"Who's the other headstone? Lydia Smyth?"

"I'm not sure," Sam admitted as Lloyd hurried back to the car for the paper, "but I'm betting it's the aunt."

Sam made a rubbing of all three headstones, and as he started to get up, his hand brushed the base of Lydia's. He stopped and wiped the dirt off a small rectangular brass plaque affixed to the base.

"Look at this."

Sam read the plaque. 'Thank you for everything. I'll love you always. Charlie.'

"If Lydia is the aunt, then this matches the stories about Charlie West's growing up." Lloyd shrugged. "She was here, her parents, and the aunt. And C. Bassett, or now Charlie West, owns the place."

Friday, June 9

"I know I shouldn't ask," Norman said as he sat on the edge of their bed in their dark bedroom, "if you've had second thoughts and want to come."

"Of course I want to come," Celia commented emphatically, "but I have to stay focused and serious about studying."

"I know." He pulled her sheet down and stretched out

beside her. He kissed her long and tenderly. "And I'm being too much of a distraction. I just hate to go without you." He sat back up. "I'll call when I get there."

"You better." She smiled as she watched him head for the bathroom.

"I was surprised when Bill Strong called and asked me— us—to go and play sleuth for them," he noted as he dressed.

Celia yawned and stretched; he hesitated and watched how the sheet clung to her lovely form. "They wouldn't know who to look for if one of us didn't show them."

He kissed her again and then grabbed his overnight duffel.

"I'll get something to eat on the road," he conceded as he reached the door and started down the stairs, suddenly realizing it would be the first they had been apart since he had gotten back to New York before Memorial Day weekend. It had only been a couple of weeks since that time, but leaving without her tugged at him more than he had expected. He sighed; at least it was only an overnight.

A little after one, he parked in the crowded parking area set aside at the Durango-La Plata County Airport. He was surprised at the amount of activity there was for a Friday as he walked to the bannered gate and called Celia.

He was studying the various airplanes when he heard the announcer alert everyone to the arrival of the Ghost Ranch's Grumman F6F, *Steppin' Out*. He walked to the parking slot in front of the equipment van with the Ghost Ranch banner stretched across one side of the box to wait.

He recognized the man at the van as one of the mechanics he had seen in Reno the previous year, but couldn't remember his name. He stopped to one side and watched as the Hellcat taxied in and shut down in front of the assigned parking area.

When the pilot climbed down, the man with the van hooked

an electric tow cart to the tail wheel and pulled the Hellcat backwards, into its parking spot.

From the size of the van and the reserved space, Norman knew they would only have the one plane and suspected the two men were all the crew that was coming.

He found a food tent and bought a burger and a beer for a late lunch. Then he spent the rest of the afternoon snapping pictures of the planes, the many kiosks of aviation items for sale, and a few of people wandering from one place to another. It was half past six when he saw the two men from Meadow Lake, casually walking through the crowd, stopping often to check out one tent and then another. He watched as the men circled around, passing the Hellcat more often than any of the other planes.

Making notes in his phone, he turned to the two men at the back of the van behind the Hellcat. He chose to talk to the taller man that was there before the plane had arrived.

"Good afternoon," he greeted pleasantly, and looked at the man's embroidered name on his coveralls, "Lenny. I'm Norman Kent and I was wondering if I could talk to you a minute."

Lenny got up and shook his hand. "You look familiar. Do I know you?"

"Not really, but we met last year under dubious circumstances," Norman acknowledged, knowing his face was turning red. "I'm the one that mistook Mrs. West for someone else in Reno."

"Aah," Lenny said, and looked at him. "And why do you need to talk to me now?"

Norman held his phone so Lenny could see the face, and selected the photos he had taken.

"Last Sunday, my fiancée and I saw these two men at Meadow Lake Airport asking Will Little about Mr. and Mrs. West. We think they were more interested in information about Mrs. West."

"And you're saying they're here today?"

"Yes. I just took this series of pictures this afternoon, and they've walked by your exhibit numerous times." Norman showed Lenny his notes. "I know Mr. and Mrs. West are not here, but I think these guys are following the fly-ins hoping to find them, or one of them, at one of the airshows."

"Why?" Lenny asked. "Why are they looking for the Wests?"

"You'll have to ask Mr. or Mrs. West," he evaded. "I was just asked to see if they are here and to let you know if they are. If you'd like, please send these pictures and notes to your phones so you'll know what these men look like. Then please erase your number from the Recent Calls so I won't have it."

Norman set the phone to send the pictures and handed it to Lenny. "Just add your number and touch send and you'll have them."

When he was finished, Lenny looked at Norman.

"I also know they've been asking a lot of questions trying to find out where the Ghost Ranch is," he continued when Lenny handed his phone back. "For what it's worth."

He stepped back and glanced at the airplane.

"I know I've taken a lot of your time, but could you show me the airplane? I'm going to have Will help me get recurrent and I've never been around any airplanes like these," Norman admitted, explaining his need for some flight recurrency training before starting to fly again.

"Sure." Lenny gestured for Norman to follow him.

Saturday, June 10

Friday night passed without fanfare. Bump slept in the van and watched the plane, but all was well. Saturday was clear and began with the promise for another good day for an airshow.

Lenny brought Bump a hot breakfast from the hotel and Norman stopped by while they were eating to say goodbye and thank them again for showing him the Hellcat. He wanted to get back to the Springs before it got too late, saying he had things to do and that he didn't like leaving his girl alone any more than he had to.

Lenny and Bump enjoyed the day, interacting with the crowd, explaining the many facts and stories about the Hellcat and its superiority in the Pacific Theater. Bump flew *Steppin' Out* in the noon heritage flight with a local North American SNJ and an Oregon-based P-51, and gave a mini-show, demonstrating the plane's acceleration and maneuverability. Lenny told him later how much the crowd appreciated his show.

More than a few times during the afternoon, Lenny saw the two men Norman had pointed out. He made sure Bump was aware as he rearranged the equipment in the van.

"I'll go in and get some takeout," Bump said as they draped the engine cover over the huge cowl. "It'll take me a bit if I go into town. You okay with that?"

"Yeah." Lenny fastened the straps on top.

"Burgers?" Bump asked, and fastened the lower straps.

"Sure," Lenny chuckled. "Hey, better yet. Stop at that place just before you get on Highway 160. Won't take so long, and we are off the clock; just night watchmen now. So see what they have on their menu and grab a cold six-pack. Good stuff. West doesn't mind if we don't get crazy and aren't scheduled to fly."

Bump threw the canopy cover up to Lenny, and together they secured the straps. Lenny jumped down, went to the van, set two plastic lawn chairs out, and closed the overhead door. "So, go on and I'll watch for critters." Lenny gestured for Bump to go.

Bump climbed into the airport's courtesy car and Lenny settled into a chair and watched as he left the airport going north to pick up Highway 172 to 160.

Except for the folding table between the two chairs, Lenny was sitting in the same chair and looked like he hadn't moved when Bump pulled in behind the van and parked. Mostly, he had just watched the other exhibitors close up their displays. The crowd had dwindled quickly as the airplanes and sunlight retired for the day, leaving a few like Lenny and Bump to the memories whispering on the breezes in the warm night.

After they ate and had a beer, Lenny walked the ramp to get a feel for the number of people that might be sleeping out as well. There were quite a few, and he liked that. When he got back, he and Bump had a second beer and Bump made a walk around.

"I guess I'll go in and get some sleep," Bump said softly, and folded the table as Lenny opened the back of the van.

"You should do that." Lenny stowed the table and one of the chairs.

"Are you going to sleep in the back or up front?" Bump asked before Lenny jumped down.

"Neither." Lenny gestured to the van. "I tied the hammock under the side of the box. I'll sleep outside in case we have visitors."

"No one came around last night," Bump said matter-of-factly.

"Well, West and Charlie didn't come today"—Lenny sat back down in his chair—"so I think these two will start thinking about how to find the ranch. My hunch is they'll make a move tonight since it's our last night here."

"You want me to stay?"

"Nah," Lenny passed the suggestion off casually. "Get some sleep. We'll get breakfast from one of the tents when you come out."

"Okay, I'll see you in the morning."

Lenny glanced at his watch when he heard two men talking. It was 11:47 and the voices did not sound close, but he thought they were coming toward him from the other side of the Hellcat. He looked around the dimly lit ramp as he rolled out of the hammock onto his knees. He looked under the plane and could see the men still a couple of airplane lengths across the ramp.

He got to his feet, quickly crossed the short distance to the plane, and slipped under its tail. Another check on the men, and seeing they were occupying each other, he moved forward and up the steps placed in the side of the fuselage. But instead of standing up like he would to get into the cockpit, he stretched out on top of the left wing where its curvature joined the fuselage, far enough forward so he could look down and see the ground.

Lenny listened, and slowly the voices came closer. He glanced down under the front of the plane and studied the mixed shadows cast by the multiple lights around the edges of the ramp. The men had stopped in front of the other wing and he could hear their conversation clearly.

"You do have it, don't you Tommy?" one of the men asked.

"Yeah, yeah," Tommy answered. "It's here somewhere. I put it in my pocket before we left the car."

Lenny saw a flashlight beam switch on and streak across the ground and disappear.

"Does this help?" the first man asked.

"Shit! Put that out!" Tommy hissed. "Someone'll see us if you flash that around. Here it is."

"Do you know where to put it?" the first man asked, and Lenny saw the shadows move closer to the airplane.

He sat up and slowly slid down over the left landing gear door and strut. His foot stopped on the tire and he let himself gently down to the ground. He ducked under the engine and stood up behind the two men; one was watching the second with his head up in the wheel well behind the strut.

He leaned forward and grabbed the back of the nearest man's collar and pushed the barrel of his Colt .45 caliber army-issue pistol against the man's head.

"I wouldn't do that if I were you," he commented in a quiet but unmistakably firm voice.

The man's head turned and Lenny knew he saw the pistol and felt its muzzle pressed hard against the side of his head.

"Oh hell, Tony!" the other man shouted, ducked, and ran for the main gate.

Lenny jerked his man down and fired a shot; the boom shattered the crystal serenity of the night, echoing and rattling around the hangars and buildings as it faded. The shot hit the ground just in front of the running man. "Come back here!"

Lenny knelt on his man's back and bound his wrists with a cord as he watched the second man stop without turning, hands in the air, trying to decide what to do.

A crowd was gathering and Lenny yelled, "Someone call the county sheriff. And the rest of you bring that man back here."

Sunday, June 11

Bump walked with Lenny up the ramp and stopped at a food vendor's tent. Lenny ordered a breakfast burrito with hot salsa and a large black coffee. The man at the stove waved and greeted Lenny by name. Lenny stepped to one side and thanked him for his help.

Bump looked at Lenny and then ordered the same.

"What was that all about?" Bump asked when he took his coffee and stood beside Lenny to wait.

"Bunch of the guys helped me out last night," Lenny admitted casually as he picked up his order. "Thanks. And thanks again for last night." The man and another nodded.

When Bump had his burrito and they started back toward their exhibit area, he started inquiring again.

"So you had a little trouble? And you haven't told me anything?"

"I wanted breakfast first," Lenny remarked, and took another bite. "Our two men from Meadow Lake stayed around last night and showed up about quarter till midnight."

"Well, what did they do?" Bump asked when Lenny paused

to sip his coffee and take another bite.

"I hate to say I was right"—Lenny smiled—"but when they couldn't get to West or Charlie, they must've assumed West and Charlie lived at the ranch and wanted us to lead them back there."

"They tried to plant a tracking beacon on the plane?" Bump was wide-eyed.

"I let them stick it in the wheel well," Lenny noted. "Then I collared the taller one, called Tony. The other tried to run, but a well-placed shot stopped him and woke everyone up. They helped corral him and we let the sheriff give them a place to stay for the night."

"Can you charge them with anything that'll stick?" Bump asked, and tossed his wrapper and empty cup into a trash barrel.

"No," Lenny admitted. "But they got the whole spiel on federal law and penalties for tampering with or damaging an airplane. Maybe they'll get the message. But the transmitter was a stick-on and the worst it could do would be interfering with avionics. They'll be out tomorrow morning, but the sheriff did say he'd give me a copy of everything they find out about them so we can give it to West. The sheriff is also aware these men are on the verge of being charged for stalking by West or Charlie."

"Too bad they can't keep them penned up," Bump commented as they stopped beside the van.

"We know who they are now. Maybe we can figure out how to put a tracker on them."

"I wish," Bump laughed.

Lenny looked at his watch, and Bump followed him as he walked back to the Hellcat, slipped around the right wingtip, and stopped in front of the right main landing gear strut. Lenny ducked under the wing, stood up in the wheel well, and pried the small module off the structure.

"This is the beacon they affixed last night," Lenny explained with a sly smile. "Watch the plane. I have to talk to a man about a trip."

"Huh?"

"Hey, Lenny," West said when he answered his phone. They had finished breakfast and everyone was heading off to enjoy their day. He and Charlie had just reached their office when West's phone rang.

"Stirred up some action for you," Lenny's voice said as West put the phone on speaker and sat down at his desk. Charlie settled cross-wise on his lap to listen.

"How so?"

"The two guys from Meadow Lake were here Friday afternoon and yesterday," Lenny explained. "It looked to me like they were looking for you and Charlie to show up. But of course you didn't."

"Were they pointed out to you?" West asked.

"Yup. Just like you hoped. That Norman fellow arrived about one or two Friday, and around dinnertime he stopped and told me they were here. Gave me his phone and told me to send the pictures he took of them to my phone, and told me to erase my number when I was done."

"Good, good. Did he say why he was there?"

"Only that he was asked to see if those guys were there, and if so, to let me know. He didn't say who asked him or why, just that he was."

"How did he introduce himself? Was he alone?" Charlie asked.

"Oh, good morning, Charlie. He was alone and said he was in a hurry to get back to his fiancée when he said goodbye Saturday morning. He introduced himself as the one that inappropriately mistook you for someone else in Reno last year. Nothing more."

"Looks like he can be trusted," West admitted, and smiled at Charlie. "Did you get a positive ID on the guys?"

"More than that," Lenny confirmed. "I figured right, that

111

when they couldn't find either of you, they'd try to get us to lead them to the ranch. They hid a tracking beacon in the wheel well of *Steppin' Out*." West felt Charlie stiffen, and then she got up and slowly left the room. "I slept with the plane last night and collared them after they had planted it. One's called Tony, and the other, Tommy. The sheriff has them for the day and will give me a copy for you of what he can find out about them before we leave."

"Very good." West smiled. "Can you deactivate the beacon and bring it back?"

"No," Lenny admitted softly. "It's fully encapsulated and operating, so I talked with Lucky Bingham. He has his Fifty-One, *Trust Me*, here and will take our beacon for a ride on his way back to Oregon."

"Tell him we owe him."

"I did. He seemed all too happy to help."

"Yeah, he would, after having his plane tracked a few years ago. Best the authorities could figure was his plane was targeted by a group of plane-nappers."

"Well, that's all I have. Bump will fly in the heritage flight and give his little demonstration around noon, and we should be heading back around three or so. That should get me in before midnight."

"Do you have the scanner with you?"

"Yeah. Nothing showed up on the van."

"We'll be looking for you when you get in. Stay safe and thanks. Same to Bump."

Cold fear suddenly wrapped its fingers tightly around Charlie's shoulders and she shuddered, listening to Lenny recounting the events of the previous evening. Surprised, she thought she had pushed her fears far enough aside to control them, but the thought of the tracking beacon and the fear suddenly returned. She had to get up. She had to move. She could not sit or stay in one place.

She slipped off West's lap and tried to look nonchalant, but she could not get out of the office quick enough. She tried to control the rising panic, but it was pulling her just like it had so many times before—Indianapolis, St. Louis, Des Moines, Kansas City—forcing her to move on, convincing her she had been someplace too long. And now, the search for her had expanded to jeopardize the ranch. Charlie did not know what to do, but she could not let her being there endanger the ranch and the people. Tears started rolling down her cheeks. It just was not fair. Not now.

Stepping into their bedroom, she pushed the door closed and the uncontrollable urge to run swept over her. Wiping her eyes, Charlie grabbed her duffel bag from the shelf in the closet and began stuffing it with underwear and socks from the dresser drawers, and blouses and tops from the hangers in the closet. She was folding her jeans and spreading them in the duffel as fast as she could when West pushed the door open and stood, staring at her.

"What's going on?" he asked as he watched her throw her clothes into her old bag.

"You know I can't stay," she sobbed, the tears welling up anew and running down her cheeks as she tried to close the bag's zipper. "I have to go..."

"What? What are you talking about?" West hurried around the foot of their bed.

She felt his body against her back as he bent over her and slip his arms around her. He drew her up in front of him, refusing to submit to her squirms, refusing to let her go.

"You are staying here with me," he encouraged softly, and held her tight. "You're okay."

"Let me go! You heard Lenny..." She slowly stopped trying to break free and turned in his embrace to face him. "I'm putting the ranch and the family in danger. If they can't find me somewhere else"—the tears were relentless—"they'll try to find our home, and everyone, everything you've worked so hard to protect will be in danger. All because of me."

He refused to relax, and she let her arms wrap around him and buried her face against his neck. The tears kept coming even as she felt his hands spread out on her back, holding her tight.

"Charlie, Charlie. It's okay," West consoled softly. "Someone is always trying to find the ranch. They have tried since I flew our first plane to its first airshow. We can handle them trying. It's usually because I'm here, I have money, I have many very valuable airplanes, and of what I have done with the restoration business that makes people try to find us. And someday they may, but we will know when they get close." West squeezed her tighter. "You are safer here with me, with us, than anywhere else, but I hope you want to stay because you love me. I love you and would rather die than let anything happen to you. Every person here will fight to keep you safe. This is your home."

"I want to be here," she whispered, forcing her ragged breath to calm. "But I can't put you or the ranch or any of our family in danger."

"We'll face this together, love," he encouraged. "We're here for you, just like I'm here for you. If there's any possible way, we won't let anything happen to you or the ranch. You're part of us now. You have a family that cares and will do anything to help you."

West turned, sat down on the edge of the bed, and pulled her onto his lap. She looked at him and he wiped her eyes.

"I can only imagine how very afraid this situation makes you," he comforted softly. "We're all afraid for you, but we're here. I'm here. I'll stand beside you and with you in whatever you do. You must know that. I'll protect you as much as I possibly can."

"Why will you do that? It makes no sense that you would do that, want to do that."

"I love you, Charlie. You're part of me and I don't want anything to hurt you. We all love you as part of our family. You have to see that, love."

She nodded her head slowly. "You keep telling me that, but it's so hard to believe I really have you and a real home with many friends. It's so different than how I grew up, so different than what was literally beat into me and my sister. My fears, my memories of how it was, still wake me in cold sweats, and I get up and sit outside to keep from waking you. I've been running for so long, it's hard to accept that I'm home now and I don't have to run anymore.

"That night in Reno, I almost ran again, but the thought of leaving without telling you stopped me cold. You have to understand that most of the time it's you that keeps the fears away, but my doubts let them back in. Don't stop reminding me, West. Please don't stop reminding me."

"I won't. You're 'my' Charlie and 'my' Charlotte," he soothed, and kissed her. "And I'm 'yours.' In every way. I *need* you too, and together we can weather anything. Please remember that and don't run away from me."

Nineteen

Woody stopped the jeep beside the sixth hangar and got out.

"Go give *Box Car* a preflight, Dani." He opened the people door to the hangar and held it for her. "I'll lower the ramp and open the main hangar door."

He followed Dani inside and went into the locker room between Hangars Five and Six to change. Dani went to the rooms between six and seven.

Dressed in his flight suit, Woody emerged and started the sequence of opening the hangar doors, first lowering the external ramp, and when it locked into place, the main door folded in two halves, upwards. He walked across the hangar to the Beaver parked in the space in front of *Hell Raiser* and *The Lady*, glancing at the T206 nestled in the corner behind *Lucky* on the near side of the hangar.

"How's the inspection?"

"Just finished," she replied, checking the last flap hinge on the pilot's side. "I had to replace a cotter pin on the elevator trim rod. Luckily, the nut had not spun off."

"Very good." He turned to the tug. "We'll get it out in the light, check the sumps, and then see how much you've forgotten since Friday."

After forty-five minutes of reviewing the basic flight maneuvers and airplane systems and controls, significantly different from the 172, Woody had Dani execute a wheel landing, a soft field takeoff, and then a full stall landing.

Dani stopped the Beaver in front of the open hangar and Woody smiled.

"Well, you have met my evaluation satisfactorily, again. Now, I would like for you take a half an hour or so and spend some time alone with the Beaver. Do some takeoffs and landings to feel settled before we top the tanks and fly up to Colorado Springs to pick up your parents and sister. They're expecting us to bring them home this afternoon."

"Certainly." Dani nodded and Woody got out and closed his door.

The P-51 *Trust Me* took off from the La Plata County airport behind *Steppin' Out*. Both planes turned west, and just past Basin Mountain, Lucky Bingham turned north with a wave and Bump turned south. *Trust Me* carried Lucky north across Grand Mesa, and in less than forty minutes, descended into a secluded mountain valley, eighteen miles northwest of Walden, Colorado. The long runway of the unregistered airport lay just a mile inside the state line west of Bear Mountain.

Lucky taxied *Trust Me* to a stop in front of an abandoned Quonset hut hangar set back beside the newer, currently used, tightly locked, four-plane-sized hangar. He climbed out of *Trust Me* and walked into the cluttered building full of derelict aircraft and farm equipment parts, pieces and otherwise neglected contents, found an old coffee can on a dusty shelf in a dark, back corner. He dropped the beacon transmitter into it and put the can back on the shelf. Lucky returned to *Trust Me*, restarted, and taxied out to the nearest end of the runway. In another two minutes, he was climbing west just north of Buffalo Ridge.

"Hey, Cee," Norman called from his chair on the upstairs

terrace. Since they had moved and begun living together, Norman had started calling Celia by her first initial, Cee, as a more intimate nickname. Celia had responded by doing the same for him. "Looks like my trip was for a good purpose."

"Oh? Well, En, you should come and tell me about it," Celia answered from the master bedroom but did not come out.

Norman slowly got up, reading the article as he walked back inside.

"It's a pretty evening tonight, En." She stepped out onto the back deck.

Norman looked over the section of the Sunday paper he was holding and saw her waiting in her panties.

"Hot tub's ready." Her expression was asking if he was. She disappeared toward the tub.

Norman tossed the paper on the bed, quickly shed his shoes and T-shirt, and followed her. He threw the rest of his clothes on the chair beside the tub and joined her.

"I knew I was missing something today." He stretched out in the water and slipping his arm around her, pulling her length against him.

"Now what were you talking about that was so urgent?" She kissed him.

"I can't remember," he teased, and squeezed her.

"Come on. You sounded like it was important."

"Okay. I hate to interrupt what you've started, but there's a short article about the fly-in in Durango—the one I was asked to go to. Seems the two men we saw at Meadow Lake were there, like I told you when I got back, but it also seems they were caught tampering with the Hellcat that the Ghost Ranch had on display."

"Tampering?"

"The article doesn't say what they did, but both of them were taken to jail by the La Plata County Sheriff and held for twenty-four hours."

"Aah." Celia nodded. "They didn't charge them."

"Obviously they didn't do anything to damage the plane, but it might have given them a scare. You remember it's a federal offence to do harm to a flyable airplane?"

"Yes, I know that."

"Well, I can just hope giving Lenny those pictures helped him catch those guys."

She thought about what he was saying. "What do you suppose they would want to do to the plane?"

"I'm not sure," he admitted softly. "Neither West nor Charlie were there. So I wonder if they tried to put something on the plane so they could follow it back to the ranch."

"I understand there are tracking devices that can do that." She playfully splashed his face. "But I bet Lenny already had that figured out."

He smiled and splashed her back. "Probably so." He rolled toward her. "I think I'll let them worry about that for now. It is a beautiful night and I'm with my beautiful woman and all is well."

Monday, June 12

Howard took the chair behind the table to one side of the restaurant's dining room, nicely secluded from the murmurs of the other patrons. Waiting for Monte to join him for lunch, Howard had just finished ordering coffee when his phone chimed. He answered and the waiter returned and poured a cup.

"Mr. Collingsworth," Tony's voice greeted him.

"Morning. What do you have to report?"

"Mr. and Mrs. West were not there this weekend," Tony explained. "They had an airplane there with a pilot and a mechanic, but no Mr. or Mrs. West."

Tony continued to explain how the weekend had progressed, including being caught just after they put the tracking beacon on the plane.

"Did they find the transmitter?" Howard asked.

"I don't know. We're still getting a signal, but it's weak. We'll see where it is and then let you know."

Howard was on his second cup of coffee when Monte came in and took the chair across from him. He smiled and asked if Howard had ordered yet.

"No," Howard admitted. "I was talking with my men in Colorado."

"Did they talk to her?"

Howard shook his head and looked at the menu. "She wasn't there, so they will try to follow the plane back to their base."

The waiter returned and he said they were ready to order. He gave his choice and Monte made a quick decision and ordered the pork chop special.

"I got an email from Sam and Lloyd this morning, the men I sent to Jackson Hole to check out the woman Charlie's story," Monte added. "They said the names and the dates they've found all agree."

He spent some time explaining what they had gone through to find the family home and its cemetery.

"Hmm. So the information agrees?" Howard questioned. "They've confirmed her parents' names?"

"Yes. They talked to the city clerk and verified the family lived in the area, the work her father did, when they died, and they have rubbings from their headstones. They verified the aunt and that Charlie owns the property now."

"So you're convinced this woman is just a lookalike," Howard said.

"Yes. We've verified her birth certificate data," Monte continued. "We have a reasonable list of the places she's worked and have visited with a few to confirm she actually worked there. The city clerk even said his parents knew the Bassets and their daughter. Everything checks out."

The waiter stopped beside their table, set their orders before them, and refilled their drinks. When he left, Monte continued.

"I know this means you haven't found Emli yet"—he leaned closer—"but it's good to know, so you don't do something improper, like mistaking Charlie for the wrong woman."

"Humph," Howard muttered. "Maybe so."

They ate lunch and changed the topic to other aspects of the business: the progress of their European project and construction resources they needed for the land development requirements.

When they finished, Monte said his goodbyes and started back to his office. Howard pondered what Monte had said, and then he activated his phone and accessed his email server.

Monte got into his car and pulled out onto the street. Once he was comfortable with the traffic, he pulled out his phone and tapped a speed dial icon.

"Cat," he greeted when she answered. "Are you alone?"

"Yes," she replied. "The kids are next door."

He explained what his men in Jackson Hole had told him. "I just told your dad and I can't tell if he's really accepting the news. At least we haven't uncovered anything that indicates that woman Charlie is your sister Emli."

"You told him," Cat emphasized, "but don't trust him."

Howard watched Monte leave the restaurant as he tapped an email message to Tony.

> Find out where the plane went and follow it.
> Bring me the woman. Do whatever you have to
> do to get her, then bring her to me, alive. Take
> her to the place I told you about in Port Huron.
> Email me when you have her. HC

Howard reread the message and accessed the server account. He marked the message for deletion once it was sent. Then he tapped Send.

Tuesday, June 13

West was waiting for everyone to settle at the breakfast table when his phone rang. He glanced at it and immediately touched Charlie on the shoulder, gesturing for her to follow him.

"Excuse us, we need to take this," he said as the phone rang a second time. "Please go ahead and start without us."

He caught Charlie's arm as he headed for the veranda and answered the call.

"Ham and cheese. Encrypt," Jessie's voice said, and he touched the icon.

He stopped at the far end of the veranda and sat down on a loveseat, motioning Charlie to sit beside him. He switched the phone to speaker and lowered the volume as he held it between them.

"Morning. It's early for you," he greeted. "What's up?"

"Morning," she answered. "Is Charlie with you?"

"Yes. Good morning," Charlie answered.

"Good, good. I have a little good news and some news I'm not sure about. I was away from my computer last night but I downloaded yesterday's and last night's traffic this morning and read through it while I'm getting ready for work."

They waited while she formed her thoughts.

"The good news, I guess," Jessie started again, "is that someone named Monte you mentioned sent a team of two, a Sam and a Lloyd, to Jackson, Wyoming, to verify facts they found from your birth certificate and city cemetery records. The good news is they reported back that everything checked out, as if they were expecting it not to. I guess I don't understand."

"Jess," Charlie said heavily, "they saw a picture of me and

123

think I'm someone else. We think they are looking for some way to prove that I am the someone else."

"Aah, well, then you might not be surprised at my next bit of news."

"Go ahead," Charlie urged.

"There was an incomplete email marked for immediate erasure, from that Howard to someone named Tony, telling him to find out where some airplane went and to follow it. Do you know what that's about?"

"Yes," West admitted softly. "We had a plane at a fly-in this weekend, and this Tony and his accomplice, Tommy, tried to sneak a beacon on board so they could follow it to the ranch."

"O-kaaay," Jessie responded, slowly emphasizing the word. "Then he told this man Tony to find and bring him the woman... From what you're saying, I...I...think he means you, Charlie. The message cut off there." Jessie paused a minute. "Charlie, I'm sorry to bring you something that sounds so ominous, but I had to tell you as soon as I could."

"Thanks. I'm glad you did." Charlie caught West's hand, squeezing it gently.

"Thank you," West repeated. "Keep listening. We'll step up our guard. Send us the copies?"

"Sure. Coming your way in just a minute," she acknowledged softly. "I'm so sorry."

"You're helping more than you know," Charlie encouraged. "Keep in touch."

West disconnected and slipped his arm around Charlie's shoulder, pulling her close.

"Well, you always feared he'd try to come after you," he whispered. "But to try to take someone he can't prove is his daughter is completely unacceptable. If Tony or his buddy show up around the Broomfield fly-in, I think I'll have them detained under a charge of stalking. That could buy us thirty days or more before they could get a hearing. If they actually try anything, they might get themselves wounded or worse. But if you want to stay here and not go to Broomfield, I'll understand." West kissed her and cocked his head. "What I want to know, though, is how Charlie Basset's inheritance came about and how she got the land her 'parents' lived on in Jackson."

"There was a little mix-up over the ownership of the land," Charlie said, and smiled tightly. "Charlie's aunt did not get the papers signed correctly before she passed away and Charlie had to petition for ownership, using her birth certificate and a few other legal papers to get the filing done. It did cost her a little, but after a few months and a few flights back out there, it worked out. Charlie Basset, now Charlie West, is the legal owner of her parents' homestead and a suitable amount of the surrounding hillside. If necessary, she has somewhere else she can hide."

He kissed Charlie again and helped her up. "Are you okay? I don't want you hiding anywhere except here."

"Of course I'm not all right." She hugged him tight.

West returned her embrace and held her for a long moment.

"This is *our* life. And I'm not going to miss living a moment of it. If you're flying, so am I. Where you go, I'm going."

"When you're flying or away from the ranch," West said softly, before he let her go, "keep your nine millimeter in your pocket. I'll do likewise. And after breakfast, I want you to go with me and Ratchet out to stores. You need to know what kind of airplane mods I'm doing."

"Okay," Charlie agreed with a deep sigh. "Now, take me back to breakfast, love." She kissed him, took his hand, and led him back into the house.

Saturday, June 17

Charlie rode in silence beside West as he drove the jeep past the hangars to the northeast. She understood, but was uncomfortable with the truth behind what they were about to see. He had taken the possible need to protect her and the ranch to a new height and it scared her almost as much as the relentless search for Emli did.

As they rounded the new Hangar Eight, she saw *The Lady* and *Hell Raiser* poised side by side on special jacks to hold the planes level. They stopped behind and between the two planes, and studying the space in front of them, she saw two white squares in the distance.

West got out and helped her as Ratchet and Woody walked up to them.

"Looks like you're all set up," he observed. Charlie stood solemnly beside him.

"Yes." Ratchet nodded. "Targets are set at nine hundred feet, bore sighted to converge at that range. That's just over two seconds at three hundred miles per hour. Bump's down range."

"Very good." West smiled. "Lenny and Dani are coming. Charlie, I want you in *The Lady* and Ratchet will take *Hell Raiser.*"

"You sure you don't want to be in one or the other?" Ratchet asked.

"I've been there, Ratchet," West admitted softly as Lenny drove up and stopped his jeep beside West's. "Looks like everyone's here."

Charlie studied West briefly, a curious frown crossing her face as she wondered when he would have fired a plane's machine guns, but she did not have long to wait.

"I remember." Ratchet nodded. "That fighter pilot training school you went to in Florida, what? Five years ago?"

"Four," West replied absently as he led Charlie behind *The Lady.*

"Lenny"—Ratchet pointed to *The Lady*—"you take the left guns, and Woody, the right guns. Dani, take a seat up on *Hell Raiser*'s left wing, near the tip."

"I really don't like you doing this," Charlie admitted. "It's dangerous to bystanders."

"I know." He squeezed her hand gently. "We won't have any ammo on board unless we need it. The ammo will be in the van or in the semi, close by but securely locked up."

"That helps a little." She forced a smile.

126

"And we should not have to sign off any maintenance items," he added, "while the guns are installed. If we do, I will install breach plugs to render them inoperable."

Charlie smiled again.

"I know you and Ratchet can't sign off the airplane in its, I'll say, 'experimental' condition," he confessed, and helped her up on the wing.

He followed her up and helped her into the cockpit.

"Feels odd to get in with *The Lady* up in level attitude," Charlie commented, and settled into the seat.

"Helmet and seat belt at least," West stated, and reached down and handed her the buckle. "In case she slips off the tail stand."

"Got it. Thanks." She fastened the lap belt. "What do I do?"

"We've loaded two hundred rounds on each side," he began. "When Bump gives us an 'All Clear' on the radio and you're ready to fire, give the gun trigger a short squeeze. Each gun fires about eight rounds a second, so a short one-second burst will give a picture of where the bullets are hitting versus where we think the guns are aimed. We'll work on getting *The Lady* harmonized and then move to *Hell Raiser.*"

"Harmonized? Making them converge at the range of the target?"

"Yup, that's it." West smiled and stood up and looked at Ratchet over the cockpit. "Charge the left gun."

Then he looked down range and saw Bump in the third jeep, driving off to their left. He stopped well to the side and turned the jeep around to face the targets.

"The range is clear," Bump called over the radio.

"Okay," West continued softly. "Break the brass wire on the guard and flip the 'Gun Master' switch up." He watched as she followed his instructions. "Next, switch the Sight Gyro on, then select Guns, Camera, and Sight."

She flipped the gyro and selector switch and glanced up at him. He nodded, then looked up over the cockpit again.

"Guns are live!" he shouted. Then he looked at Charlie as he knelt down beside the cockpit. "Tell Bump you're live."

"Ghost Two and *The Lady* are live," she announced softly into her mike.

"Roger, Ghost Two. The range is yours."

"Look at the sight and the circle of diamonds with the very small dot in the middle. The target is the white square," he said in a loud whisper. "If we calculated right, the bullets should fall to the center of the circle, the dot at that range."

"I can barely see the target." She stared at the gun sight.

"Rotate the handle on the throttle to bring the circle in to match the width of the target, and hold it for one second."

"Aah," she whispered.

"She's yours, anytime," he urged, and gently touched her shoulder.

She inhaled and steadied her stare through the reticule. Slowly, she rotated the handle with her left hand and squeezed the trigger with her right forefinger.

The brilliant morning sun broke over the horizon in unison with the sudden cackle of the left fifty cal piercing the silence, a different rooster crowing to herald in the suddenly different morning.

"Low and to the left," Ratchet said loudly from his place on the right wing beside Woody, his feet dangling over the leading edge as he studied the white square through his large binoculars.

"Switch the selection from Guns back to Off," West commanded gently, and waited as Charlie absorbed the moment. Then finally, with a twitch of her head, she reached up and flipped the selector switch.

"Ghost Five, *The Lady* is secure. Making an adjustment," she announced into her mike, and slowly turned to look at West.

He smiled as Lenny opened the left gun bay, bent down,

and made an adjustment. Finally he looked up, gave a thumbs-up, closed the bay cover, and sat down on the left wing near the tip.

West nodded to Charlie. "Again."

"Ghost Five, *The Lady* is ready for a second run," she announced.

"The range is clear," Bump answered.

She went through the routine again and called Bump as she flipped the gun selector switch to Guns. "*The Lady* is live."

"Roger."

The short cackle wasn't as much of a surprise this time, and she let herself smile. She remembered buying her 9 millimeter from her uncle and having to sneak out to learn how to shoot it, but this was different—not filled with so much hate and anger. She flipped the gun switch off and called Bump.

Then she sat back and put her hands on the windscreen frame and looked at West.

"Not so bad?" he asked.

"Not so bad, love," she answered, suddenly feeling less stressed over the situation.

"Left looks good," Ratchet announced.

"Charge the right gun," West shouted loudly.

She repeated the process and was pleased when Ratchet announced, "The right looks good. Set up both."

"Confirm both left and right guns are charged," West said, again in a loud voice.

"Left's charged," Lenny shouted, followed by Woody's, "Right's charged."

With a nod, Charlie repeated the procedure and fired. Both guns rattled the morning and Ratchet studied the target. Then he lowered the binoculars and smiled.

"Both are on the money. Everything's well inside an eighteen-inch circle."

Howard turned to his computer, opened his mail server, and checked his business inbox. He browsed the normal clutter of messages, scanning and discarding any that were unimportant. Others he filed in folders assigned to relevant business topics. He stopped and studied the two remaining messages, both from Tony.

Howard was certain they would not have anything to report that would further his case, but he did wonder about the mysterious ranch. He clicked on the subject line of the first message, time stamped late the previous night.

> Mr. Collingsworth. We have tracked the beacon up near the northern Colorado state line. It is late, dark and we are going to stop in Walden at the Chester Inn and start again in the morning. Will send more information then. Tony.

Howard opened a map program to see where Walden, Colorado, was, and then he clicked on the second message, timestamped midmorning.

> Mr. Collingsworth. We located the beacon at a small landing strip a mile from the Wyoming border, in a mountain valley about eighteen miles by road northwest of a town called Cowdrey. There were two hangars there, one new and locked up and one old, abandoned Quonset style full of airplane and farm junk. The beacon is stashed in that one but we cannot put our hands on it. Too many hiding places. Could not tell how many or what kind of planes are in the other, small hangar, but I think it's safe

to say this is not the Ghost Ranch with many
restored fighter airplanes. We are returning to
the Denver area. Tony.

Howard slapped his desktop and turned his chair to face the
bookcase across the room. He was not expecting Tony to find
anything useful, but not finding anything did not make him feel
any better; he still wanted that woman. When he got through
with her, she'd admit to being Emli! He was certain of that! And
then she'd pay doubly, for hiding from him, for the lost monies
she had cost him, for the long delays and penalties he had to
pay for not being able to fulfill his arrangements—and once he
had her, he would not have to face the rider on his contract. Yes,
he thought. He'd make her pay, all right. And he'd enjoy every
minute extracting that payment.

Howard turned back to his computer and clicked on a reply.

Tony. Find that woman and that ranch! Find
someone that knows where it is! And go get her!
I am running out of patience! HC

After lunch, West led Charlie out onto the front veranda and
sat down on the loveseat.

"Are you more comfortable with the guns on the planes than
you were this morning?" West asked, and took her hand.

"Some," she admitted. "The reason still scares me a lot, and I
really don't like the idea that you, we, might have to use them."

"The reason scares me too, love," West confirmed. "But
this effort to find you, and the ranch as a means to find you,
is a lot different than we've seen before. And I am going to
do everything I can to keep you safe, even if I have to shoot
someone."

"I know you will"—he squeezed his hand—"but I don't have to like that you might have to do it." She sighed and looked down the valley. "But if I think about it logically, like all of the other mechanical systems on the plane, the guns are just another system. They're like a big rifle, and getting to shoot them is a real treat. They make you feel so very powerful." She thought a minute. "Does the ATF know you have real machine guns?"

"Yes." He smirked. "They're part of the authentic equipment these planes had. Of course, the law is that one can't fly around with operational guns and live ammunition. And we'd *never* do that. Technically, we have to put the breech plugs in the guns if we have them installed in a flying airplane."

"Of course not," Charlie agreed softly, and held his eyes. "Not unless there was some kind of an emergency or serious threat to life and limb."

"That's why we have a few plugs that can be removed"—he nodded with a smile—"in case that emergency happens."

West turned at a soft knock behind them and saw Belle standing in the doorway, holding one of the doors open.

"May I interrupt?" she asked, and West smiled at her.

"Certainly." Charlie gestured to a chair. "Come and join us."

"Thank you." She smiled and moved to the chair.

"We were just reviewing the morning," he explained. "What can we do for you?"

Belle looked nervously at West, and then glanced at Charlie before she swallowed and straightened her shoulders.

"I was talking with Helen a few days ago, and this morning she told me I would have to talk to you," she started softly. "I don't want you to think I'm ungrateful for all you've done for me and our family, and especially the things you've let me learn and do here on the ranch."

West waited while she glanced from the wall to the floor, trying to put her words together properly.

"You're very welcome," Charlie encouraged. "But if there's something you'd like to change, please let us know."

"Thank you, ma'am, er, sorry, Charlie." She swallowed again. "It's just that I never thought you'd consider it and then you came, and that changed everything. And now Rose is working with the planes and has learned...Well, we didn't think she'd ever get the opportunity and now she's a pilot and all, and..."

"Belle?" West asked when she paused. "Do you want to learn to fly also?"

Her head bobbed slowly but words did not come out at first. "I...I really appreciate being able to learn what Helen does and talking with the pilots and watching them come and go, and I know it's important and that Helen needs the help, especially when we're busy, but...well, yes. I'd like to try to become the ranch's third woman pilot."

West winked at Charlie and then rubbed his chin.

"Let's see." He thought for a moment. "You're seventeen, right?"

Belle nodded slowly.

"And your birthday is in the fall?"

"I'll be eighteen on September twelfth," Belle said softly.

"Hmm," West uttered, and glanced at Charlie's dancing eyes. "And you want to be a Ghost Ranch pilot?"

"Yes, sir. I'd like to earn the right to be called Eddie, the third in line, and to have a Ghost designation and fly where and when you need or want me to fly." Then she stopped and looked down. "I know I'll still need to help Helen, but if there's time, I'd like to fly."

"Well," West continued with a huge smile, "I think we can get Helen some added help so you can have time to learn."

"Really?" she asked, her disbelief obvious in her pitched voice and wide eyes.

"Yes," West said, and reached for her hand. "I will talk with Helen and Woody and get a plane arranged. Consider yourself a student, and Woody will make an announcement at dinner tonight. By the way, you'll be sitting at the dining room table for your meals from now on, starting tonight."

"Thank you." She jumped forward and hugged West tightly,

and then turned to hug Charlie. "Thank you. I can't wait to tell Rose, er, Dani and Mama." She stood up and regained her poise. "I will try to make you proud of me. Thank you."

"I'm already proud of you," West said softly. "You follow Woody's instructions and learn what you're taught, and you will do fine. Now, git along and share your good news."

Belle smiled and hurried back into the house.

"They almost treat you like a father," Charlie noted with a chuckle.

"I guess I'd have to say sometimes I feel like I am. I'm as proud of them as any father could be." West smiled. "Helen has her flight suit almost finished."

Charlie chuckled again. "You were right when you said she'd ask soon."

West nodded. "Once Rose started, I knew it wouldn't be long, so I talked it over with Mom and Madra to be sure everyone would be okay with it." Then he looked at Charlie. "You know you've started something here. Camilla will be next, but she has to wait a few years. She's only fourteen now, but that doesn't mean we can't get her ready early."

"I'm surprised the boys haven't asked," Charlie admitted.

"I am too, though Philip has inquired but hasn't started." He took her hand as he got up. "Let's tell Mom officially and then go up and talk to Woody."

West stood at the head of the dinner table beside his chair, like he always did, and watched as Charlie took her place on his left and Helen took hers on his right. He noticed Becky had added the wide extension in the table as Bump and Dani took their places on Charlie's side of the table, leaving a space for Woody between them. Lenny and Ratchet took their places down from Helen, leaving the last chair on that side empty.

"Before we start," West said to everyone, "Woody has an announcement."

West turned to the doorway behind him and Woody

134

stepped in with his arm through Belle's. He walked down Helen's side of the table, pulled out the empty chair, and Belle sat down, trying to remain calm and to act proper. Woody then stepped to the end of the table and turned to face everyone.

"May I present our newest student pilot, Miss Belle Ventura. I have arranged for a plane from Will Little again and a flight physical for Belle next week on Wednesday. I will need Dani to fly us up to the Springs Wednesday morning. As you know, once Belle solos, we will bestow her nickname and Ghost identification." Then he looked at her with a wide smile. "Your training will begin on the trip home, so read your part ninety-one to be ready. I'll answer any questions you may have. Charlie, can you make time to teach the ground school again?"

"Yes"—Charlie nodded and smiled at Belle—"I'm happy to do the ground school."

"Thank you." Woody nodded, then walked around and took his chair. He raised his water glass. "To Belle."

Monday, June 19

Monte bathed and got ready for bed as usual and noticed Cat had donned her long pajamas again, even though the weather was warm, like she had since the first of the month when he had confronted her about the missing pages in Michael's airshow booklet. He regretted how he had handled his questioning, how he had treated her with the way he asked, making her feel like she had done something unthinkable. Afterwards, Monte had realized how much of Cat's past he did not know, never thought to ask her about, and how much it had shaped her perceptions, her likes and dislikes. He had never realized how different her childhood had been from his.

He felt he was closer to her before their "discussion," when she was more afraid of him, but now...He wanted her to want him rather than just having to be with him. He had to admit it was something he had never thought about, thinking a marriage meant a couple would go through the motions, even intimate motions, and would eventually come to like and even love each other, no matter how the marriage came to be. But, he realized, it did not work that way. Not like he thought. It would be so much better to be in love first.

Cat had been more serious that night than he had ever seen her. She was not angry nor was she apologetic. She had finally gotten to a point where she had made up her mind, and the reasons and position she took were not open for negotiation. She was suddenly different, stalwart, and he had to admit he liked seeing her that way.

"I talked to your father today," he said by way of making conversation.

"Did he have more for you to do for him?" she asked as she slipped her light robe on and sat down on the edge of their bed with her back to him.

"No." He forced himself to not rise to her challenging tone. "I gave him more information that my investigators have found out about the woman, Charlie. He seemed almost uninterested in hearing it."

"I told you," she reiterated. "He already has his mind made up and you won't be able to change it."

"Maybe not"—Monte sat down beside her—"but short of locking him up, I don't know how to keep him from going after her."

She turned, looked at him, and held his eyes with a blank stare. He knew he should know how, but he did not.

"You may have to take a more pro-active role," she finally stated, and stood up. Her tone made it obvious that she thought he ought to know what to do. "I'm going to fix myself some tea and read for a while. Get a good night's sleep."

Monte watched as she went to the door and slipped out into the hallway. He suddenly missed her goodnight kisses. Even if they may have been fakes or forced before, he missed them.

Cat warmed a kettle of water and poured it into a teapot with a tea basket to let it steep. She carried it, a cup, and a saucer into her craft room and sat down at her desk. With only the small desk lamp turned on, she took a small flat key from the lap drawer and walked over to the wide closet. There, she lifted the bottom edge of a stack of printed cloth and unlocked a flat metal box hidden beneath the stack.

She laid the ten cards and one envelope on the desk and poured the tea into her cup. Then she slid the envelope from the bottom of the stack and pulled the card from within. She inhaled the vague perfume, remembering it was Emli's favorite; she had only received the one scented card.

She removed the card from the envelope and looked at the small slip of paper that slid out with it, remembering how she had rediscovered it when she had gone back to study the cards a few months earlier.

"What were you trying to tell me, Emli?" she asked herself in the barest of a whisper as she spread the piece out under the light.

She remembered the sketch of a trunk, angled to look at the top and corner with the lid open. A dotted line indicating the rectangular bottom of the trunk, but the arrow pointing up from inside confused her. She studied the picture and sipped her tea. She knew the trunk was their grandfather's trunk because the key Emli included had worked in it. She had found the .45 caliber army pistol Emli told her about and she had found the other pistol, the 9 millimeter she said was there as well. Because of Emli's example, she had "borrowed" the 9 millimeter and still kept it under her own mattress, just in case. She was still afraid Monte might turn out to be too much like their father.

She sipped her tea and reread the simple note Emli had included: "If you're strong enough, everything you need to stop father is here. Be very careful if you try and do not let him find what I have hidden. You know what he would do."

Yes, she realized, she did know what he would do. And dying was something she wanted to avoid as long as she possibly could.

Suddenly, she looked at the picture and realized the floor indicated in the sketch was not the "bottom" of the trunk, but drawn higher. Maybe a false bottom! Her heart jumped and she started to get up, but quickly stopped herself. She did not know if she could actually trust Monte, but thought most likely not. Then she realized she would have to figure a way to get into her parents' house without them knowing, and check out the trunk—again without them knowing.

"That's going to be difficult," she whispered to herself again.

She slipped the card and paper back into the envelope, replaced it in the stack, and returned them to the metal box. She locked the box and slipped the key back into her lap drawer as she sat down at her desk again.

She inhaled and picked up a novelette she had started, and read a while as she finished her tea. Then she picked up her teapot, cup, and saucer and took them to the kitchen. She washed, rinsed, and dried them and put them away. As she went back to her craft room to turn the lamp off, she saw Monte coming down the stairs.

"Everything all right?" she asked.

"No," he said with a sheepish smile. "I don't like going to bed alone. After sleeping with you all of these years, I find I don't like sleeping without you."

She waited, knowing she also missed him, but she did not move or say anything.

"Please?" he asked. "I may not be able to change your father's mind, but maybe I can figure a way to stop those he has searching for her. I'll really try, Cat."

She nodded. "Okay, Monte. I'll come to bed, but that's all. If you want more than that, it's going to have to wait until you've earned it."

He held out his hand and she looked at him a long moment before she took it.

"I'll try."

Twenty
Tuesday, June 20

Monte sat down at his desk, and set his deli coffee cup on a coaster and his bagged breakfast sandwich on the desk. He glanced around the room and at the clear desktop, but he was not actually looking at anything. His mind was on Cat and her changed manner and attitude. In the fifteen years they'd been married, this was the first time she had taken such a determined stand.

But the content of their discord brought him back to his dilemma: somehow, he had to figure out how to keep Howard or his men from finding and kidnapping the woman, Charlie West.

Monte switched his computer on and took his sandwich and napkin out of the paper bag. He ate it and drank his coffee, thinking about his options. Then he turned to the computer and opened his emails. He sorted the incoming messages into various business folders and deleted those that had no significance.

One from Lloyd and Sam held his attention and a thought crossed his mind: if he met with them, maybe they could find Tony and Tommy and get them to stop their search.

Monte got up and went to the lobby and asked his secretary, Alice, if she had any coffee made yet. He was pleased when she did and filled his regular mug for him.

Back in his office, he sat down and stared at the screen. He didn't think he could dissuade Tony, but he had to do something and at the moment, talking face-to-face with Lloyd and Sam was the best he had come up with. He opened Lloyd's message.

Mr. Williamson. Sam and I are back in Denver,

waiting for your next request. Contact me at
your earliest convenience. Lloyd.

Monte reached for his desk phone, picked up the handset,
and tapped the speed dial button for his home.

"Cat?" he asked when the connection was made.

"No, Dad. It's me. Mel," Melony said with a giggle. "Just a
minute."

He heard her tell Cat he was on the phone.

"Hello," she answered, sounding cautious.

"Hey. You know Mel's starting to sound a lot like you. I was
thinking about what you want me to do, and I'm going to go to
Denver and meet with my investigators," he explained. "I was
wondering if you and the kids would like to take a few weeks
and go with me."

"You're going to be gone for a few weeks?" she asked,
startled.

"Only if you and the kids go," he clarified. "Otherwise I'd
only be gone overnight."

"When?" she asked, and sighed. "What would we do?"

"I want to go out on Friday, and there are a lot of things
to do," he said, and read things off the Denver website he had
called up while they talked. "And I see there's an airshow there
for the Fourth of July weekend. Mike and Mel would like that.
Call it a vacation, Cat. We haven't taken a vacation since the
kids were very young."

"I'm sure they would enjoy it," she agreed. "Are you going to
work all the time, or can it really be a vacation?"

"I will limit my work to the problem at hand. I'm hoping
my investigators can head off your dad's guys. I don't know if I
can make it work, but I'm going to try. And the rest of the time
I'll be on vacation too."

He waited a long moment while she thought about his
suggestion.

"Okay," she relented. "I think the children will enjoy it a lot."

"Good"—a spark of hope could barely be hidden in his tone—"and I hope you will too. I'll get tickets and make hotel arrangements. Do you have any preferences?"

"Probably just someplace with a pool and a hot tub," she admitted, thinking a moment. "I'll get things around here ready."

"Would you like for me to come home early and help?" he asked.

"I'll leave that up to you." Her tone was still unemotional. "I'll be happy if you get the travel arrangements made."

"Okay," he agreed. "I'll see you this afternoon."

He hung up after the connection broke and turned back to the computer. He composed a short message for Lloyd.

> "Lloyd. I will be in Denver Friday on a family vacation. My plan is to meet with you and Sam Saturday morning and discuss our next move. Plan to be available. I will call you when I get in and arrange a time and place. Monte."

Monte reread the message and clicked the 'Send' icon. He exited the mail server and returned to the hotel listings for Denver. After a few minutes, he turned and tapped his intercom.

"Alice, will you book four tickets for me and the family to Denver on this Friday? Return on the ninth."

"Yes, Mr. Williamson," she replied. "Do you want me to make hotel reservations?"

"I will, but show me what my choices are. I want a place the kids and Cat can enjoy and relax in—pool, hot tub, maybe water rides, nice restaurant, those sorts of things."

"I'll get right on it," she said, and closed the connection.

Before West and Charlie could join the others for lunch, Helen caught them as they came in the side door.

"You received another 'interesting' email this morning," Helen said softly. "It's from someone named Jessie."

"Was it marked 'Urgent?'" he asked as they stopped just inside the door.

"No," Helen admitted. "Didn't you hire a Jessie once?"

"Yes, Mom." He smiled. "She's the same one. Remember when Charlie and I went to Austin a month ago? We met and talked to her then."

"You didn't say, or I'm getting forgetful." Helen shook her head. "Go eat now. I'm sure it'll wait. I just wanted you to know so you can check it out before you go back up. How's the TF coming?"

"Very nicely," Charlie admitted. "It might be ready for engine runs in another couple of weeks."

"Very good." Helen pushed them toward the dining room. "Soon you'll have two of your own planes to fly. Go eat now."

"I wonder what sort of an update Jess has this time," he pondered absently as he took his chair in their office, pulling Charlie onto his lap as he sat down.

"Can't be too urgent if she didn't call," Charlie supposed optimistically.

West clicked the mail icon and then Jess's message.

> Good morning West, Charlie. I would have called, but these seem to be repeats of the information you have already received. Saturday, that man Howard received a message from and

replied to Tony and Tommy who had followed a 'beacon' to someplace in northern Colorado. Their message said it wasn't at the Ghost Ranch. Howard's answer was angry and demanding they find the woman.

This morning, the man Monte contacted Lloyd and Sam, the two he sent to Jackson Hole to check out your family names, Charlie. He says he's going to Denver on Friday and wants to meet with them on Saturday. Did not sound too urgent to me, so I sent the copies rather than call and cause any undue concerns.

I will keep listening. Let me know if I need to do something else. Jess.

They reread Jess's message and West saved it with the others they had received from her.

"Monte's going to be in Denver? On Friday?" Charlie absently asked, trying to understand. "And his investigators are there now?"

"What is it?" he asked softly, hearing the rising concern in her voice. "I don't understand."

"They're all here! Monte and his investigators are just up the road in Denver."

"Yes. People often go places for business meetings—"

"Will they be at Broomfield?"

"Maybe. I don't know." He squeezed her waist, pulling her closer. "Remember, these are the ones that verified your past, not the ones trying to capture you."

"Yeah, you're right," she sighed, and squeezed his free hand. "But if Monte shows up at Broomfield, and sees me, I don't know if I can hide knowing him."

"Maybe we can just keep him from seeing you."

"You know he'll see me if he's there and I'm there. He's

coming because Emli's lookalike is here."

"Yeah, you're right." He laid his head against hers. "We'll just have to do the best we can."

"Easy for you to say."

"Come on. We'll read the details of Jess's cache later, tonight, before we go to bed. But now, we have work to do." He stood her up and took her hand. "Back to the TF?"

"Yeah." She forced herself to smile. "I'm getting excited about that, getting closer. I think I am starting to see the end of the tunnel."

"You spend much more time up there," he chuckled as he hugged her, "and I'll have to put a cot beside your desk. I'm jealous."

Karl deVon, Deputy Minister of Rural Development, closed the door behind him as he entered the large office of Elrich Voster, Deputy Minister of South Africa's State Security. "You asked to see me?" deVon asked as he stopped in front of the large, ornate desk.

"Yes," Deputy Minister Voster said, and laid the papers he was reading on his desk. He looked up. "Have you heard something concerning Howard Collingsworth?" He gestured to the chair beside the desk.

"Some," deVon answered as he settled onto the chair. "Your man Collingsworth sent two men to the state of Colorado. His emails to them indicate he thinks his long-lost daughter is there somewhere. He said she had been seen a little more than a month ago, and again at an airport near the city of Colorado Springs about two weeks ago. "

Voster's eyes went wide. "He thinks he has found her?"

Minister deVon nodded. "His communications imply he may have. He has them looking for 'that woman.' He hasn't been on a hunt this serious since she disappeared."

Voster rubbed his chin. "I have not heard anything from the men I sent to follow Howard. Get in touch with them and see what they know. You have their contact information."

"Very good," deVon said, and stood up. "I'll let you know what I find out."

Wednesday, June 21

"I don't think I've ever seen Belle so excited," Charlie admitted.

"To tell you the truth," West agreed as he drove past the open ramp to Hangar Seven, "I don't think I have either. She was eager to learn the traffic control work that Mom does, but that was nothing like this morning."

"I think everyone could see the difference," she chuckled, "why she's more excited. Living here and growing up here in the shadows of airplanes—and not just any airplanes. She must've had many discussions about the dream of flying with her sister." She sighed at a thought. "There are times when it would really be nice to have a sister to talk to."

"I can only imagine," he admitted. "Looks like they got an early jump after breakfast."

"They did, didn't they?" she admitted. "Looks like they took the T206 instead of *Box Car.*"

"Yeah." He continued driving to the people door for Hangar Two and the TF. "I imagine Woody will give Dani a little more Dual on their way up to the Springs and she'll practice on her way back."

"I'm sure. Do you know which airplane Will has for Belle?"

"No," he admitted. "He has four or five 172s around his place. We'll know soon enough."

"You know," she began softly as she got out and he opened the people door, "what you're doing for the girls, maybe all of the kids, is really great. Besides the cost, it really shows your continued faith and belief in them."

"Thank you." He smiled. "Like I said, they make me feel a little bit like a father, and I want them to have the best and succeed in what they want to do in life."

Charlie looked at him as she walked down the stairs at his side. "I think you'd make a wonderful father."

"I'd like to try"—he nodded in agreement—"once our current dilemma has been put to bed and our life has settled down, when you feel like you're ready to try being a mother. I think raising a family with you would be a wonderful experience." He stopped and kissed her, then turned to the hangar and switched on the lights.

Saturday, June 24

"The paper doesn't mention the Ghost Ranch," Tommy said as Tony drove up Horizon Drive into the Grand Junction Regional Airport.

"They don't always announce when they're going to be someplace," Tony explained as he looked around.

"Looks like the airshow entrance is over to the right," Tommy noted, "and they're parking in the dirt in between."

Tony took the first right at the roundabout and followed the line of cars onto the dirt. A man with a bright-colored vest directed him to a row in the middle of the parking area.

"Since Mr. Collingsworth is paying for us to see all of the shows," Tony commented with a heavy tone, "we should go check out what's here."

"Yup. Never know," Tommy agreed. "You might see something you like."

"They're airplanes, Tom. Just airplanes." Tony led the way.

"I know," Tommy admitted, "but they're very nice airplanes. Most of them anyway. Especially those from the Ghost Ranch."

Tony paid for their wristbands and they walked down Navigation Way, past the hangars and T-hangars to the display area along the taxiway beside Runway 04-22. They took their time and slowly walked the length of the exhibit area to the southwest and then back to the northeast, noting the many beautiful airplanes, sport and recreational models, light sports category and many amateur-built models.

In an area reserved for restored warbirds, a Boeing-Stearman Model 75—also known as a PT17 trainer, Tommy noted from the sign in front of it—and a North American T-6 Texan were on display. When Tony inquired, the owners said they were the only exhibits expected for the weekend.

For lunch they ate with many others under an open-sided tent spread over a number of picnic tables in front of three food kiosks: Mexican burros and tacos, Italian sausage and meatball sandwiches, and Southern fried chicken and corn dogs.

Later in the afternoon, they split up and visited with the various exhibitors, asking about their planes or products and occasionally asking about the Ghost Ranch and wondering aloud why they had missed coming to the airshow. Sometimes an exhibitor gave a speculation in return, but mostly, people just did not know why the ranch chose one show over another show.

With the sun low in the western sky, walking back to the car, Tony admitted to a little possibly good news.

"The fellow with the aluminum polishing booth," Tony stated, turning down the row to their car, "had a little bit of information. He gave me the name of an attorney that has quietly, on occasion, admitted to doing work with the Ghost Ranch."

"Really?" Tommy asked, and looked at Tony. "Think he could be legit?"

"I think we'll go and ask him. His office is in Denver."

"I'll try to make this short," Monte said as they waited in the hotel lobby.

"You could've gone to their hotel." Cat was still skeptical of Monte's behavior, and she watched the front doors for two men entering together. That had been all the description she could muster.

"I told you, I'm not going to run off and do a lot of work," he insisted. "I want to be close, and if you need anything, you'll know where to find me." He smiled at her. "Maybe you could take the kids swimming and I can join you when I get finished."

"Can we do some of the things on your list this afternoon?" she asked.

"We sure can," he agreed. "Pick something out, you or you and the kids, and we'll go do it."

She smiled at him, letting a little of her skepticism abate. "Okay. We'll find something interesting. We might have to do something for Mike one day and something for Mel another. There are so many things on your list."

"And that list's paraphrased. There are a lot more things to do, so if you find something you want to do that's not on the list, add it."

"Okay."

"Aah, I think this might be them." He gestured as two men spun the revolving door and entered.

He stepped forward and asked, "Are either of you Lloyd?"

"Yes," the taller man answered. "Are you Mr. Williamson?"

"I am. Monte please," he greeted, extending his hand. "And this is my wife, Cathy."

"Nice to meet you ma'am." Lloyd nodded. "This is Sam."

"Nice to meet both of you," she returned the pleasantries. "I was just on my way to check on the children, so I guess I better go on."

Monte smiled at her and held her eyes a moment longer than necessary, then turned to the men. "Gentlemen, I have a conference room reserved, so if you'll follow me."

When the men were clustered around one end of the ten-place conference table, Monte explained what was happening and how Howard was pushing to capture the woman named Charlie West, claiming she was his daughter Emli in disguise.

"But we know that's not right," Sam said emphatically.

"Yes, we do," Monte agreed. "That is why I needed to meet with you. I need to find a way to stop his investigators, Tony and Tommy, from going after her."

"That won't be easy," Lloyd said. "Tony has very few scruples and those can usually be bought."

"Obviously, you know them," Monte surmised, pleased.

"Yes, we know them," Lloyd admitted. "Do you have anything in mind?"

"Not much, I'm afraid. I know Howard has them following the airshows around Colorado, looking for planes from the Ghost Ranch in hopes this woman Charlie shows up. I'm thinking I need you two to go to the next airshow and see if they are there. If people from the Ghost Ranch show up, we need to interfere with anything Tony or Tommy try to do—specifically anything against that woman or any other Ghost Ranch people."

"Okay. You do know the next one is here in Denver?" Sam asked.

"The July Fourth weekend airshow? Yes, we're planning on attending that one. Do either of you have pictures of Tony or Tommy?"

"No, I don't." Lloyd looked at Sam.

"Me either," Sam admitted. "When we see them at the airshow, we'll point them out to you. We can get pictures there."

"Okay. I have your cell number and you have mine," Monte confirmed. "I'm sure we'll get there early, especially if my son has any say in the matter. Call me when you get there and we'll join up and see who's about."

"Okay," Lloyd agreed. "If I may ask, why are you so

concerned about what this Howard does to this woman Charlie?"

"My company, along with my father's, has work dealings with Howard's operation," Monte explained, "and if Howard goes through with this criminal act, it will look very bad for us by association. Kidnapping and worse are not things we want to be a part of. And secondly, I don't want any of this to reflect on the good character of my wife or my family. They do not deserve any bad press or embarrassment due to Howard's unscrupulous actions."

"I'm sorry, Mr. Williamson, but how would what he does be an embarrassment to your wife and family?"

"Howard is my wife's father," he admitted softly. "And neither one of us can condone what he is about to do. If I had any hard evidence that he's done this before, I'd have the police involved, but unfortunately, I don't."

"I see. That does make this more difficult." Lloyd slapped his knees. "Okay, Mr. Williamson, we'll see you at the airshow and show you what these guys look like, and let you know if we hear anything else."

Monday, June 26

"Where's Dani?" West asked as everyone settled at the breakfast table.

"She had an early flight this morning," Woody said as he spread his napkin. "Paul already had a ten o'clock so he gave her an eight o'clock ride."

"Ride?" West whispered, and looked at Charlie's wide smile. "Is it that time already?"

"You've been too busy to notice." Woody chuckled. "She has her hours and I've run out of things to give her dual on. We've actually started instrument work while she finished building her time."

"So she's taking her 'commercial ride' this morning?" West asked, to confirm he was hearing right.

"Yes." Charlie chuckled and laid her hand on his arm. "She took the T206 and had to be there by eight."

"Wow. I must be getting absentminded." He shook his head. Then he glanced at Belle. "And I'll ask how our newest is doing before I miss something else."

"Belle is progressing very well. Will provided us with a very nice 172N with modest avionics. Just right for a new student."

"Thanks." He nodded and looked at Helen. "I presume you're up to speed and have a party planned for Dani?"

"Of course, dear." Helen patted his other arm. "The women have it under control."

Someone laughed and West saw Belle's smile. He assumed Ratchet was the culprit.

"Very well." He smiled and shook his head again. "Any special tasks this morning, Ratchet?"

"Nothing special." Ratchet smiled at Charlie.

"Mr. Taylor, good morning," Tony said as he entered Carson's Denver law office. "I'm Tony and this is my colleague Tom. Thank you for seeing us."

"Good morning," Carson greeted, standing before his desk. He extended his hand and shook theirs as they came in and took the chairs he proffered. "Tony, Tom. I'm Carson. May I get you anything? Coffee? Water?"

"No thanks," Tony said.

"Then what can I do for you?" Carson asked as he settled into his chair behind his desk.

"We're looking for some information on the Ghost Ranch," Tony said bluntly.

"Well, I think you may have come to the wrong place," Carson admitted. "The only information I have is the same public information you can get through the social media sources."

"Now, now, Mr. Taylor," Tony pressed softly. "I understand that on a few occasions you told friends of yours that you were the legal counsel for the ranch. And if you were legal counsel, you have more information than social media sources."

Tony noticed Carson was beginning to perspire.

"Any client information I have is protected and not available for discussion."

"I believe at one time," Tony continued, "you told that same friend that you thought the Wests' name was not their real name. You indicated there was something more going on than just pretty airplanes. Why would you tell your friend that if it's confidential?"

"Speculations over drinks is not viable information," Carson rebutted. "Anyone can search the Wests on the internet and come up with questions."

"Hmm. So it's okay for you to debase," Tony continued, "or cast aspersions on a 'possible' client in public over drinks with friends? Why would you do that to someone that pays you to represent them?"

Carson did not answer immediately. "A few years ago I was intrigued with things about the ranch and the Wests that didn't have a clear definition," Carson admitted. "Since then I have discovered it is best to stick with the facts and leave the speculations to others."

"Is that why you no longer represent the ranch?" Tony asked.

"I will leave it that I do not represent the Ghost Ranch or the restoration business," Carson said, "and you can draw your own conclusions from that. Now, is there anything other than information on the Ghost Ranch that I can help you with?"

"Only your comments about the name thing," Tony pressed.

"You will have to do your own research," Carson responded firmly, "and come to your own conclusions regarding the validity of the names."

"Then I guess we have no more questions, Mr. Taylor." Tony

stood up. He extended his hand and Carson shook it. "Thank you for your time."

Tony and Tom left without looking back, and once outside, Tony commented, "He must've really gotten into trouble. Maybe threatened with disbarment."

"Why do you say that?" Tom asked.

"Carson was sweating and would not confirm any hearsay about the ranch," Tony said. "But he did give us some things to check on, like the Wests' name and that he thinks there is more to the ranch operation than pretty airplanes."

"Then we should do a little surfing?" Tom asked.

"I think so."

Thursday, June 29

Woody and Belle walked into the dining room and quickly took their seats as West watched them.

"Sorry we're late," Woody apologized, and smiled at Belle.

"I take it," West questioned, "it was a good afternoon?"

"Yes, it was. Belle, would you tell everyone what happened today?"

Belle looked surprised and slowly looked at each of them. Then very softly, she said, "I... soloed." Then much louder, with a bounce in her chair: "I soloed!"

Everyone cheered and clapped, and Woody raised his water glass in toast.

"Very nice." West repeated the toast gesture with his glass. "Congratulations. Looks like we need to plan another party." Then West gestured to the serving plates. "Dig in before it gets cold."

As they ate, Ratchet asked about support for the Broomfield Heritage Days Fly-In.

"I'm thinking of sending two planes for the show," West answered. "Is the semi loaded, Lenny?"

"Yes. If I leave at daybreak, we can be in place a little after lunchtime tomorrow. Woody is going to ride with me."

"Going from here," he continued. "Charlie will fly the Corsair and I will ride with Ratchet in *The Lady*. When we're finished, Ratchet will bring the Corsair home and Charlie and I will bring *The Lady* back."

"Sounds good," Ratchet agreed.

"Whose turn is it in town this weekend?" West asked.

"Gracie's family's turn," Dani said. "I'm supposed to fly them out and drop them in the Springs at Curt Kullet's and pick them up on Monday about noon."

"So you can support the fly-in after you drop them off?" he asked.

"Yes, I can," Dani agreed with a wide smile.

"That leaves us one unaccounted for," West admitted, and everyone looked at Belle.

"Belle can ride with me and get familiar with the Beaver," Dani said.

"Very well. Now, that reminds me. Belle told Charlie and me that she wanted to be nicknamed 'Eddie' when the time was right and she had earned the privilege. She wants to be the third woman pilot and named accordingly: C – D – E." West smiled and pointed to Charlie, Dani, and Eddie as he spoke. "If you all concur, I would like to bestow that nickname, since she has soloed and—if Woody agrees—is definitely on her way to her private ticket."

Everyone nodded and smiled. Woody gave him a thumbs-up.

"Very well," he continued with a nod, and turned to Helen. "Mom, can you put her new name on her coveralls and her flight suit?"

"Certainly," Helen agreed, and smiled at Belle.

"Then Belle will be known among us as Eddie." He looked at her. "Your call sign is Ghost Eight and you will support us in Broomfield tomorrow through the weekend. Since you will be in your last year of high school this fall, I will talk with Robert and Madra about future support. I would also like you to

154

support us in Reno this year."

Eddie's smile grew as she absorbed what West was saying.

"At the fly-in," Charlie added, "we'll show you what you will need to do to help and what you'll need to learn."

"Thank you, West, Charlie," Eddie said, and nodded to each of the others. "Thank you."

"Okay, Dani," he continued again. "Gracie's family is six, and with you and Eddie, *Box Car* will be full up. Bump, you'll have to ride with Lenny and Woody if you're planning on going."

Bump and Lenny nodded.

"Dani?" Charlie asked. "After dinner, can I borrow you and Eddie for a little bit? I need your help with something."

"Sure." Dani smiled and Eddie nodded vigorously.

Monte tucked Melony in bed, kissed her cheek, and then tucked Michael in and kissed his cheek. He said goodnight as Cat came in and told them goodnight, kissing each of them.

"Thanks for taking us to the museum and the aquarium," Michael said as she turned out the light.

"You're very welcome, dear," she added. "Get a good night's sleep and tomorrow we'll pick some other things to go and do."

She closed the door all but a crack, and joined Monte on the balcony. He was pouring two flutes of wine as she sat down in a chair beside his.

"Thanks," she said as he handed her one. "I think I can use this. We should end our days at home this way. Ooh, my feet feel like I've walked across the whole state."

Monte pulled her feet up onto his lap, slipped her flats off, and began gently rubbing the balls and arches, one foot at a time.

"I hope it wasn't too strenuous." He sipped his wine with one hand and rubbed with his other. "I think the kids had a lot of fun."

"I think they did," she agreed. "I actually did too. Thanks for taking us."

Monte nodded and smiled. "I'm glad. What do we have on the agenda for tomorrow?"

"I told them we'd pick something out in the morning." She took another sip of wine.

"Sounds good." He leaned back in his chair, continuing to massage her feet as they talked.

"You know, between you doing that and the wine"—she smiled—"I'm probably going to fall asleep in this chair."

"That's okay." Monte took another sip. "I won't let you fall over."

"You didn't say how your meeting went Saturday," she noted absently. "I thought you might've mentioned it."

"Aah, I guess I haven't talked to you about it," he realized as he thought back. "Sorry."

He pulled his cell phone from his pocket and unlocked it. He touched the icon for audio messages and handed it to her. "Pick Saturday's recording and you can listen to the whole meeting. I can get you earbuds if you want them."

She shook her head and tapped the selection. She listened, and when the recording stopped, she handed the phone back and watched him as he put it away.

"Do you really feel that way?" she asked. "About us?"

"Certainly. I told you, when I first saw you, I was hooked. If our marriage wasn't already arranged, I would've pursued you and tried to win you. In the long run, I think it would've been better that way. Less confusion and a lot less doubt and fear. But once I saw you, I knew I had to be with you."

"I'm sorry it's been so hard for me to accept things." She watched him for a long moment. "But it's been hard for me to figure you out."

"Cat, it's okay. You had no way of knowing me when we got married, and I certainly didn't know what you've been through.

156

You don't see me at work to know me outside of the house. After we talked, I feel like I pressured you into having kids and that you've resented me some for it. Not knowing how to please you, I've tried to give you your space. I tried to stop imposing on you too much. I'm surprised, a little, that after all of these years you still feel the way you do, but I believe you when you tell me how you feel, that you don't trust me.

"And yes, you are right. I've let your father push me to gather information for him—some I don't like." He held her eyes for a moment. "And you were exactly right when I asked—well, more like confronted you about the missing pages in Michael's booklet. I'm sorry for how I came across. He does have lists of who has useful single daughters. When he asked me to review and amend that list, I did. But I told him I disagreed with what he was doing and I also told him I knew how he fixed his South African 'deals' and a couple of others. He didn't like that, and he did threaten me—or I should say you and the kids."

Cat stared at him. "You've never told me that that was going on."

"Of course not. That isn't the sort of thing a man wants to come home and tell his wife about her father when she asks how his day went. I can't prove to you that what I'm saying is true. You have enough doubts about my integrity that I don't expect you to understand or accept how I feel or how I am just because I say that's the way it is. I am, after all, the guy your dad picked and forced you to marry. I am, in your eyes, what he trained you to see, to dislike when you look at a man. Maybe I'll always be that man you see that way, with only one demeaning thing on his mind. I am—"

"Stop!" she insisted sharply. "I had five years before Melony came along that I could have run away. I could've—"

"Maybe. Now you could, and can," he continued softly, "but back then, I'm not certain you were really able, or ready to defy your father. He would have found you and made your life a living hell. Now, knowing what I do about him, I'm not sure it wouldn't have been even worse than that."

"He would've killed me," she whispered, barely out loud.

"Just like he intends to do to Emli, if he finds her, or this woman Charlie, if he gets his hands on her."

"That is my fear too," he admitted, and slowly closed his eyes, still gently rubbing her feet. "And if he figures out I'm trying to stop him, he might try to do something to you or the kids. I can't let that happen."

"Thanks, Monte. I really want to believe you. We don't have anyone else to turn to."

"You really are very important to me, and I'll do everything I can to keep you and the kids safe." He gently squeezed her foot. "I just hope I'm good enough."

Twenty-One
Friday, June 30

As planned, the semi left the ranch just before daybreak and dropped south into New Mexico, skirting the larger mesas. They drove through Branson and up to Colorado 160, then took the more-traveled 160 into Trinidad and on to Interstate 25. Dani and Eddie went straight from breakfast up top to check on the airplanes and start the preparations for the trip. Charlie, West, and Ratchet arrived a few minutes behind them and pulled *The Lady* and *Bad Luck* out of Hangar Six. Dani towed *Box Car* out of Hangar Seven and down to the fuel farm. There she filled the tanks while Eddie cleaned the windscreen and side glass.

Ratchet pulled *The Lady* up beside *Box Car* and fueled her from the higher-octane pumps. West cleaned *The Lady's* windscreen and the canopy and wiped the dust off the wings and cowling.

Towing the Beaver back to the hangar, Dani passed Charlie towing the Corsair to the fuel farm and Eddie waved.

When the three planes were arrayed in a line before Hangar Seven and the tugs were returned and parked in their spots inside, Ratchet made his rounds and secured Hangar Six's door.

A little before eleven, Dani and Eddie drove two jeeps down to the main house, collected Gracie and her family, and brought them up for loading. West and Ratchet drove the jeeps back down and left one for Helen and the house.

With Eddie close on her heels, watching everything she could, Dani completed her walk-around of the Beaver and signed the release form. She checked that her passengers were secure, strapped in as they should be, and then closed the large side door.

"We're ready." Dani waved to Charlie. "We'll see you in

Broomfield." Then she turned to Eddie. "Get in and let's go."

She climbed the strut and slipped into the left seat, closed the door and belted herself in. Checking again that everyone was ready, she started down the checklist and started the Pratt and Whitney R-985.

"Ghost Ranch"—Dani keyed her mic—"Ghost Seven and *Box Car* are departing. Trinidad to Florissant to the Springs, then on to Broomfield."

"Ghost Seven, Roger," Helen acknowledged. "Have a safe trip. Bring me back some souvenirs."

"Definitely, Ghost Ranch." And Dani pushed the throttle forward.

Box Car was airborne at 11:10.

West stood in front of *The Lady* and off to one side so he could see Ratchet in the front seat. He waited with the fire bottle as Ratchet went down the checklist steps and finally started the Merlin. Then West walked over and stood in front of the F4U-5, *Your Bad Luck*.

Charlie had strapped herself in, secured the parachute straps and the shoulder harness, and had raised the seat to its highest position to help visibility for taxiing. She was a smaller build than the average pilots, slighter in frame, but the huge Vought and Grumman cockpits made her feel like a mouse in a living room, the sole attendant in a symphony hall. Now all she needed was for the band to start playing.

She visually checked the wing lock indicator pins to confirm they were flush with the wing skin and the wing folding control was pulled aft, secured in the Spread position detent, and the wing locking pin lever was pushed forward into the Locked detent. A misstep there could result in an unwanted, inadvertent wing fold during flight—not a good thing to happen.

She checked her fuel quantity indicator and confirmed the fuselage fuel tank was full. With the main tank and the two drop tanks, *Bad Luck* had a cruise total of five hundred useable gallons, nearly sixteen hundred miles' worth. She selected the fuel selector to draw from the main fuselage tank.

Going down the checklist, she adjusted the rudder pedals, checked the controls for freedom of motion, uncaged the horizontal and directional gyros, set the altimeter barometric pressure, set the arresting hook up, and tested the oxygen mask and verified oxygen flow.

She confirmed the ignition switch was rotated full right to Off, Mixture lever set to Idle Cut-Off, Fuel Transfer switch was set to Off, Cowl Flaps switch was set to Open, Oil Cooler and Intercooler flap switches were both set to Automatic, Propeller lever was full forward to Maximum rpm, Supercharger selector to Neutral, the throttle set to the red mark, approximately one inch open and the Battery switch set to On. She glanced around the airplane and switched the Boost Pump switch to Emergency and held the Primer switch On for about ten seconds. Then she turned the Boost Pump switch Off.

She yelled, "Clear!" and rotated the ignition switch to Both, and raised the guard and engaged the Starter.

The 2100-horsepower Pratt & Whitney Double Wasp R-2800 coughed and belched gray smoke and she pushed the Mixture to Auto-Rich. The engine quickly settled into a fast idle and Charlie adjusted the throttle to steady the engine at 1000 rpm. She waved West aside and watched the oil pressure and temperatures as the big engine slowly warmed. She happily sighed; the band was finally playing.

West put the fire bottle in the hangar, secured the doors, and raised the ramp, transforming the welcome sight of the hangar into a mere mound of grassy dirt to the casual observer. When West was secure in the back seat of *The Lady*, Ratchet keyed his radio.

"Ghost Two, lead the way. We'll follow in your four o'clock."

"Thanks, Ghost Three." Charlie waved and gave him a thumbs-up. "Ghost Ranch. Ghost Two and Three departing as a flight of two for Broomfield, via Trinidad, Cotopaxi, Grant, and Nederland."

Charlie pushed her throttle forward and taxied away from the hangar before turning southwest into the light wind.

"Have a good flight, Ghost Two," Helen replied. "Ghost Ranch on standby."

Charlie waved to West and Ratchet and lined up for her takeoff. She locked the tailwheel, set the flaps, the rudder trim, aileron trim, and elevator trim.

"Ready when you are," Ratchet announced, and Charlie switched the boost pump to Emergency, lowered her seat to her normal position, and pushed the throttle forward. She checked the engine instruments as they stabilized and then concentrated on the takeoff. Once airborne, she retracted the landing gear and the flaps, and glanced back to see *The Lady's* gear coming up. She closed her canopy as they passed over the rim of the mesa and immediately had a thousand feet of ground clearance. Smiling, she turned west and led the parade up the valley between the mesas.

Norman closed the library reference book and sat back in his chair.

"Cee, I think you have it." He smiled when she looked up.

"Yes, maybe." She leaned back and stretched her arms high above her head. "Ooh, I'm stiff." She looked around the nearly empty room lined with tall bookcases and file drawers: a very typical reference library room.

"Are you getting hungry?" he asked, and arranged the three books near him into a single stack. "I am."

"I think a break would be good. Especially for my shoulders and back."

Norman picked up his stack of books and returned them to the shelves he had gotten them from, even though the signs all said to leave them on a cart. He knew they would need them again, soon.

"Are you coming back here this afternoon?" he asked as she helped put her stack away.

"I think I need to." She stopped to look at him. "And you have that Miller file to work on."

"Yeah," he admitted. "I need to spend two or three hours making some progress for them."

"Can you drop me off and then come and pick me up when you're finished?" she asked. "Otherwise, I could—"

"I can drop you off," he interrupted with a feigned pout. "And pick you up when I'm done. We don't need to go back to get your jeep."

"Thanks." She picked up her notepad and grabbed her purse.

"But it'll cost you." He smiled. "You have to take the weekend off and go to the fly-in with me. Up in Denver."

"I really should—"

"Yes you should! I already have a nice hotel room for us."

"Not at the Valley Lodge again." She eyed him. "That was wonderful, but—"

"No, nothing that nice," he insisted, "but it does have a hot tub on a secluded, private deck."

She sighed and smiled. "Okay, okay. I guess I can use a real break."

He kissed her and gently pushed her toward the door. "Thank you. Now, what are you hungry for?"

Saturday, July 1

West's phone alarm buzzed softly and he gently squeezed Charlie, her back nestled tightly against him.

"It's time, love," he whispered in her ear.

"I know," she replied, and turned to face him, stretching her length against him and returning his embrace.

He held her to him as he rolled onto his back. She wrapped herself tightly around him and kissed him fully as he responded to her caresses and needs.

"We better get cleaned up," she finally whispered, happily awake and ready to face the day, and then pushed herself up. "You have to get the fellows out to the airport and I have to meet the girls in twenty minutes."

She threw the sheet aside and hurried to the bathroom and West swung his legs off the bed and followed.

Showered and dressed, West stopped and watched her as she finished dressing and brushed her hair.

"Go on," she urged. "We'll come down for breakfast when you get back. Call me when you're here."

"Okay." He smiled, stole a quick kiss, and went to the door. "I'll be about a half an hour, depending on traffic."

West called when he got back and the waiter had just suggested a table near the front windows when he saw Charlie lead Dani and Eddie into the hotel restaurant. He stopped and smiled. He knew they were planning something special, but had no idea what until they walked in and stopped at the table.

"What do you think?" Eddie asked, gesturing to Charlie.

They were each dressed in a Ghost Ranch's embroidered, fitted blouse with an American flag on the back, dark gray slacks, and they each sported matching hairdos—except for Charlie's bright hair color—pulled back on one side with bright red, white, and blue swaths of color.

"I think she looks beautiful. You all do, and you will make a lasting impression," he complimented brightly. "I like the colors. Perfect for the weekend's theme."

"We thought so," Dani said as Charlie stole a kiss from him and let him help her into her chair.

Dani and Eddie took the other two chairs and they all picked up a menu as their waiter stopped for their drink orders.

"They sure don't give up easy," Lenny said as he folded up *Bad Luck's* canopy cover and nudged Bump. He gestured to the string of people entering the main gate.

"They certainly didn't take the hint," Bump agreed when he spotted Tony and Tom in the group spreading out onto the ramp and among the numerous airplanes on display. "Did you show Ratchet and Woody their pictures?"

"Yeah, but you probably ought to let them know we've seen these guys this morning. I'll call West and Charlie."

The morning went quickly and Charlie tried to lose herself in busy work to keep her mind off the two men Ratchet had alerted them to. When she had to, she fielded questions—about the Corsair for a while, and then she traded with one of the men and covered the TF, explaining its specifications and features. Dani and Eddie helped and periodically took a turn wiping the cowlings and belly panels to keep the planes spotless and presentable. Occasionally the showgoers asked for a picture of Charlie, Dani, and Eddie in their matching outfits, posing in front of one plane or the other.

"Now that is something you don't see very often," a familiar voice greeted, and Buck Troy stopped beside them.

Charlie turned and smiled. "Buck. It's good to see you."

"It's been a while," Buck admitted, and Charlie gave him a hug. "You three sure look nice."

"Thanks. Have you met Robert and Madra's daughters, Dani and Eddie?" Charlie asked, and turned to the girls.

"No"—Buck smiled—"I don't believe I have."

"Dani, Eddie, this is Buck Troy," Charlie introduced. "He helps us gather parts and pieces. Buck's a very good friend of

West's."

"Nice to meet you both." Buck extended his hand.

"Dani is our newest full Ghost Ranch pilot. Commercial, studying for her instrument ticket, and she's learning to become a mechanic," Charlie continued to explain. "And Eddie has just soloed and is on her way to being another Ghost Ranch pilot."

"My, my." Buck smiled wider. "Things have most certainly changed since I was out last. And for the better, I must say. And a warm congratulations to you, Charlie. I was so happy to hear you and West had tied the knot."

"Thanks. Sorry we didn't invite anyone outside the family."

"I understand. Now that I've had my morning sufficiently brightened, can you tell me if that husband of yours is around?"

"He should be in the trailer." Dani gestured over her shoulder. "He was talking with Ratchet a minute ago."

"Thank you. I need to talk to him about his next shipment."

Charlie gestured to the trailer. "And thanks for the TF parts. It'll be flying in a few weeks."

"You're very welcome." Buck patted her shoulder and turned to find West.

Charlie stood in the wide trailer doorway, watching Dani and Bump as they discussed the Corsair with two couples, one with a toddler and stroller in tow. Eddie was helping Lenny and Ratchet with *The Lady* and she wasn't sure where Woody had gotten off to. She glanced at her watch and decided it was close enough to noon to grab a bite.

She slipped around West and Buck, still discussing the parts and pieces he had found that might help various rebuild projects, and collected a sandwich and soft drink from the refrigerator. Food and drink in hand, Charlie climbed the makeshift stairs and settled on a plastic chair under the large beach umbrella.

Charlie propped her feet up on a second chair and watched

the visitors as they milled around the displays while she ate. She saw Buck as he left, and waved when he looked back and saw her on the roof of the trailer.

West climbed the stairs and joined her, bringing her a soft drink and himself a lunch.

"Doing okay?" he asked as he slid a chair beside her and sat down. He glanced at the soft drink she already had and set the extra beside his chair.

"Yeah," she admitted, and caught his hand. "Just needed a break. Has everyone else had lunch?"

"They're grabbing a bite in shifts," West said, and took a bite of his sandwich. "I brought you an extra pop if you want it."

"Thanks. Did Buck have good news?"

"Yes, he did," West said. "He found cowlings and another set of main gear for the Mosquito. And a few P-38 parts."

"And I presume you're going to take them." She chuckled and glanced across the ramp.

She suddenly turned toward the visitor's gate, eyes wide, and her hand quickly covered her mouth and slowly slid down to her throat. "Oh shit! No!" She leaned forward, scanning the crowd as they walked past from the gate. "Did Jess's email say Monte was coming to Denver to talk to his investigators, or Monte and his family were coming?"

"Jess told us Monte was coming, but the actual email she forwarded said family. Why?" West asked, and tried to follow Charlie's urgent gaze.

"Damn! Damn! I missed that," Charlie admitted. "Oh God, no! He brought his wife and...and...two children. I didn't know they had children..."

"What? Where?" West looked across the ramp, trying to locate the object of her discomfort.

She described where they were relative to the tents and the kiosks in front of Jet Services and he finally spotted them and quickly focused on the brunette that looked strikingly like— He glanced at Charlie.

"Dark-haired man, broad shoulders? Accompanied by a

'Charlie' with light brown hair instead of blond? Only longer than yours? A ten- or eleven-year-old boy and a little older girl?"

"Yes..." she answered very softly, her breathing heavy. "That's Emli's sister Catherine."

He noted that she referred to Catherine as Emli's sister, and her being there was definitely affecting Charlie—a lot.

Charlie sighed and he took her hand.

"Are you sure you're going to be okay? You can stay out of the way and we can talk to them if they stop to chat. You can stay in the trailer."

Charlie shook her head. "No. I never expected this day to come, but when Jess said Monte was coming to Denver, the thought did cross my mind. I guess I should have mentioned it to you. It's...it's a test I have to get past. And they wouldn't be here if it wasn't for Emli's lookalike."

"At least Monte's investigators aren't disputing who you are," West urged encouragingly, and squeezed her hand.

"I'll try to remember that." She let the barest of a smile cross her lips.

Later in the afternoon, Charlie was standing between the two planes facing the trailer, talking with Dani and Eddie, when West stepped up behind her.

"Take a deep breath, love," he whispered in her ear, and kissed her cheek. "Emli's sister and family are approaching on your six o'clock."

"Okay." Charlie took that deep breath and squeezed her eyes closed. *You can do this, Charlie. You can do this.*

Dani saw Charlie's discomfort and obvious preparation for something abnormal, and then she saw the couple and slipped around West and Charlie, tugging on Eddie's sleeve as she went.

"Good afternoon," Dani greeted as she stopped in front of the couple, trying to hide her sudden surprise when she looked at the woman. "Any questions I can answer for you?"

Eddie stared at the woman and then glanced back at Charlie.

"Sure," the boy with the couple said quickly. "What kind is it?"

"It's a trainer version of the North American P-51," Dani explained, "called a TF-51. The factory modified the regular fighter by putting a second seat and controls behind the pilot's seat, where a fuel tank was."

"Do you teach in it?" the girl asked.

"When we qualify our pilots, we do," Eddie said, forcing herself to focus on the girl instead of the mother. "Dani will be learning one day soon and I'll learn when I've gained the experience I need."

"Very interesting," the woman said. "So you're not like a flying school?"

"No." Dani smiled. "Our planes are to show our history, and the training we do is to qualify our pilots."

Eddie glanced around and saw Charlie climb up the left main strut.

"Eddie," Charlie called when she stood up on *The Lady's* wing. "Would you get two pair of those booties for the children? They might like to look inside."

"Wow. Can we?" the boy asked, and looked at his parents.

"I guess," the man said, "if it's all right."

Eddie hurried to the trailer and returned with the booties.

Charlie motioned to the boy to come to her side of the airplane. When he did, he stared at Charlie a long minute before he heard Charlie telling him where to grab and step.

"When you get up here, turn around and Eddie can put the booties on you," Charlie explained. "And while she's doing that, your sister can climb up."

The boy hurried to the strut and followed Charlie's instructions.

"I'm Charlie. What's your name?" she asked as she helped

him up and turned him around to sit on the wing with his legs hanging over the leading edge.

"I'm Michael. Most call me Mike, and that's Mel—short for Melony," he explained as Eddie brushed his shoes off and slipped the booties over them.

"Nice to meet you, Michael," Charlie said as Dani helped Melony up on the strut. Charlie lifted her onto the wing and turned her around. "This is Eddie. She's learning to fly. She soloed on Thursday. And this other young lady is Dani. She just received her commercial pilot's license and will soon start flying the fighters too."

"Do you fly the fighters?" Melony asked as Charlie stood them up and guided them to the cockpit.

"Yes, I do."

"Both of these?" Michael asked.

"Yes. We have eleven airplanes we can fly right now," Charlie explained, "and I fly all of them. At different times, of course. My husband and the mechanics also fly all of them."

They laughed and looked inside the cockpit. Charlie moved between them and the trailing edge of the wing and began pointing out the various controls and switches.

"Would you like to sit inside?" she asked, and lifted Melony over the canopy rail when they both nodded vigorously. "Sorry, Michael. Ladies first."

"I know," Michael said. "That's what Dad always says."

Charlie leaned closer and Michael peered in. Charlie put Melony's hand on the stick and slowly moved it around, pointing to the ailerons as the stick went from side to side, and the elevators as the stick moved from front to back. After many questions about everything she could see, Charlie finally asked her if her brother could have a turn.

In moments, Charlie had switched their places and Michael started with a myriad of new questions.

When Charlie pointed out the various instruments, Michael immediately stopped and stared at the airspeed indicator.

"Does it really go seven hundred miles per hour?" he asked

with wide eyes.

"No," Charlie laughed. "See the red marks and the extra needle pointing to about five hundred miles per hour?"

"Yeah," Michael answered.

"Those marks tell the pilot where his limit is," Charlie said. "The extra needle will come down to a smaller number at high altitude and lower the maximum speed we're allowed to go."

Then she continued around the cockpit, being sure Melony had room to see also. Finally, Charlie lifted Michael out of the cockpit and walked them back to the leading edge above the left strut. They sat down and Eddie removed each of their booties and handed them to them.

Melony turned her head and looked up at Charlie, asking in a low voice, "Do you know you look a lot like our mom?"

"I did notice that," Charlie agreed, surprised by her frankness, "when you walked up."

"Are you related?" Mike asked when he heard Melony's question.

"No, Michael, I'm not."

"How do you know?" Michael persisted. "Could be related by a brother or sister—"

"No, Michael. I don't have any brothers or sisters. I'm all there is left of my family. Now, if you look at the Corsair," Charlie said, changing the subject as she knelt down between them, "there's a man there with the name 'West' embroidered on his shirt." She touched her nametag in reference. "That's my husband, and he will show you everything about the Navy Corsair." She stood up and looked across at the Corsair. "West! I have two coming to see you."

"Thanks." Michael slid forward. His dad caught him and set him down and then helped Melony.

"Thank you, Charlie," the little girl said when she turned around.

"You're very welcome, Melony."

She inhaled deeply as she sat down on the leading edge to

171

survey the crowd and watch the children and their dad walk to the Corsair. *Hang in there, Charlie. Just a little longer.* When she looked back, the children's mother was still standing there, looking at her.

"Sorry." She smiled, hoping she was not giving any indication that she recognized or knew who Cat was. "Did you have any questions? I got so wrapped up helping Michael and Melony, I didn't stop to think you might have some also."

"I...just wanted to say thank you for taking the time with them. I'm Cathy and that's my husband Monte. The children are so excited to get to come, and your explaining everything means a lot to them. I'll never get them to sleep tonight."

"I'm very glad to be of help, but I'm sorry if they don't."

"If you don't mind me asking," Cathy continued, "when did you start flying? You don't look old enough to have been flying very long."

Charlie smiled, knowing where Cat's question was coming from, but she let it pass as a compliment.

"No, I don't mind. I was in high school when my aunt passed away—she raised me. I found work in a local garage to get through school and stay fed. Then, when I graduated, I started helping at the local airport, learning how to work on airplanes. I would sweep the hangars and take out the trash for airplane rides. When my inheritance from my aunt came, I could pay for lessons and the serious learning began. I wasn't twenty yet when I got my ticket."

"I guess that means you have a lot of hours by now. Sorry, I don't know how to say what I'm trying to say."

"That's okay." She grinned. "Some say I'm older than I look, but I do have a lot of flight time and I have been lucky to have very good teachers and opportunities."

"I was just curious. It seems like it would take a lot to learn."

"Determination is what it takes." She climbed down the strut. "I need to get something to drink. Would you like a bottle of water?"

"Oh, no thanks." Cathy glanced at her husband and kids on

the stand beside the Corsair. "I really should catch up with the rest of the family. Thank you, though."

"Sure thing. Come back by if you want to climb up and take a look inside. And be sure to check out the other displays." Charlie smiled and Cathy turned to leave.

Charlie brushed past Dani and went quickly into the trailer and got a bottle of water from the refrigerator, wishing it was something a lot stronger. She clung to the refrigerator for many minutes, trying to stop the trembling in her arms and legs. And when she could stand upright without the crutch, she slowly turned and squeezed into the corner behind the R-2800 engine and sat down on the upturned bucket.

Her face buried in her palms, she began to cry, shaking all over again at the suffocating feeling of being inches from Cat and unable to touch her, unable to feel her embrace, unable to tell her she was still alive. The urge to tell her how sorry she was for leaving her was overwhelming, stronger than she could have ever imagined, and more than once in their brief conversation she wanted to gush everything, suddenly feeling like she needed Cat's forgiveness.

The children's start when they had seen her haunted her. They saw their mother's familiar face in hers and were confused, questioning. And all she could do was to ignore their concerns as if she did not see them.

Her tears kept coming and became breath-stealing sobs. The tremors uncontrollably shook her body and she fought to regain control, wringing her fists and willing herself to stop shaking. She never expected that day to actually come, but it did, and she had to get control of herself.

With the rag from her hip pocket, she wiped her eyes and blew her nose just as Dani stepped into the trailer, calling her softly.

"Charlie? Charlie? Where are you?"

When she saw Charlie's sneakers and pantlegs behind the engine, Dani stopped and knelt down in front of her.

"Go away, Dani. Please," Charlie said in a hoarse voice, angry that she did not sound normal.

173

"What's wrong?"

"Nothing," she lied. "I just want to be alone."

"It was that woman. The one that looks—"

"Please, Dani. Not now. Please..." Charlie's voice was but a soft whisper.

Dani left quietly, but less than a couple of minutes later, West stepped in and knelt in front of her.

"I told Dani I wanted to be left alone!"

West tried to shush her, and reached for her hand. Where she had squeezed into, he could not get his arms around her.

"Come out here so I can hold you. It's okay."

"It isn't okay!"

He pulled her hand and she resisted. "You don't need to hide from me. I'm on your side, remember? We both knew this was going to be hard."

Slowly, she gave in and reluctantly moved out of the tight corner to him.

"I'm here, love. Take your time and let me help."

Monte poured wine into Cat's plastic flute as they watched Michael and Melony playing in the hotel pool.

"Thanks." She took the flute. "You're sure that was 'the' Charlie West that Father's trying to drag back to Detroit or wherever?"

"Yes. That's her. There's only one," he confirmed. "Seems like a very likable woman."

"She does. And that makes me even angrier when I think about what my father is trying to do. Did your men say anything today?"

"They showed me pictures of Tony and Tom, and then they saw them and two other men around ten or ten thirty."

Monte rubbed his chin and slowly shook his head. "I'm thinking they're definitely up to something. Did Charlie act like she knew you?"

"No." Cat shook her head as she sipped her wine. "She looked at me and talked like I could've been anyone. She said she liked talking with the children, but it was so strange to look at her and talk to her. She really does look like how I would expect Emli to look now, but there was nothing in our conversation that would make you think she is. I still wanted to grab her and hug her and blurt out how glad I was to see her again. It was strange, her feeling so familiar. I guess it's the looking-alike thing."

"You said you asked her how she got started flying?"

"I did, and she explained how she survived after her aunt died and how she used her inheritance from her aunt to learn to fly. Sounded just like the information about her that you found—"

"Hey, Mom?" Melony asked from the edge of the pool. "Can we go back to the airshow tomorrow?"

Cat looked at Melony. "I would've thought you'd seen all there was to see today."

"No. The Corsair and the...the TF...TF-51, yeah that's it. They're flying in the Heritage Flight at noon tomorrow," Melony explained. "Mike and me, we want to go and see them fly. I'll bet Charlie will be flying one of them."

"You think she'll be flying?" Monte asked. "Why would you say that?"

"Well. Her husband, West," Michael joined in, "he said she's their best pilot. Didn't you hear him, Dad? West said she's qualified in more than forty different airplane types. I'm not sure what that means, but it's a lot of airplanes, I think."

"No, I didn't hear him say that," Monte admitted, "but you are right, that's a lot of different airplanes."

"He said she used to do delivery flights too," Michael continued. "Like when someone buys an airplane, she would take it to them for the company that sold it."

"He had really nice things to say about Charlie," Melony added, and smiled. "Like the nice things Daddy always says about you, Mom. I think that's really nice."

Cat stared at Melony and slowly smiled as she looked at Monte. "That...that is nice. If your dad thinks it's okay, I guess we can go again and see if she's flying."

"Thanks, Mom," Michael and Melony said together, and splashed back into the pool.

"Did you see that man Tony?" Norman asked Celia as he scanned the area inside the banquet tent. Dinner was over and they were enjoying an after-dinner drink.

"I see his sidekick Tom." She followed Norman's gaze. "But I don't see Tony now."

"Me either." He took her hand. "Let's walk around the outside for a few minutes. I could use a little air."

She got up with him and let him lead her to the nearest opening in the banquet tent. He stopped outside and inhaled the cooler evening air, then slowly walked around toward the front of the tent.

"I don't see anyone." She glanced one way and then another.

"No, I don't either." He stopped and turned to her, slipped his arms around her waist, and pulled her to him. "But I'd hate to waste a beautiful moment like this." He kissed her slowly and felt her respond.

He released her lips and saw a cigarette lighter flash across the space to the next kiosk. "Again. I think they're behind you."

He kissed her again, tenderly and tried to listen.

"Did you hear anything?" he asked when he released her.

"Hear what?" She smiled. "When you're doing that, I can't hear a thing."

"Okay." He slowly turned so she could see across the ramp.

She glanced to her right and saw the men. "It looks like Tony and two others. Tom's inside, so who are they?"

"I'm not sure, but I think we'll stick around for a little while—at least until the Ghost Ranch folks call it a night."

"I heard a couple of West's men talking about sleeping with the planes. Is that normal?"

"They did at Durango," he admitted. "That's how they stopped Tony and Tom that night. So I guess it might be becoming more normal than it has been. If we see Lenny, I'll let him know what we've discovered. Now, let's go back inside slowly"—he inhaled and smiled at her—"like the two lovers I feel we are."

He caught her hand and she squeezed it as he led her back inside through the nearest tent opening.

West led Charlie into their hotel room and closed the door behind them.

"Come and sit a few minutes," he said, and stopped beside the overstuffed chair.

"I love these outfits," she admitted as she stopped at the bathroom door, "but I think I'm going to get out of it and into something more comfortable first. I'll be right out."

"I'll be right here."

He slipped his shoes and socks off, then his shirt and pants, and threw a robe on before he settled onto the chair to wait. He listened to the sounds of her washing and getting comfortable and thought about how well she had done in the face of an extreme test of her capabilities and endurance, seeing Catherine again, face-to-face, after all these years.

She finally came out of the bathroom, fastening her robe. She walked over to West in the chair, sat down across his lap, slipped her arms around him, and wilted with her head on his shoulder.

"I hope you know I am very proud of you," he admitted, and held her tight.

She nodded, gently pressing her head against him. "Thanks," she whispered. "I wasn't sure I could do it." She took a deep breath. "I wanted so much to run and hold her, to tell her I'm really alive. It was much, much harder than I expected, to see her, standing right in front of me. And I have a niece and nephew. I mean, Emli has a niece and nephew. I didn't even know."

"You couldn't have known, love, but I hope it wasn't too disturbing to talk with them."

"It wasn't," she whispered. "Only once, while we were talking, did I come close to losing it. It was after..." She took a deep breath. "I told myself they just looked like someone I once knew, and that they weren't really them. But the kids were genuinely interested, I think." She sighed. "I'm sorry, West. I can't think of myself as Emli anymore and had to keep reminding myself. Emli was someone else and she's dead. I'm Charlie, and I'm alive."

"I know. I also think the children were very interested," West agreed. "They couldn't stop talking about how nice you were to explain things to them. You were really great."

"I hope I was convincing."

"I hope so too." West squeezed her again. "If they have doubts, we'll probably know tomorrow, and we'll deal with it then."

"Show me we'll be all right, Griff," Charlie whispered, and kissed him. "Charlotte needs some of your time with her."

Twenty-Two
Sunday, July 2

"What's going on, Tony?" Tommy asked. "You look like you just ate the whole cherry pie."

"I don't like cherries," Tony said as he walked back toward the line of displays and Tommy fell in step with him. "But I did arrange a second opportunity to try to find the Ghost Ranch."

"Really? That's great. What did you arrange?"

"We'll know when it works. In the meantime, keep a watch on that Charlie woman. I have to talk to Benny and Larry."

Monte led Cat and the children through the main gate, bought them wristbands, and proceeded down the rows of displays stretching northwest along the taxiway.

"Dad?" Melony asked. "Why are we coming all the way down here?"

"To see the planes, dear," Cat explained. "We have time and we thought you might like to see them all. Don't you?"

"Sure," Michael interjected. "We just want to be sure to see Charlie take off and then see the Heritage Flight."

"We'll get back in time. Maybe grab a sandwich at that stand just past the main gate."

"Yeah," Michael and Melony agreed together. "Those were good."

They spent the rest of the morning working their way back down the taxiway to the southeast toward Jet Services and the Ghost Ranch display.

"Monte?" Cat asked as they walked, watching the children

as they investigated the various displays and kiosks along the ramp. "Do you think the children have heard you talking about Charlie at home sometime?"

"I don't know when," he admitted softly. "Her name has only come up when I talk to your father and he brings her up. I honestly don't know of any time when they might have. Why?"

"Just their sudden preoccupation with her." She stopped and looked at him. "Michael seemed to fix on her when he saw her picture, and Mel's doing the same."

"Well, since Charlie looks a lot like your sister"—he smiled—"I suppose they might have picked up on how she looks a lot like you."

"Like me?" She slowly smiled at the realization. "I suppose that's possible. I'd never thought of that."

"Well, there is a striking resemblance." He smiled, catching her hand. "She couldn't be a lookalike and not have some resemblance to you. You were almost twins."

"We've got about a half an hour to engine starts," West said as he stepped back up into the trailer. "Charlie, why don't you fly *The Lady* and Ratchet can fly *Bad Luck* for the Heritage Flight?"

"Okay." Charlie nodded at Ratchet. "We have the flight-planning sheet from the briefing."

"It'll be a nice flight with Lucky's P-51 and Dan's P-38 joining in," Ratchet admitted. "We're covering both the Pacific and the European theaters of operations."

West stepped down from the trailer and stopped, checking on their coverage of the display, pleased to see Woody in front of *Bad Luck*, talking to visitors, and Eddie sitting on the wing, listening. Bump was discussing *The Lady* with a small group of men and Dani was cleaning the canopy and windscreen.

He smiled as Charlie stopped beside him. With Ratchet inside, that left Lenny free to wander around and watch for Tony and his growing group of "friends."

"Did you see Emli's sister and family come in this morning?" Charlie asked as she hugged West's arm.

"I did," he replied. "They went up the ramp to the west, so it looks like the children didn't get enough airplanes yesterday."

"I think you're right and I don't think they've been to many airshows," she added. "They acted like everything was new to them."

"Yeah." West smiled. "It's always nice to see someone with so much interest and enthusiasm."

Celia stopped at the kiosk west of the exhibitors' gate and looked at the displays of aviation themed jewelry. Norman glanced at the displays and then turned to watch the aerial routines.

"Hey, En," she asked, and caught his arm. "Which one of these do you like best?"

She was holding two different themed earring pairs and he knew he really could not afford to choose wrong.

"Are you trying to set me up?" he asked, and looked closer at each pair. "Hmm. I think the silver P-51s inlaid on the thin turquoise stones are more striking than the combination of polished and satin silver ones." He held them up to her ears and smiled. "Yes, I think these are better, and they go with your ring."

Celia smiled and squeezed his arm. "I agree. I like them too. Can I get them?"

"Certainly." He stole a kiss. "I think they will look fantastic."

Celia paid for the earrings and joined Norman as he spotted two familiar figures walking along the displays, back toward the main gate. He pointed.

"Looks like Tony and his sidekick are back." He caught her hand. "I haven't seen the guys we saw last night."

"It was pretty dark," she reminded him. "Are you sure you'd recognize them in the daylight?"

"Probably not by themselves," he admitted. "I was hoping to get another look at them with Tony so we could recognize each one when we see them again or by themselves."

"We'll just have to keep our eyes open," she commented as they walked slowly back toward the gate, stopping to check on the different displays and kiosks as they went.

When Charlie, helmet in hand, followed Ratchet out of the trailer and stepped around the wingtip of the TF, two children ran across the ramp toward her, calling her name. She paused and smiled when they stopped a few feet away.

"Let me see..." She made a show of trying to remember their names. "Melony and... Michael. Right?"

"Yes," Melony said brightly. "Would you sign our brochures?"

They both held out the paper brochures they got at the gate when they had arrived that morning.

"I think I can do one better than that." Charlie turned back to look at the trailer. "Hey, Dani," she called. And when Dani looked out, she continued. "Will you bring me two of those autographed posters we had made on Friday?"

It only took Dani a minute to arrive with the posters in hand.

"Well, hello again," Dani greeted, remembering the children. "Here you are, Charlie."

"Thanks." Charlie took the rolled and tied posters, bent down, and handed one to each of them. "These are a picture of all eight of us in front of these two planes, and we've all signed it. So, now you have a great picture you can put up in your rooms, with all of our signatures."

"Oh, wow!" Melony exclaimed. "Thank you."

"Yeah. Thank you!" Michael said excitedly. "This is really great. Thank you."

"Now, I'm going to get in and start *The Lady*"—she gestured to the plane behind her—"so you'll need to stand back and give us room. Are your parents close?"

"Yes, just over there." Melony pointed.

"Maybe you should stand with them," Charlie suggested, "so you won't be too close to the propellers."

"Okay. I knew you were going to be flying today," Melony said.

"You knew?" Charlie asked, surprised.

"Just the way West talked about you and how good of a pilot you are," Michael admitted. "Mel figured he'd be letting you fly today."

"That's why we came back," Melony said. "We wanted to see you fly. Thank you for the posters, Charlie."

"Thank you very much," Michael said again. "Come on, Mel. We're keeping Charlie from her work."

They waved and Michael led Melony across the ramp. Melony waved again and Charlie turned to *The Lady* and mounted the left strut.

She quickly strapped herself in, watching the children as they walked back and joined their parents. She caught Cat's look as she glanced up after the children reached her, and their eyes locked for a second before she donned her helmet, shaking her head to clear their images away as she plugged the communications umbilical in and waved to Ratchet. She took a deep breath and selected the Ghost Ranch frequency and called Ratchet.

"Sorry to keep you waiting, Ghost Three."

"No problem, Ghost Two. Your fans needed you. Signal when you're ready for start."

She stepped through the checklist and held her arm up when she was ready to start. She looked at Ratchet, and when he nodded she dropped her arm and switched the starter on.

The TF and the Corsair's propellers began turning at the same time, and both engines started on the first try. Charlie cycled the flaps and checked the hydraulic system pressure, and with a gesture to Ratchet, released the brakes.

Watching as she turned toward the taxiway and away from the crowd, Charlie glanced again and saw Melony and Michael waving enthusiastically from the sidelines. She looked at them, waved, and quickly turned back to the business of taxiing *The Lady*.

When they landed at Broomfield after the Heritage Flight, Charlie taxied to the ramp in front of the Ghost Ranch display area and slowed to a stop. She waited until Ratchet taxied up on her right and stopped, and then she raised her arm and they both pushed their throttles up to clear the engines. She dropped her arm and they both cut the ignition and the fuel, and the two engines spun down together.

Bump was hooking up the tow bars to the Corsair when Charlie and Ratchet removed their helmets and stood up to climb out of the cockpits. The crowd nearby clapped, and Charlie waved as she climbed down the left strut and walked around the propeller to help. Dani smiled as she stood up on the tow bars for Bump, holding a propeller blade for support.

Charlie chuckled as Bump began to back away, pulling *Bad Luck* with him. Ratchet joined her.

"Are you going to wait for Bump?"

"Yeah," Charlie admitted, watching the Corsair swing around in front of its parking spot. "Looks like they'll have *Bad Luck* spotted in a minute."

Ratchet waited with Charlie as Bump and Dani parked the Corsair and returned to tow *The Lady* in. West rode out on the tug and told them how much the crowd liked the four-plane flight.

"I think it was a big hit," West said as Bump hooked the tow bars into the landing gear rings.

"That's good to know," Charlie conceded, then turned to Dani. "Walk with me? I need to drain the sumps before I feel like getting something to eat."

"Sure. Bump, can you get this?"

"Go ahead, you two." Bump chuckled. "I think we can spot *The Lady* for you."

"Thanks." Charlie led Dani across the ramp toward the sanitary station beyond Jet Service's street gate.

Charlie heard Eddie holler from the trailer and waved as Eddie started to catch up at a trot.

Eddie reached the sanitary station after Charlie and Dani had already chosen portable toilets and gone in. She stopped and waited, scanning the area around them and the few spectators entering and leaving other modules. She noticed the utility van behind the sanitary station and two workers at its open back doors and then glanced absently down the ramp.

When Dani and Charlie stepped out, Eddie was completely unprepared when the two workers darted out from behind the portable toilets and grabbed them. One grabbed Dani, covering her mouth and dragging her backwards, and the other grabbed Charlie in the same manner.

Eddie charged, yelling at the top of her lungs for them to let Dani and Charlie go. She saw Dani slowly go limp and she jumped at the man holding her, but he hit her across the face, knocking her to the ground.

Eddie rolled over and saw the man throw Dani in the back of the van. Charlie was struggling and Eddie was getting to her feet to charge again, yelling into her mobile phone for West to hurry, when she heard two loud bangs. Then Charlie wilted and Eddie saw her pistol fall to the ground just before the man threw her in the van and closed the door. He stumbled and half ran to the van's passenger door and jumped in.

Eddie screamed and charged the van as it started to move, suddenly heading off toward the exhibitors' gate near Jet Services.

Norman and Celia were approaching the sanitary station, talking about her new jewelry purchase and deeply enjoying each other's company when they heard a woman's persistent scream. Startled, Norman looked around and saw the struggle near the portable toilets.

"Cee! Stay here and call the police!" he shouted, and took off on a dead run.

He reached the back of the van as it started to move, but he could not catch the handle on the back door. Quickly recovering from a stumble, he started diagonally across the grassy verge to head the van off before it could get to the exhibitors' gate.

Running as hard as he could, he cut in front of the van as it tried to turn into the gate. The driver saw him lunge and instinctively jerked the steering wheel, overcorrecting, and the van slammed head-on into the solid concrete abutment supporting the gate.

Norman, realizing the van had stopped, spun around to the driver's door, jerked it open, reached in, and grabbed the man behind the wheel. He unceremoniously hauled the man out and slammed him onto the ground as someone else opened the passenger door and pulled the other man out and threw him down.

When Norman's man tried to roll over, he slammed his head against the asphalt and yelled at him to lie still. He banged his head again, wondering how he was going to keep him there while he tried to help the others. To his relief, an airport police car stopped and one officer hurried to his aide, and the other hurried to the other side of the van. Two Broomfield police cars stopped on the other side of the gate and the two patrolmen quickly assisted.

Norman stood up and reported that the man on the ground

was the driver of the van, and he proceeded to explain what he saw and did. Then he saw the doors at the back were open and he glanced around the door on his side to see West lifting a limp Charlie out, and one of his mechanics lifting the other woman. They sat down a short distance away, and a third woman in Ghost Ranch attire—the one he had heard yelling—knelt down in front of them.

Norman noted the airport's emergency medical ambulance's arrival. The techs quickly began checking Charlie, the second woman, and the two men pulled from the van. Suddenly, the man he knew as Lenny hollered to West and the EMT.

"Here's what they used," he said, and picked up a bottle with a rag around the neck. He walked over to the technician and held the bottle for them to read.

The woman asked West questions about allergies or medical problems, and when West said he knew of none, she gave Charlie and Dani each an injection.

"This will counter the anesthesia and speed their recovery," the med tech explained encouragingly. "They'll start coming around in fifteen to twenty minutes."

A hand on Norman's shoulder startled him and he turned to see Celia, concern coloring her face, standing next to him.

"I think they'll be all right," he said, and stepped back from the door.

"This one's been shot," a voice from the other side of the van said, and Norman and Celia looked around the door again to see two techs carrying the passenger on a stretcher and another man walking beside them. "Twice in the stomach."

Norman looked back and saw the police had taken the driver to a patrol car. He smiled and looked at Celia. "I think they can finish up here without our help," he said, and slipped his arm through hers and led her away from the van where they could quietly meld with the gathering spectators.

Monte heard the woman screaming from where they

stood in front of Jet Services. He looked in the direction of the screams and saw the struggle and the van at the sanitary station. When he saw the driver get in and the second man trying to get someone in the back, he suddenly realized who they were after.

"Shit! They're trying to take Charlie! Stay with the kids." He immediately started running toward them. "Call the police!"

He saw the van start moving and hurried, but was surprised when he saw another man jump in front of it, forcing it to swerve and collide with the concrete abutment beside the gate.

He reached the van and jerked the passenger side door open. He saw the other man quickly pull the driver out and slam him to the ground. Monte agreed that was the appropriate way to handle them and followed the example; he pulled the second man out and threw him down.

The man groaned but did not resist, and Monte waited, knowing the police would be coming.

Knowing where Charlie and Dani were going, West instantly started running when he heard the screams and got Eddie's urgently pleading call.

"Woody, watch the planes!" Ratchet shouted as Bump and Lenny joined him behind West.

West saw a man running ahead of him on his right, charging the oncoming van, and then he saw it swerve and crash.

Eddie ran toward him as he reached the van. She was crying, fearfully beside herself. "In the back!" she shouted through her sobs. "They put them in the back."

West grabbed the handles and wrenched the doors open, letting them swing wide. He curled his arms under Charlie and Bump quickly lifted Dani into his arms. West led the way to one side and slowly sat down on the open asphalt ramp. He ignored the people quickly gathering behind them as he cradled Charlie and checked her pulse.

Bump lowered himself down beside West and held Dani in his lap, following West's example.

Eddie knelt in front of them and leaned close, wiping her eyes. "Charlie dropped this before they could take her." She held the pistol out to him. "You should keep it for her. I think she shot the one that grabbed her. Two shots."

"Thank you, Eddie." He forced a smile. "She's always been prepared as much as she could be. I'll keep it for her. And thank you for calling and yelling." He reached out and cupped her chin, looking at her face. "Who did this to you?" Her cheek was puffy and redder than it would have been from crying, and a dark bruise was forming behind her eye.

"The one that took Dani," Eddie said in a low voice. "I tried to stop him, but he knocked me down, so I called you and kept screaming. I tried to get to Charlie, and that's when I heard the shots. I saw her drop the gun where she struggled."

"Thank you, Eddie." West squeezed her shoulder. "You're a very brave woman and both Charlie and Dani will be proud to know you tried. And I'm very proud of you."

"Thank you, but I felt so helpless," Eddie admitted softly. "I couldn't stop them..."

"I know. It's okay, Eddie. You did help. We got your call and someone heard your yelling. Without you, no one would've known there was trouble. You helped as much or more than anyone could. Do you understand? You did help."

"Yes, sir." She smiled and wiped her eyes again. "Are they going to be all right?"

"I hope so." He gestured to the ambulance and the EMTs crowding around them. "We'll know in a few minutes. Just remember that you did really well. Did I tell you, I'm very proud of you?"

A technician knelt in front of Charlie and another knelt in front of Dani. They started asking questions and West heard Lenny: "Here's what they used."

Lenny held a bottle with a rag and showed the label to the woman. She nodded and dug into her bag, then gave Charlie and Dani an injection.

"This will counter the anesthesia and they'll start coming around in fifteen to twenty minutes," she explained. "It won't be long."

"This one's been shot," a tech announced as two of them carried the man from the passenger's side of the van on a stretcher. "Twice in the stomach."

The woman tending to Dani looked up. "So one of these two gave him what he deserved."

West recognized the man walking beside the stretcher as Catherine's husband from the previous day. And he remembered the name from Charlie's explanations and Jessie's eavesdropping. West waved him closer.

"I assume you helped stop the van," West surmised, "and got this guy out."

"Monte." He extended his hand. "The other guy stopped the van. He jumped in front of it and made the driver swerve."

"What other guy?" West asked.

"The guy that pulled the driver out." Monte looked around. "He talked with the police officer that took the driver."

"Thanks. I'll talk to him in a few minutes, once Charlie is awake and can stand up."

"I am sorry this happened, Mr. West." Monte knelt down on West's open side. He nodded to Eddie. "There are two fellows that have been following you two, Tony Bellini and Tom Laker. These two were accomplices I discovered this weekend, but I didn't think they would try anything here."

"We knew they were here also, Monte" West admitted. "A friend of ours tipped us off, but I didn't plan well enough for Charlie or Dani's protection."

"I sent two private investigators to watch Tony and Tom," Monte continued. "I was thinking we could head them off, figure out what they were going to do. But I wasn't prepared enough either."

West decided to wait to comment and let Monte talk. It was becoming obvious to him that Monte, without actually saying it, was becoming an ally. But before Monte could go on, Charlie started to twitch and move her arms.

As she became more animated, obviously remembering her struggle, West leaned close and softly talked to her, hoping to keep her from waking and thinking she was still in the clutches of her captors. Charlie shook, rolling to him, and curled her legs as she slowly woke and opened her eyes. West held her close and smiled, watching her.

"Hey, love," he greeted softly. "You're safe, now. Everything's okay. Eddie called us and got help."

"West?" Charlie whispered a sigh and slipped her arms around him, pulling him tight against her. "You're here."

"Yes, love," he encouraged. "I'm here and you're going to be all right. And Dani's going to be all right too."

"Dani?" Charlie slowly looked around and saw Bump holding Dani in his lap, watching her with a deeply concerned face.

"They tried to take both of you," West said softly, and chuckled. "They are obviously color blind. They didn't know you were the blonde and Dani the long-haired brunette."

"Oh, West..." She squeezed him again. "What if—"

"Sssh," West said, and gently put his finger on her lips, "we'll talk about that later, love. Right now I need to see if you can stand up and show everyone you're okay." He glanced at Eddie. "Eddie, give us a hand, please."

Charlie looked around at the crowd of curious spectators that had gathered a short distance away. Eddie took her hand and West turned her and helped lift her, and together they slowly stood up. Surprised, Charlie looked at the crowd again as they began to clap. A medical tech asked if she could get her standing blood pressure.

"How's Dani?" Charlie asked when the tech was finished. She took a step closer, with West holding her arm tightly so she would not fall.

"She's starting to move a little," Bump admitted, and smiled.

"Good," West conceded in a loud whisper.

"What do I do?" Bump asked meekly.

"Talk to her," Charlie said softly. "She knows you, Bump. Let her know she's okay, that she's safe and that you're here."

Slowly she responded to his voice, and before Dani opened her eyes, she slipped her arms around him and pulled herself tight against him.

"Hold her, Bump," Eddie whispered, leaning close. "You know she likes you, so hold her like she means something to you."

Eddie looked at Charlie and West and smiled.

He nudged Charlie and gestured to Eddie. "Eddie was the one that sounded the alarm and got help."

Charlie quickly caught Eddie in a bear hug and squeezed for all she was worth. "Really? Thank you, thank you for me and for your sister."

"It was all I could do," Eddie confided. "I'm so very glad people heard me. West, Lenny, Bump, and that man from yesterday came running."

"I know this will hit me and I'll fall apart in a few minutes, but thank you, Eddie. From the bottom of my heart."

"Thanks, Officer." West took the copy of the police report. "I hope you can find the other two and who they work for."

"We'll certainly do our best, Mr. West," the patrolman replied. "I've got yours and Charlie's statements and I don't think there will be any questions about Charlie shooting the kidnapper in self-defense. Your conceal-carry permits check out, so I think I have everything. Someone in our office will call you when we get the judge's comments back."

"Thanks."

"Please let us know if there is anything else you need help with. You have my card. I've recorded that you're pressing charges and we'll be letting you know what's next."

"Thank you, again." West shook his hand.

The officer stopped and chatted with his partner before they went through the gate and got into their patrol car, and West turned back to Charlie where she was talking with Dani and Bump. He explained what the patrolman had told him.

"So it was Norman?" Charlie asked in a surprised whisper. "And he jumped in front of the van?"

"That's what he said," he chuckled. "I hope he knows you're both okay."

"Why didn't he say something? Or talk to you?" Charlie asked, looking around and then back at West.

"You said no personal contact. Remember?" West said, and held her eyes. "Your stipulations."

"But this is different...isn't it?" Charlie asked. "I only meant he could work for us on the business side of things if he respected our privacy. I didn't want him nosing around like Carson did."

"And the few times he's contacted us with very important information, he has respected our privacy and your stipulations. He kept us informed by telling Lenny or by asking permission through Bill Strong. He hasn't broken his promise—not even now, after he basically saved both of your lives."

"We'll have to think of some way to say thank you and show our gratitude," Charlie declared. "There has to be a good way and not embarrass him."

"I'm still not clear why you wanted to leave so early," Celia admitted as she hung her blouse in the niche across from the sink in their hotel room.

"It was time, Cee," Norman stated simply, and stepped up behind her and hugged her. "We saw that they were both okay, the medics were happy and the police had their reports, and I figured we should go and let them get back on their feet. Besides, I suddenly felt like I should be with just you, and maybe the hot tub."

"I see." She held his arms around her. "I think it's admirable that you don't need to tout about how daring and brave you were, and I won't mention how scared I was when you jumped in front of that van, or when I thought about what could have happened." She exhaled slowly. "Is the water ready?"

"Yes, my dear Cee. It most certainly is."

"Then unfasten me, En, and help me finish getting ready." She lifted her arms and waited.

He followed her request and she returned the favor.

Relaxing in each other's embrace, they spent most of an hour after their passionate interlude letting the hot water vaporize the last of the tensions and disbelief of the afternoon's incident. Finally, Norman broke their comfortable silence.

"I don't want to sound impatient, Cee," he said softly, "but today reminded me of how fragile our time can be, and I'd like to set a date to give you the other half of your ring."

"Hmm," she murmured. "I'd like that too. How about a week after I take my exams? That will give me time to shift gears."

"I like it. That's only a month away. Do you have a preference where we have the ceremony? I'm sure we can find a *padre* that will conduct the service."

"Do you remember that place, sort of in the middle of the Garden of the Gods? It's in between the two big rock formations—the ones called the Three Graces?"

"Yes. That's a very pretty place, and I believe they allow weddings there."

"Yes, they do. Let's have the ceremony there late morning and then do a lunch and reception at that restaurant Bill Strong sent us to after we got here, 'In the Aspen Grove.'"

"That will be grand. May I call our folks and siblings and tell them the news? Then I can start making arrangements while you study."

"Let's call them together," she agreed brightly. "Once I finish with you here." She let her hand wander in explanation.

West sat with Charlie in the front of the semitrailer, each on a stackable chair facing each other. They were leaning to each other, foreheads touching, and he held her hands gently between them.

"How's Dani holding up?" she asked, and squeezed his hands.

"She's shaken up but doing okay. Robert, Eddie, and Bump are with her. We can go and check on her in a few minutes, but first, how about you?"

"I'm really okay. Between Eddie and you and Lenny, Bump, Monte, and especially Norman, we're both okay and will live to fly another day." She tried to chuckle, but coughed instead.

He tipped her head back and kissed her. "I know you are okay physically, but I am worried about you emotionally. I'm so sorry I let it hap—"

"You didn't let it happen. I wasn't alone. I followed your warning and it still happened. You know me well enough to know I'll bounce back. I have to."

"Actually," he continued, "there were enough people with you to keep them from getting away."

"I know, but now it scares me more than ever. It was too close. I always figured I could defend myself and keep them away, but..."

"...but we're learning. And now, we have the police watching more closely and we have taken two of Howard's men out of circulation. We won't let our guard down and I'm not going to leave your side."

"Thanks. But you can't do your job and follow me around all

day."

"Okay. We'll work something out."

"Right now, the only thing I want you to work on is spending some very private time with me when we get back to the hotel. I need you to remind me I have a life now—one that is worth living for. That I have you, and how that makes all the difference in the world."

"I will do my best, love."

"Why did those men want to hurt Charlie and Dani?" Melony asked as they sat quietly eating a late lunch under the tent in front of the food stands.

"Sometimes bad people do bad things to others," Cat said softly, uncertain of how to answer.

"When people are wealthy or famous," Monte continued in an attempt to explain and soften the impact on the kids, "sometimes bad people will try to find ways to extort money from them. Sometimes they will try to kidnap someone important to the wealthy people and then demand a large ransom."

"Are Charlie and Dani wealthy and famous?" Michael asked.

"Sure they are," Melony said, and bumped shoulders with him.

"That's right," Cat agreed. "Charlie and her husband own the airplanes they brought, and apparently they own many more. They have to have a lot of money to do that."

"And," Melony continued, "they are famous because everyone knows them and likes it when they come and bring their airplanes to the airshows."

"Did Charlie really shoot one of them?" Michael asked.

"You heard that? That one of the men got shot?" Cat studied

Michael's face.

"Some of the people in the crowd said one of the medical people said the man on the stretcher had been shot. Was he really?" Michael looked at Cat and then Monte.

"I believe he was," Monte said with a sigh. "Apparently Charlie or Dani tried to defend herself."

"I didn't know pilots had guns," Michael persisted.

"Aah. Let me try to explain it this way." Monte glanced at Cat. "Look at the country around us here. You see mountains on one side and desert or grasslands on the other. If a pilot has airplane trouble and has to land out there, he, or she, might have to take care of themselves for a while before help can get to them. They might—"

"You mean like defend themselves against snakes, or wolves, or coyotes, or bears?" Michael interrupted, and Melony giggled.

"Yes." Monte smiled. "Like snakes, bears, coyotes, and who knows what else. Back where we live, you wouldn't expect pilots to need guns, but here...maybe."

"I see." Michael nodded and returned to his burger.

Cat smiled at Monte and covered his hand with hers.

Twenty-Three
Monday, July 3

Tony and Tom ate an early breakfast in the restaurant connected to their hotel. When he had finished, Tony forced himself to go back to his room and make the call.

"Mr. Collingsworth," he said dryly when Howard answered his office phone. "Tony here. I need to talk to you."

"One minute." Tony could hear Howard get up, walk somewhere, and then close a door. "What do you have?"

"It's what I *don't* have that's the problem. The two 'helpers' you sent have cost us, both the prize and the advantage of surprise."

"I'm sure it isn't that bad, Tony," Howard argued. "Maybe they're a little overzealous, but I'm sure—"

"They would not listen to my orders," Tony explained in a dusty voice. "Yesterday, they decided to attempt kidnapping Charlie and another woman, on their own, in broad daylight!"

"In broad daylight, you say?" Howard asked with a hint of a smile in his voice. "A bit daring, but—"

"But nothing!" Tony shouted. "People came out of the woodwork to stop them! There were people everywhere! One man jumped in front of them and caused them to crash into a concrete barrier! Larry was shot twice and died last night in the hospital, and Benny is in the city jail being charged with two counts of kidnapping. Since they had the women in their van and were trying to escape, the charges will stick!"

"How?" Howard whispered, suddenly at a loss for words.

"How?" Tony asked in dismay. "Stupidity! That's how! You sent me incompetent help, and I'm betting you told them to do whatever they needed to do to get it done." Tony's voice was getting drier by the word. "So they ruined all of our planning and put that Charlie woman on high alert! It's going to be ten times harder to catch her now! And one of them died in the trying! All because of your meddling! Either you let me do this or we're out. Get someone else to finish this."

"Now, now, Tony," Howard started to soft talk.

"No. You heard me," Tony stated firmly. "In a week or less the Colorado Police will be looking for Tom and me, and they will probably know you set this up. It's going to be really hard to pull this off now, and you better watch who comes to your front door."

The phone was quiet for a few minutes and finally Howard sighed and said, "Lay low for a while and see if this cools off. Is there another fly-in in the near future?"

"Of course we're going to lay low! I'm checking on the next fly-ins," Tony shouted. "But you stay out of it! You set me up to fail again, and I'll come and deliver my message to you in person! And you won't like what I have to say! Goodbye, Mr. Collingsworth."

Tony hung up and Tom looked at him.

"Well?" Tom asked. "Is he going to hold you responsible for Benny and Larry's actions?"

"He may try," Tony sighed. "But maybe we can redeem some of the weekend."

"You mean your other opportunity?"

"Maybe we'll get lucky and find out where the ranch is. If we can, maybe, and it's a long shot, but maybe we can get her there, when they least expect it. Like I told Howard, it's going to be a lot harder now." Tony got up and went to the door.

"Let's go back out to the airport and see what's happening. Maybe we can hear something useful."

Monday awoke bright and sunny with high, thin clouds slowly gathering on light winds through the morning. Many people that had witnessed or heard about the previous day's incident stopped by the Ghost Ranch display and said how happy they were that Charlie and Dani were doing well and not injured. Many stopped and bought the autographed posters and asked if they had ever thought about selling Ghost Ranch T-shirts.

"Not just the normal fly-in T-shirts," Ratchet said as a group of teenaged girls walked away. "They wanted shirts with autographed pictures of Charlie, Dani, and Eddie. Together and separate."

"Really?" West asked in surprise. "Well, things have definitely changed since Charlie came aboard."

"What's changed?" Charlie asked as she, Dani, and Eddie stopped to listen.

"Everything about the Ghost Ranch, I'd say," he replied, and Ratchet repeated his comments about the requests.

"Seems you girls have woken up a number of young girls," West remarked, "to the thrilling experience of flying."

"We had a few even asking where they could learn to fly," Lenny commented from his chair. "I told them where to look and what to look for to get a good teacher or school."

"I'm surprised," Charlie said with a smile.

"I'm not," West admitted. "The ranch never had a woman on the team, not that anyone could see at the airshows, until Reno last year. At Alamosa we had two women representing us, and now three. And you're pilots. I'm not at all surprised the female spectators are noticing and thinking, 'why not me?'"

"I'm not a pilot," Eddie said, "but you said they asked about shirts with pictures of me?"

West turned and hugged Eddie's shoulders. "They certainly did, and they know you're learning to fly and will be a pilot very soon. That's what matters. You're walking the walk and know what it's all about."

Eddie smiled at West, then at the others.

"You're part of the team," Charlie reiterated, with pride coloring her voice. "Don't ever forget that. And soon you'll be flying the fighters just like us."

"When we get home," West continued, and smiled at Charlie, "I think we all need to sit down together and think about this new T-shirt request and decide if we want to do anything about it."

Everyone nodded and West looked at Dani. "And how are you doing this morning?"

"Better, much better." Dani grinned and glanced to where Bump was wiping the Corsair's belly behind the cowling. "I had a lot of moral support last night, and of course I'm very thankful for everyone that jumped in and helped stop those men."

"It scared us all, but I am glad you're doing okay."

Dani smiled. "And how are you doing, Charlie?"

"Okay I guess. Like you, I'm coping."

Dani nodded as Ratchet stood up from the table.

"Half an hour to engine start," West said, and turned to go back to the trailer.

Charlie turned to follow and Dani slipped into to a chair at the poster table when Ratchet got up. Lenny stood up and gestured for Eddie to take his place while he helped get the planes ready.

Charlie got her equipment duffel down from her shelf and West quickly stopped her.

"Are you sure you should fly the routine today?" he asked, and Charlie stared at him, questioning.

"Why not? I feel fine," Charlie challenged.

"Are you sure? Yesterday was—"

"Yes I am!" she snapped. "Sorry. Other than you helping me iron out the wrinkles, my worries, like we did last night," she said in a gentler voice, stepping close and wrapping her arms around him, "flying is the most therapeutic thing I can do. If I wasn't feeling okay, I'd tell you."

"Sometimes"—West grinned and squeezed her tight—"I'm not sure you would. Go on. Get ready. You'll just make my life miserable if I try to keep you on the ground."

After the Heritage Flight was finished and the planes respotted, they all gathered in the trailer and ate a lunch catered by the Italian food tent across the ramp and paid for by the airport. West said that it was the airport's way of saying they were sorry for the incident and for Charlie and Dani's discomfort and duress.

"They've also offered to fill the planes for our return trip home," Ratchet said. "On their nickel."

"I think they like us and want us to come back again," Bump chuckled.

"Ratchet"—West looked around the front of the trailer and the stacks of boxes—"when we get home, pull the trailer into one of the hangars and let's refit the front end as a crew lounge—chairs or sofas, refrigerator, lighting, windows. Make it a nice place to eat, relax, or to discuss our plans and objectives, or whatever else we need to use it for."

"Sure, boss," Ratchet agreed with a wide smile. "We can rearrange the storage so the boxes are properly stowed or use smaller, maybe plastic bins on steel shelving and redo how we place and secure engines in the back."

"Also, with that in mind," West continued, "look into the trailering laws for dual trailers. We could put the engines and 'special' parts in a second, half-length trailer. Our crew is getting large enough that we need space for you guys and not just airplane parts. Plan seating for twelve."

"Twelve?" Lenny questioned in surprise.

"Yup." West smiled. "Philip has asked to learn to fly, and I think we'll start Camilla with familiarization. She's too young to get her tickets but not too young to learn. And Mom has expressed an interest in coming on occasion—especially to Reno to see her old friends."

"That will be nice," Dani admitted softly, looking at the front of the cluttered trailer. "May I ask that we look at a new set of stairs to the roof, like spiral to save floor space, and maybe a railing around the top?"

West smiled and looked at Ratchet. "You heard the woman. Put it on the list. Let's put plans together and make it happen."

It was midafternoon when the fuel truck finally left after refueling *Box Car, The Lady,* and *Your Bad Luck.* Lenny stepped back up into the trailer and stopped to talk to West.

"Didn't detect a tracker beacon on any of the planes," Lenny acknowledged. "I went over them twice and didn't find any signal."

"Very good." West patted Lenny's shoulder as he stepped out of the trailer. "I think we'll stow our duffels and head back in a little bit, and Dani should be about ready to go pick up Gracie and her family in the Springs."

He saw Eddie conducting the Beaver's walk-around, flashlight and mirror in hand and an oilcloth in her hip pocket. He chuckled at her appearance: all business and no worry about what people might think about her look. Dani had thrown their duffels in the luggage compartment and was securing the side door when Bump stopped to talk to her. Two days earlier West knew he would have been surprised, but he was not surprised today when Dani threw her arms around Bump's neck and pulled herself up to him, holding him for a long moment. Bump returned the embrace, holding Dani with just her toes touching the ground.

"Did you know?" Charlie asked softly, stopping beside him and smiling at Dani and Bump.

He slowly shook his head. "Not until yesterday."

"I thought I saw Bump taking a special interest at Alamosa"—she nodded—"but I wasn't sure. Do you think it will be a problem for Madra? Robert has to know."

"They're fair folk," he confirmed, but wasn't completely convincing. "If Dani and Bump are really serious, they'll have to talk about the age difference. Hopefully eight years won't bother them too much. If they're not really serious, I just hope no bad feelings come out of it."

"I'm ready to stow our bags." Charlie took his arm. "Do you have everything you need packed in yours?"

"I do." He smiled at her. "I'll walk out with you."

Together, Charlie and West carried their duffels out to *The Lady* and West stowed them behind the second seat. He glanced at the Beaver and saw Eddie climbing into the right seat and Dani climbing the opposite strut to the pilot's seat. Bump stood at the wingtip until Dani had started the engine and began taxiing out. He waved and turned back to the trailer as Dani swung *Box Car's* nose toward the taxiway.

It was 4:35 when *The Lady* broke ground heading northwest. West followed the runway heading until they were nearly to Nederland, where he turned to a southwesterly heading and started a climb to 13,500. He flew to clear the gap west of Roger's Peak and Mount Bierstadt, and then south over Grant.

As the mountains gave way to the high plains, Charlie called from the back seat.

"We have a bogey. The modified APS-13 indicates a non-propeller type at four or five miles behind us. Too bad it can't tell us elevation or azimuth."

"Aah, I see it. We're doing about three thirty true and he looks like he's holding a steady distance," West confirmed as he watched the gauge. "At that range, he must be a little below us to have a visual. I don't know of any civilian airplanes with targeting radar."

"He might be using the ATC radar hits to see where his traffic is," Charlie offered. "Maybe we should drop down and turn, to see if he's following us visually or not."

"I think we will do just that. Selecting Transponder Off. We're going totally VFR and dark."

He started a descent, leveling at 11,000 feet, relatively low as they approached the high prairie and turned southeast around the two Twin Cone Peaks. He decelerated, waited thirty seconds, and then turned back west. At forty-two seconds, a Cessna Citation Mustang passed a mile and half in front of them, coming from behind the North Twin Cone Peak. West shoved the throttle forward and turned to an intercepting course.

"He's slowing and descending," West noted. "He's obviously lost us and should start looking around in a minute. Thirty seconds and we'll join up. Get his N-number for future investigation."

"Roger that," Charlie agreed, feeling the excitement of the hunt. "Too bad you don't have those acetylene show cannons on board. We could make him think he's being shot at."

"You do have a wicked streak, don't you?" He chuckled and slowly adjusted power. "Forming up. He'll know we're here in a moment or two."

He held *The Lady* off the Cessna Mustang's left wing to give maneuvering room and slowly edged forward until he could clearly see into the cockpit; there were two men, the left one flying and the other one searching with large binoculars. West and Charlie both waved when the pilot of the jet scanned the horizon and suddenly saw *The Lady* beside him.

"Got a very nice picture," Charlie commented with a chilling laugh. "Too bad we can't get a picture of both of us, two different generations of Mustangs in formation."

West gave the jet's pilot a 'what now?' gesture, shrugging his shoulders as he waited.

"He's not on plane-to-plane UNICOM," Charlie said.

"Well, he hasn't decided to tell us what he's up to. So I think we'll just leave him here and watch a few minutes. Try to keep an eye on him. I'm going to roll over and then drop in behind him."

"Okay," Charlie said brightly. "I'm ready. Remember you have drop tanks on."

West waved goodbye and pulled *The Lady* up and rolled right, making a forty-five degree turn and continuing the roll, returning to their previous heading. The Cessna pulled ahead three-quarters of a mile during the maneuver and West matched his speed until the jet finally started a turning climb to the left.

West stayed in his blind spot and followed him around until he rolled out on a northeasterly heading, back to overfly the Twin Cone Peaks.

"I think you busted his bubble," Charlie said as West slowly reduced power and let the Mustang disappear into the distance. "TF-51 bests the modern private jet."

"I think we did, but only in playing hide-and-seek. I wonder how he'll explain the encounter to the guys that hired him." He chuckled and turned toward the mountains behind Como.

They flew southwest, skirting the east face of the range, passing Fairplay and down to the junction of Highways 285 and 24. Then they followed Highway 24 across the ridge, turning south in the Arkansas River Valley at Johnson Village, south of Buena Vista. They continued south, past Poncha Springs, through the 8,999-foot Poncha Pass and down into the San Luis Valley.

Staying low at 11,000 feet, West flew east, crossing the mountain ridge just south of the 9,513-foot La Veta Pass and then south to Trinidad as they rounded the two Spanish Peaks. He slowly descended to 8,500 as they passed Trinidad and dropped to a thousand above ground level as they turned east toward the ranch, skirting the feet of Fishers Peak to the south.

Charlie called the ranch and Helen's happy voice answered.

"*The Lady* is eight minutes out, inbound," Charlie announced.

"I'll have Philip open your hangar," Helen stated. "Good to have you back home."

"We'll see you in a few minutes, Mom," Charlie added. "We'll put *The Lady* away and then I think we have a lot to tell you. Better turn the 'drinking lamp' on."

Tony was surprised, watching the planes departing Rocky Mountain Metropolitan Airport after the airshow, when the Cessna Mustang approached and landed. He was certain they had not been gone long enough to locate the elusive Ghost Ranch, but maybe... He held a moment of hope that the ranch might be closer than they thought, but quickly shook the notion away. They had not been that lucky in anything they had tried so far.

He walked over to the exhibitors' spaces as the Mustang taxied in and turned, slowing to a stop. After a long moment, the engine's whine decreased and then it spun to a stop, and the cabin door slowly swung open and the two men stepped down. The owner spotted Tony and slowly walked over to where he was standing. The other man went to the exhibitors' trailer and disappeared inside.

"Well, Mr. Bellini," the man said when he got close. "It seems Glen is as cagey as I've always heard he was."

"Cagey? How's that, Mr. Long?" Tony asked, unsure of his meaning.

"He knew we were following him," Long said. "Or he certainly figured someone would be. We lost him a little south of Interstate Seventy when he dropped below the horizon and mixed in with the background. And then he shows up on our left wing in as pretty of a formation as you please. Nice and polite, but I couldn't raise him on the radio. So after a few minutes, he pulled up and we lost him again."

"Did you look for him after that?" Tony asked.

"No use," Long said with a smile. "He could've led us all over western Colorado without showing us anything. Once he knew we were there following him, the game was his to control. He seems to know how to disappear when he wants to and pop up on your wing when he wants you to know where he is."

"But how am I supposed—"

"You'll just have to try another day, Mr. Bellini," Long said. "Now, you paid me the thousand, so you only owe me for the fuel I used. Since I didn't find the ranch, you don't owe me the finder's bonus. You keep that for your next attempt." Long started to turn away, but stopped when Tony hesitated. "Come along, Mr. Bellini. John has called the fuel truck."

Charlie and Philip were up top when Dani and *Box Car* entered the landing pattern. Philip had the hangar doors up and they walked up the ramp to watch as she turned final, heading almost straight at them. A quarter mile away, Dani let the Beaver settle and gentle clouds of dust billowed up behind the tires.

Philip drove the extra jeep up beside the plane as Dani climbed down the strut and Eddie quickly opened the right-side door. He unloaded Robert and Madra's luggage and the new bags of items they had purchased, and when they had settled in the jeep, he drove them down to their house.

Charlie drove the tug up out of the hangar and Dani and Eddie hooked the tow bars to the gear rings. Eddie guided and Dani rode the tow bars as Charlie turned the Beaver and backed it into the hangar.

Once inside, Dani stopped Charlie and stepped away from the plane. "I'm sorry I made you angry," she confessed softly, so Eddie wouldn't hear. "I didn't know what to do after you talked to the children and that other woman, the one that said her name was Cathy."

"I know," Charlie said, and forced a smile. "It was a shock and I didn't handle it very well. But thank you for caring."

"I think seeing someone that looks like yourself, face-to-face, would be very unsettling," Dani agreed. "I'm your friend, Charlie. If there is ever anything you want to tell me, I'll listen. I don't like seeing you like that and I had to do something. I hope it was all right that I went and found West."

Charlie nodded and took Dani's hand. "That was the best thing you could've done. Thank you. There is so much I cannot explain, but he was who I needed. Thank you."

Dani smiled a weak smile and nodded. "If you ever..."

"I know, Dani. I know..." Charlie turned and went back to put the tug away.

With the plane put to bed and feeling better in the moment as they walked to the jeep, Charlie nudged Dani.

"So tell me," she asked softly, "how long have you and Bump been an item?"

Dani looked at her and grinned. "I guess it was pretty obvious, wasn't it?"

"In Alamosa, or when he comforted you after the kidnapping?" Charlie smiled to ease the memory of the incident. "Or when you said goodbye this afternoon? Which one wasn't obvious?"

"You noticed in Alamosa?" Dani was surprised. "We'd only realized we liked each other the week before Alamosa. I mean, I knew I liked being around him and how he'd take the time to explain things to me, but I didn't know how I felt until I asked Helen about learning to fly and saw how excited Jim was when he heard I was going to start lessons."

"She wasn't sure how he felt," Eddie added, "until I pointed it out to her."

Charlie smiled when Dani scowled at Eddie.

"No matter, Dani," Charlie said again, nudging her shoulder. "I wish the best for you, but for your sake, both of you, don't rush it. You haven't had the chance to date or be around other men, maybe more normal men, and I don't want you two to get hurt."

"You think we'll get hurt?" Dani asked, surprised.

"No. Not necessarily." Charlie smiled. "That sounded too presumptuous. I guess Bump is as good of an example as any of what 'normal' men in aviation are. And he definitely cares for you and that's obvious. That's also very important."

"I keep telling her to be careful," Eddie added.

"Like you have a lot more experience?" Dani shot back.

"Now ladies, no bickering." Charlie chuckled, realizing she sounded like a mother hen, and laughed at their antics. "Love is wonderful. Just be honest with each other in everything."

Tuesday, July 4

"Looks clean," Lenny said as Ratchet came out of the trailer. "No beacons or signals. You should be able to leave without being tracked."

"Thanks." Ratchet nodded as Bump and Woody joined them.

"Trailer's closed up and locked," Woody said. "We're ready to leave once you're on your way." Woody nodded to Ratchet.

"I'll go over the whole rig again before we head out," Lenny added.

"Okay." Ratchet smiled. "Let me know if anyone takes off behind me and seems to be heading in the same direction."

"Roger," Bump agreed. "We'll watch and let you know."

"All right, you guys, I'm off. West said they were followed by the Cessna Mustang that was on exhibition up on the west end. I don't know if they'll try the same thing or not again."

Ratchet and *Bad Luck* made a gentle right-hand turnout toward Estes Park and climbed to 13,500 feet before he turned northwest and proceeded over the Alpine Visitor Center, situated at 11,800 feet between Trail Ridge and Marmot Point.

He checked the modified APS-13 West had them install in each of the planes and saw no bogies. Past the ridge, Ratchet turned southwest to Milner Pass, then southerly, following the valley down past Grand Lake and Lake Granby. With no bogies sighted and no calls from Bump, Ratchet relaxed and descended into the long valley.

The APS-13 beeped, the annunciator winked on, and the needle swung nearly full scale! Ratchet's internal systems went to full alert, just like they had every time the F-14 Tomcat's missile warning went off, filling the cockpit with flashing red light and a loud-voiced "Missile Detected." Ratchet waited, changing his course about thirty degrees to the right. He searched behind him and saw a medium-sized business jet climbing slightly above his altitude and heading northwest; it had simply crossed his path behind him.

He laughed, let his shoulders drop, and looked back at the APS-13 indicator, the annunciator lamp dark with the needle back in its undisturbed position. He turned back on course and headed for Silverthorne.

"Dad?" Melony asked as she flopped on her back across the couch in their hotel room's sitting area. "Can Mike and me send Charlie an email to wish her well?" She lifted her head and looked at him as he set his satchel on the dark wood-look desk.

"I...don't know. Do you have Charlie's email address?"

"No. But the Ghost Ranch should have an address." Michael stated matter-of-factly as he sat down on the edge of the couch by Melony's feet. "We could send a message there."

Monte looked at Cat with a questioning look. "We really don't know them..."

"It ought to be okay"—Cat smiled at Monte—"if they just express their good wishes. Don't you think? I mean, if they don't like getting a message, they can just ignore it."

Monte smiled and sighed. "Okay. I'll see if I can find an address, and you two"—he pointed at Melony and Michael—"can go and get into your swimsuits."

"Thanks." Melony got up. "And thanks for bringing us on a vacation."

"Yeah," Michael agreed quickly. "I don't remember us ever going on a vacation before."

Monte smiled and shook his head. "To tell you the truth, you both were pretty young the last time we went somewhere together. And I admit I had forgotten how much I like going."

"Can we take vacations more often?" Michael asked.

"I think we should plan on it." Monte squeezed Michael's shoulder. "I still have to work, but we'll make plans and try to stick to them. Now, go get changed and I'll see what I can find for an address."

"Was that Lloyd?" Cat asked as Monte switched his phone off and slipped it into his shirt pocket.

He nodded as he stepped up to the empty chair beside Cat, a small end table separating them. He glanced at Melony and Michael splashing in the hotel pool. "Yes. Just an update on their surveillance." He sat down and stared across the pool, thinking. "They haven't seen Tony or Tom since early afternoon yesterday."

"That's not good, is it?" Cat asked, watching his blank expression.

"I'm not sure." Monte turned to look at her. "But it doesn't feel right. I feel like they're up to something else that we should know about."

"I hate to ask," Cat continued, "but have you called my father to tell him what's happened? That his men kidnapped Charlie and got caught?"

Monte held her eyes a long moment and then slowly shook his head.

"Why not?" Cat asked, her tone piqued.

"Take it easy," he answered softly. "I thought about that, but I figured that if I called him, a couple of things would happen. First, he would know we're using my investigators to check up on him and his progress. Right now, I think he still thinks I am verifying facts on Charlie Bassett. Second, he would know that I am openly against what he is trying to do, more than just my comments in the office, which would mean that he will start telling me what he wants me to hear and then change his tactics so I don't know what he's doing."

"Ooh. I hadn't thought of that."

"He might figure out that I'm following his men anyway," he admitted. "But if he does, I hope I'm astute enough to tell when he tests me."

"Tests you?"

"Yes." He smiled. "If he thinks I'm not on his side, he will try to confirm it, and then he'll limit what he tells me or asks me to do."

"Will that be obvious?"

"Maybe," he conceded. "Maybe not. For now, I want to see what he does next. Tony is bound to call him and talk about what they've done and what they're doing. Maybe your father will tell me enough that we can figure out what he's up to."

"Which 'we' are you talking about?" she asked as she got their plastic wine glasses out of her shoulder bag.

"First, you and me," he noted, and took the plastic carafe out of the paper sack he had beside his chair, "and then us and Lloyd and Sam second. I hope you understand that I'm not intentionally withholding anything I know from you. If you ask and I've overlooked telling you something, I'll fill you in."

Cat let a reserved smile cross her face. "I'm trying to believe that, Monte. I won't doubt you unless I have reason."

"Thanks. If you think you have reason"—Monte poured wine into their plastic glasses—"please ask me about whatever makes you think or feel that way. I don't know of anything I can't tell you."

"You think there will be some things—?"

"No. That's not what I mean." Monte set the carafe on the table, looking steadily at her. "I just don't have a crystal ball and I really do want you to know everything I know. You be the judge, but please ask if I do something you think is wrong or that I'm leaving you out."

She watched him a long moment before she picked up her plastic glass and sipped her wine. "Okay."

"I really do want you to trust me," Monte admitted softly, making certain the children were not too close.

"I know." Cat smiled. "I appreciate everything you're doing. For us and concerning the Charlie issue."

Dinner at the ranch was nearly over when Charlie asked if anyone had heard from Woody. She glanced slowly around the table at West, Helen, Dani, Eddie, and then Ratchet.

Ratchet smiled and shook his head. "I haven't heard anything. They were going to call me after I left if anyone took off and headed in the same direction, but I heard nothing then, and nothing since."

"I'm glad the mods to the APS-13 worked well." West chuckled, remembering Ratchet's telling of his trip home.

"Maybe, too good." Ratchet joined West's mirth.

"When will they get back?" Charlie asked.

"Probably between eight and nine," Ratchet answered after giving it some thought. "Driving time is about five and a half hours and they should have gotten on the road around three to three thirty.

West looked up to see Becky step through the kitchen door and stop at the foot of the table.

"Would anyone like coffee with dessert?"

"Dessert?" Ratchet asked. "Count me in. Coffee, yes."

"Sure," Eddie and Dani replied at the same time.

Helen and West nodded and Charlie shrugged and nodded.

Becky returned to the kitchen, and Gracie entered with dessert place settings and Camilla gathered the dirty dishes.

"Gracie?" West asked as she started distributing the plates and silverware. "Would you please set places for the three of you also? We have empty seats and would like for you to join us."

Gracie smiled. "Are you certain, Mr. West?"

"I wouldn't have mentioned it if I wasn't certain, Gracie." He smiled. "Please."

"Thank you." Gracie and Camilla nodded and Camilla quickly carried her collection of dishes back into the kitchen.

When Gracie came back with the extra place settings, Camilla and Becky followed her in. Becky was carrying a chocolate-iced, three-layer cake and stopped at the foot of the table. Camilla took a place beside her and Gracie stood opposite. Together, they started singing "Happy Birthday."

West caught Charlie's hand and started singing along. In a moment, the whole table was singing to Charlie.

"Oh my," Charlie said, half covering her mouth in surprise. She turned and smiled at West. "You remembered..."

"Of course, Charlie. I hope I never forget any of your special days. I also don't think you've had a real birthday party in a number of years, so we're having a party in your honor." Then West looked at Becky. "If you'll bring that down here and take a seat, I'll serve tonight."

"Oh, no—"

"Oh, yes. Please, Becky," he interrupted. "My turn tonight."

Reluctantly, Becky walked around the table and set the cake in front of West.

"Thank you." West gestured to her chair. "And, my heartfelt thank you to each of you for everything you do for Charlie, me, and Mom every day of the week." Then he turned and looked at Charlie. "And a very happy birthday to you. I asked Becky to refrain from putting all thirty-two candles on it because I didn't want to burn the place down when we lit them—"

Charlie slapped his hand. Smiling hugely and holding his eyes softly, she mouthed a silent "Thank you."

West sliced and served the cake amid happy conversation, pleased that Becky, Gracie, and Camilla joined them. And after a moment, he looked at Charlie.

"Did I show you the email we received this afternoon?" West asked as he took a folded piece of paper from his shirt pocket.

"No," Charlie questioned. "Who's it from?"

Everyone at the table looked at Charlie and listened.

West handed it to her, and as she unfolded it, her eyes went wide with surprise. "The two kids? Writing to say they hope Dani and I are doing okay after the trouble at the airport and to thank us for showing them the airplanes and giving them the signed posters." Charlie looked up and smiled. "That's very thoughtful."

"They used the email address from the ranch website," West said, and turned back to his second piece of cake. "Must have used their dad's laptop to write and send it." West raised one eyebrow, implying the significance of that fact to Charlie.

After everyone had enough cake, West asked if they could adjourn to the living room.

West guided Charlie ahead of them and she stopped in the doorway, staring at the gifts arranged on the loveseat.

"No birthday party is complete without a few gifts from those close to you," West explained. "And these are from your family."

Twenty-Four

Lenny, riding shotgun in the cab of the tractor-trailer rig as the afternoon sun settled and rested on top of the mountain ridge to their west, was still chuckling over Dani's obvious liking for Bump. Still slightly embarrassed, Bump sat strapped into the jump seat between Lenny and Woody, in the doorway to the sleeper compartment.

"I'm really happy for you," Lenny commented, "but it was a surprise to most of us."

"I said I was sorry," Bump said softly, barely making himself heard above the normal rumbling cabin noise. "We weren't trying to announce anything to anyone."

"Maybe not," Woody chimed in, "but saying goodbye the way you did in the middle of the ramp, in front of all the exhibiters, crews, and spectators, certainly didn't go unnoticed."

"Like I said," Bump continued, trying to defend himself, "I was surprised and caught off-guard until she kissed me. Then I didn't care where we were."

"Yeah," Lenny chuckled again. "We figured that out."

"Hmm," Woody said, staring at his outside mirror. "Wonder what they want."

"What?" Lenny asked, and looked at his outside mirror and the flashing lights coming up behind them. "State troopers? We're not speeding are we?"

"Nope." Woody began slowing down.

He flipped his right blinker on; they were about two miles north of Farista and the turnoff for Walsenburg. When he felt they were slow enough to not throw a hailstorm of gravel up in front of the patrol car, Woody pulled the rig onto the shoulder. "But I guess we'll find out what's up in just a minute. You can roll your window down, but don't get out and keep your door closed."

"Whoa!" Lenny shouted just as the rig stopped. "Someone just jumped off the hitch deck and is running for the fence. The troopers are in pursuit."

"What?" Woody asked, leaning forward, trying to see the chase. "Someone was riding between the cab and the trailer?"

"Yup," Lenny confirmed. "I wonder if those troopers saw him on the highway. Maybe that's why they stopped us. Aah, they got him. He ran along the fence and looks like he got tangled in the barbed wire when he tried to jump it."

"Where was he going?" Bump asked. "There's nothing out there but scrub and grass as far as you can see, until you get to the mountains."

Lenny laughed, watching the man struggle against the troopers' hold as they walked back toward the semi. "He was never going to run that far. They're walking back this way."

Woody slowly opened his door and climbed down between passing motorists zipping by. He walked slowly around the front of the tractor and waited for the troopers as they approached.

"Are you the driver of this rig?" one of them asked.

"Yes, sir. I'm Woody," he answered, and offered his hand.

"Did you know you had this man riding on the outside of your rig?" the Trooper asked as he shook Woody's hand.

"No. Not until he jumped off as we stopped."

"We spotted him looking up over the trailer a few miles back and decided to check him out," the second officer noted.

"Do you know him?" the first asked.

Woody looked at him a long moment then said, "I'm not sure." He turned to the cab. "Lenny, come and tell me if this is one of the fellas that's been following us around this summer."

Lenny opened his door and slowly climbed down. He stopped beside Woody and pulled his phone out, selected pictures, and held an image up beside the man and slowly nodded.

"Yes, sir. This is Tom," Lenny confirmed. "He and his boss, a guy named Tony"—he showed the two images to the officers—"have been following us all summer, starting in Alamosa in May. There were four of them and two of his buddies kidnapped our boss's wife and one of our pilots in Broomfield on Sunday. They were caught before they got off the airport."

"I had nothin' to do with that," Tom argued as he squirmed and tugged at the policeman's grip.

"Kidnapped?" the second officer asked absently, ignoring Tom's comments. "I heard a report on that. One of the kidnappers got shot in the act and he later died. The report confirms they kidnapped two women."

"Yes," Woody said. "A lot of people helped stop them and both women were rescued unharmed."

"If you can reach a Lieutenant Bridges of the Broomfield Police," Lenny added, "he can give you all of the details. He has copies of these pictures and he'll be very happy to hear from you. This is one of the two men he's still looking for. Tony seems to be the one making the arrangements and calling the shots."

"Why would he be riding on your rig?" the first asked further.

"I can only speculate," Woody admitted. "Maybe you can get him to tell you."

"Who were the women they kidnapped?" The first glanced at the other, who was talking to someone on his radio.

"Dispatch says a Mrs. Charlie West and a Miss Dani Ventura," the second trooper answered.

"West? That sounds familiar," the first admitted absently.

"She's the wife of a Glen West," the second said. "He owns the Glen West Aviation Collection and Restorations. Something like a flying museum of restored World War Two airplanes."

"Hmm." The first thought a moment. "This isn't the first time someone has tried to kidnap and ransom a member of a wealthy family."

"Mr. West is filing formal charges against these men and

anyone else you find associated," Woody said, interrupting their growing conversation. "He'll be very happy to know you caught another one."

"Is there a warrant out for this one?" the first asked the second.

"Yes. Issued Monday morning for a Tom Laker," the second said, and Lenny pointed to the man they held between them. "Also one for an Antonio, aka Tony, Bellini."

Friday, July 7

Howard quickly got up and closed his office door when he answered the phone and heard Tony on the line. He sat back down and picked up the handset.

"I wasn't expecting to hear from you this soon."

"I think I can safely say Benny's talking." Tony's voice was still tight and strained.

"What? How can you say that?" Howard asked, standing bolt upright, forgetting his handset was tied to the desk unit by a coiled cord. He grabbed the desk unit before it fell over the edge of his desk.

"I checked the Denver Police website this morning to see if there was anything on Tom," Tony commented, "and I—"

"On Tom?" Howard was confused.

"Yes. I sent him to follow the Ghost Ranch's semi rig to see where it goes after the airshow. And I haven't seen or heard from him since."

"So he's missing?"

"Yes," Tony admitted. "I checked the police website to see if there was any information on arrests since the weekend, and I didn't see anything listed that would tell me that. But I did find a listing for new warrants. And there, on the list, is one for me and one for Tom, issued Monday morning."

"Damn!"

"My sentiments exactly. Benny knows Tom and I are

involved in this, so I'm certain they got him talking. That probably means they know you sent us."

"Damn! Damn!" Howard muttered and tried to pace behind his desk, but the handset cord stopped him. "And if Tom's missing because they caught him, they'll most likely get him to corroborate Benny's story." Howard thought a long minute. "You said Larry is dead?"

"Yeah. One of the women didn't like him grabbing her. Two shots in the stomach and something inside of him blew up."

"Well, at least he won't talk. You better find someplace to sit tight for a while."

"You think so?" Tony asked facetiously. "Of course I will. You might want to think about finding a place too."

Charlie slipped her headphones and boom mike on and plugged the umbilical into the two jacks in the TF's left wheel well. She glanced up at Dani in the cockpit with her white helmet on.

"Dani? Are you hearing me?" Charlie asked, and tapped the side of her earphones.

"Loud and clear."

"Thanks," Charlie said, and moved under the uncowled engine and checked the hose routings one more time, running her fingers along them from the firewall to the appropriate engine ports.

She nodded to Bump standing in front of the right wing with the large fire extinguisher mounted on open-spoked metal wheels. She smiled, realizing that, more often than not, Bump found a way to work whatever jobs Dani happened to be working.

"Okay," Charlie continued. "Start through the pre-start procedures, calling off the steps as you go."

Dani followed Charlie's instructions and called off each step while Charlie looked at the various areas around the engine and firewall to visually detect any leaks. She verbally called ignition switch Off, battery switch On, and noted the voltage was showing good, throttle cracked one inch, mixture in Cut Off, propeller in High, supercharger in Auto, carburetor Air in Ram.

"Ready to pressurize the fuel system," Dani remarked, "and prime for start."

"Okay," Charlie agreed. "Go ahead."

"Ignition switch to Both," Dani confirmed. "Fuel shutoff valve On and Selector to Left Main, Boost Pump Normal and fuel pressure verified. Priming for a cold engine."

"Ready here." Charlie glanced at Bump. He signaled that he heard and she went back to watching.

Then Dani called "Clear!" to alert Charlie and Bump that she was about to swing the prop, and then she lifted the switch guard and engaged the starter. "Engaged."

The large propeller began to turn, and after seven or eight blades, the engine popped and sputtered. A few wisps of gray smoke drifted away and the engine spun down and stopped.

"Prime again for a cold engine," Charlie repeated, and Dani went through the procedure again.

The second attempt, the engine popped and sputtered three or four times before it finally spun down and stopped.

"I think you're gaining on it. We're getting the air out of the system."

"One more time. Mixture back to Cut Off, ignition still both, fuel pressure still good," Dani reconfirmed, and then primed again for a cold engine. Then she shouted "Clear!" again and engaged the starter. When the engine popped, she quickly pushed the Mixture knob down to Auto Rich and the pops began to come closer together, slowly losing their sharpness and settling into a rough purr, with short burbles as the engine settled down.

"Hold about thirteen or fourteen hundred RPM. How's the

oil pressure?"

"Oil pressure is steady just below the high limit," Dani replied without showing a lot of excitement. "Oil temp is still cold. Hydraulic pressure looks good. Generator is showing a small charge. Battery voltage is good."

Charlie climbed up on the left wing and peered down behind the engine and around the oil tank, looking at the general security of each hose and electrical cable connection. Then she turned her head to face Dani and smiled at her through the windscreen.

"I'm going back down." Charlie carefully slipped down the left strut and then stepped to the left wingtip. "Slowly advance to two thousand RPM. Be ready to cut the mixture and throttle if anything goes haywire."

"Roger." Dani complied and pushed the throttle forward. "Two thousand."

The Merlin settled down and ran smooth at two thousand.

After a minute or two, Charlie added, "Mag check."

The engine RPM sagged as Dani selected one magneto off and then reaccelerated when she turned it back on. Dani repeated the procedure with the other magneto and the engine responded in a similar manner, signaling proper operation. "Fifty RPM drop. Looks good."

"Idle," Charlie called, and Dani brought the throttle back to Idle.

They were pleased when the engine settled smoothly at Idle with no burbles or pops.

"Hold it for two minutes, check the oil pressure and temp and coolant temperature, then clear the engine and shut it down."

Charlie and Bump were waiting in front of the left wing when Dani secured the cockpit and stood up. She stepped out onto the wing and set her helmet in the seat, then turned and slipped down the left strut.

"Looks like a clean run," Dani commented with a wide smile. "Helen said the data looks good and she'll have the printouts for us when we come down."

"Amazing." Charlie stared proudly at the TF. "And the first run was clean." She looked at Bump and Dani. "Sounds like a good time for a celebratory soda."

She turned to lead them back to the hangar and ran squarely into West, standing behind her.

She chuckled and covered her mouth. "Were did you come from?"

"Hangar," West retorted with a wide smile.

"I didn't hear you come up," Charlie admitted, still trying to hide her embarrassment for running into him. "Have you been here long?"

"Long enough to know congratulations are in order." He grabbed her around the waist and spun her around. He set Charlie back down and looked at Dani and Bump. "I'd congratulate you for helping, Dani, but I don't think that would be proper under the circumstances."

Dani smiled, and West knew she remembered all of the times he used to swing her and her sister around when they were young. "I understand," she agreed. "Those times are fond memories, but"—she looked at Bump and then back at West— "I think I'm going to have to train someone else in how that's supposed to be done."

"I think that should be high on your list of priorities." West hooked his arm through Charlie's and turned them toward the hangar. "I believe someone mentioned refreshments."

Bump took Dani's hand and followed West and Charlie back inside.

As they stepped under the hangar's folded doors, West asked, "It's alive and breathing now. So what are you going to name it?"

Charlie smiled as Dani maneuvered Bump closer.

"Since you've been teasing me about the amount of time I'm spending with him instead of with you"—she jabbed his chest with her finger—"I'm going to name it 'My Affair,' with a subtitle in smaller letters, 'Charlie's Other Man.'"

"That's very nice." West leaned down and kissed her. "I like knowing who my competition is."

Monte and Cat were standing together with Melony and Michael in front of them, taking in the panoramic view of Colorado Springs and the expanse of eastern Colorado beyond. The day was bright with high, thin mares' tails drifting across the sky from the west.

"Is your jacket warm enough, Mel?" Monte asked as he leaned down to talk to her. "It's a little cold up here."

"I'm okay, Dad," Mel replied, and smiled at him.

"How about you, Mike?" he asked, looking at Michael.

"Yeah, I'm warm enough, Dad," he answered. "It looks like we're in an airplane."

"Yes, it does, doesn't it?" Monte agreed.

Cat smiled when he asked if she was warm enough. "Yes. But I didn't think Pike's Peak would be this much cooler than down in the city."

"Do you want to have lunch up here?" Monte asked. "Or wait until we get back down in Manitou Springs?"

"Down where it's warmer, Dad," Mel suggested. "It's pretty up here, but I think we should find a nice, warm restaurant when we get back down."

"I agree with Mel." Cat took Monte's hand. "And, I think we should go inside and wait for the Cog to start reloading."

"Okay." Monte turned them back to the concession building.

They were almost back to the entrance when Monte's phone rang. He pulled it out of his pocket, glanced at the face, and mouthed a silent "It's your father" to Cat. "Go on inside and I'll answer this."

Cat led the children inside and Monte turned to face the wide parking lot with four cars in it and answered the call.

"Hello, Howard. How are you today?" Monte asked, hoping the latest events did not have Howard in one of his moods.

"How's your vacation going?" Howard greeted tersely,

"Wonderful," he answered happily. "Cat and the children are really enjoying the sights and activities. Swimming every day and Cat says I'm going to have to install a hot tub when we get back."

"I'm glad you're all having a great time." Then Howard hesitated.

"Everything okay?" he asked.

"Yes, yes," Howard responded, but Monte knew there was something else on his mind. And he figured he could guess what it was. "I was wondering when you're going to be back."

"Aah, Sunday around one. We leave here at nine ten, lose an hour in the time change, and it's a two-hour-and-forty-five-minute flight."

"Thanks." Howard was still hesitant. "Mary has been thinking about you and your vacation and she wants me to take her on a trip for a couple of weeks. It's not what I want to do, but I got her to agree that I can stop off and check on a couple of my projects while we're gone. So I agreed to go."

"Really? I mean that's great." Monte was dumbfounded. "You need to take time off every now and then. Do you know where you're going?"

"Yeah," Howard explained. "New England and then down into the Carolinas. We'll fly out and then drive down the coast and fly back from Raleigh."

"Wow. That sounds better than our trip," he admitted. "When are you planning to leave?"

"Tomorrow afternoon. Mary's been planning for a couple of days and wants to know if Cat can check on the house a couple of times while we're gone."

"Sure. I'm sure she'd love to check on it for you." He was trying to hide his surprise at the suddenness of the trip. "And with your security system, everything will be fine."

"Thanks, Monte." Howard sounded more comfortable. "I think Mary will call Cat from the airport tomorrow."

"Good. Cat will like that. I'll let her know."

"Okay. Call me if anything happens that I need to know about."

"I certainly will. You have an enjoyable trip."

"Thanks. I'll talk to you later. Have a safe trip home."

"Thank you."

He stared at his phone as Howard disconnected.

Monte had to wait until they were down off the mountain and had found a suitable restaurant for lunch before he could think about Howard's phone call again. Once seated, he turned to the children.

"Grandpa said he hopes you're enjoying your vacation."

Melony and Michael smiled.

"Was that your call up on the mountain?" Melony asked.

"Yes. And"—he glanced at Cat—"it seems Grandma has talked him into taking her on a vacation also."

"They're going on vacation?" Cat voiced her surprise before she thought. "I mean, it's been a very long time since they've gone anywhere together."

"That's true," he reiterated. "Mary asks for you to look in on the house a few times while they're away."

"S...sure," Cat concurred, and Emli's sketch of the trunk flashed through her mind. "I can do that. When are they leaving?"

"Tomorrow afternoon." He waited for Cat's reply.

Her thoughts stumbled, but she held her composure and slowly continued. "That's soon. When did they decide?"

"He said your mom's been working on the idea for a few days. He blames her thinking about our vacation for her deciding they need one also."

"Where are they going, Dad?" Melony asked.

"He said New England, and then they are going to drive down to North Carolina and fly home from there."

"Will they be back before we get back from soccer camp?" Michael asked.

"Probably about the same time. Now go and wash up before the waiter comes to see what you want to eat."

"Okay," they said together, and slid out of their chairs.

"Why New England?" Cat asked when the children had disappeared down the appropriate hallway.

Monte's expression turned somber. "Do you remember me telling you about the list of names your dad had?" He watched her a moment. "The investors that had single daughters?"

Cat's face suddenly went pale. "Oh Monte, nooo."

He nodded. "It's only a hunch on my part, but two of those on the list are in the New England area—one in New Hampshire and one in Maine. I'll check my notes when we get home, but I think New Hampshire has two unmarried older daughters. There's another one in North Carolina and a resort project just inland from the Pamlico Sound on the waterway inland to Greenville."

"I don't think Mother planned this vacation at all," Cat suddenly admitted, feeling like her chair was beginning to sink into sandy ground.

He reached out and took her hand and she immediately wanted him to hold it, tight.

"Yeah, but I have a feeling she's going along with whatever he's up to. My first reaction to the call"—he glanced at the hallway to the restrooms—"was that Tony called him and for some reason he felt he needed to leave the Detroit area. Then, when he told me where he's going, I could only think of the one reason he would choose New England. Then I remembered what was in North Carolina." When he saw the children coming back, he held Cat's eyes. "I'm sorry I couldn't tell you before now. We'll talk more later."

"Thanks. There's definitely something not right here. He's setting up an alibi, getting ready to do something." She forced herself to smile and greet the children with comments about the menu as they sat down.

Charlie's story continues in,
The Price of Escape, Eight's Warning, Part 3.

Phonetic Alphabet

World War II   Current usage

A	Able	Alpha
B	Baker	Bravo
C	Charlie	Charlie
D	Dog	Delta
E	Easy	Echo
F	Fox	Foxtrot
G	George	Golf
H	How	Hotel
I	Item	India
J	Jig	Juliet
K	King	Kilo
L	Love	Lima
M	Mike	Mike
N	Nan	November
O	Oboe	Oscar
P	Peter	Papa
Q	Queen	Quebec
R	Roger	Romeo
S	Sugar	Sierra
T	Tear	Tango
U	Uncle	Uniform
V	Victor	Victor
W	Whiskey	Whiskey
X	X-Ray	X-Ray
Y	Yoke	Yankee
Z	Zebra	Zulu

Glossary

Characters:

-A-

Alice - Monte Williamson's secretary.

-B-

Baron, Richard - Owner of Jet Services in Broomfield, CO, located on Rocky Mountain Metropolitan Airport. Member of West Restorations, LLC board of directors.

Bassett, Charlie - Pilot and mechanic. Birth certificate shows parents as Arthur and Sarah Bassett, deceased. Resided in Jackson, WY. Birthdate on her birth certificate is 4 July.

Bellini, Antonio (Tony) - One of Howard Collingsworth's "investigators" tasked with finding and capturing Emli Collingsworth or her lookalike. Partnered with Tommy Laker.

Benny - Teamed with Larry, Benny is one of two additional rough-handed investigators and the individuals Howard hired to kidnap Charlie at the Broomfield fly-in.

Bingham, Lucky - Owner and pilot of P-51, *Trust Me*. Lives in Oregon.

-C-

Celia - See Gibbings, Celia

Collingsworth, Catherine (Cat) - Older of two daughters of Howard and Mary Collingsworth (32). Sister Emli.

Collingsworth, Emli Charlotte - Younger of two daughters of Howard and Mary Collingsworth (30). Birthday June 12. Sister Catherine.

Collingsworth, Howard - Owner and founder of International Opportunities, a multinational commercial land development and construction firm. Married to Mary and has two daughters, Emli and Catherine.

-D-

Doc Warren - See Warren, Doc

-E-

Eight - West's nickname when he flies pace, chase, and safety for various racing classes. Named for the eight o'clock formation position he flies.

Emli's college friends

Celia Gibbings (domestic and family law)

Norman Kent (business, domestic, and family law)

Marty Logan (archaeological law and ethics)

Ben Scroles (banking law)

Nancy Gomez (business law)

-G-

Ghost Ranch "Hands"

John "Ratchet" Powers - Lead mechanic, Ghost Three (39)

Lester "Lenny" James - Mechanic, Ghost Four (30)

Jimmy "Bump" Ashward - Mechanic, Ghost Five (27)

Norm "Woody" Stold - Mechanic, Ghost Six (50+)

Dani Ventura - Ghost Seven (19)

Eddie Ventura - Ghost Eight (17)

Jessie Miller - Security (29)

Ghost Ranch, LLC Board

Board of Directors:

Glen West (Griff Montgomery) – Chairman

Helen West (Montgomery family)

Richard Baron (Jet Services, Broomfield, CO)

Carl Henry (Henry & Sons Refining, Cactus, TX)

Bill Strong (NW New Mexico Ranching Supplies,

Clayton, NM)

Investment and Legal Support:

Thomas Grant (LLC Investment Manager)

Carson Taylor (Legal Counsel, Denver)

Ghost Ranch staff

Cappie Montez and wife, Celina, and sons Philip (20) and Peter (16).

Henry Astera and wife Gracie Astera, Celina's cousin, sons George (17), Patrick (15), Billy (13), and daughter Camilla (14) help on big weekends and holidays. Moved to the ranch when Rosita started flying.

Robert Ventura and wife Madra and daughters Rosita (19) and Belle (17).

Becky (34), the Senior Ranch Cook.

Gibbings, Celia - One of Emli's college friends at Yale Law College (32). Friend of Norman Kent. One sister, June. Father Walter. Mother deceased.

Gibbings, June - Celia's sister (33).

Gibbings, Walter - Owner and co-owner of multiple stone quarries in New Hampshire, Maine, South Dakota, South Carolina, Texas, Italy, and Brazil. Widowed father of two daughters, June and Celia.

-H-

Henry, Carl - Owner of Henry and Sons Refining, Inc. based in Cactus, TX. Has a couple of business airplanes and one personal airplane, a P 40N restored by Glen West Restorations. Carl is on the board of directors of West Restorations, LLC.

Hill, Bobby - Owner and pilot of P-51D Mustang, Six Six Tear Whiskey (66TW), named *Daylight Devil.*

-J-

Jessie - See Miller, Jessie.

-K-

Kent, Norman - One of Emli's college friends from Yale Law College (34). Norman introduced Emli to the world of flying. Also a friend of Celia Gibbings. Parents, Steve and Margaret. Younger sister Ronnie.

Kent, Ronnie - Norman's unexpected sister (20).

Kent, Steve - Norman's father. Wife Margaret (Maggie). Living in Shelbyville, outside of Louisville, KY. Daughter Ronnie.

Kullet, Curt - Owner and operator of High Plains Aviation on Meadow Lake Airport in Falcon, northeast of Colorado Springs.

-L-

Laker, Tommy - One of Howard Collingsworth's "investigators" tasked with finding and capturing Emli Collingsworth or her lookalike. Partnered with Tony Bellini.

Larry - Teamed with Benny, Larry is one of two additional investigators and the individuals that Howard hired to kidnap Charlie at the Broomfield fly-in.

Lawrence - Howard Collingsworth's lead negotiator in Paris.

Little, Will - Owner and operator of Central Colorado Aviation on Meadow Lake Airport in Falcon, northeast of Colorado Springs.

Lloyd - Private investigator. One of Monte Williamson's investigators tasked with verifying public information on Charlie Bassett. Partnered with Sam.

-M-

Miller, Jessie - Software Coder (29). Originally hired by Griff Montgomery when she was seventeen. Stayed with his company when it sold and Griff left.

Montgomery, Grifford Westfield - Internet and Software Entrepreneur (37). Founder of an internet security company. Aka Griff in family and business circles. Birthday March 19.

Montgomery, Helen - Widowed mother of Grifford. Aka Helen West. Trained and worked as a registered nurse, maintained her currency and credentials after moving to the Ranch.

-N-

Norman - See Kent, Norman.

-P-

Powers, John "Ratchet" - Ghost Ranch lead mechanic and shop foreman (39). Mechanic and pilot. Longtime friend of West's.

-S-

Sam - Private investigator. One of Monte Williamson's "investigators" tasked with verifying public information on Charlie Bassett. Partnered with Lloyd.

Setters, John - Owner and pilot of C model P-51 Mustang, Oh Seven Zulu (07Z), named Malevolent Greetings.

Smyth, Lydia - Charlie Bassett's aunt. Sister of Arthur Bassett. Buried in the family cemetery in Jackson, WY.

Sonny - Owner of Sonny's Collection Services in Melville, Michigan.

Stan - Works for Sonny.

Stewart, Mr. - An investigator hired by Howard Collingsworth to find clues to the whereabouts of his long-missing daughter, Emli. Mr. Stewart contacts Ben Scroles on March 3 in St. Louis.

Strong, Bill - Owner of NW New Mexico Ranching Supplies, Clayton, NM. Bill is on the board of directors of West Restorations, LLC.

-T-

Tommy - See Laker, Tommy

Tony - See Bellini, Antonio (Tony).

-V-

Voster, Elrich - Assistant to South Africa's Minister of State Security.

-W-

Warren, Doc – "Adopted" uncle to Grifford. A family friend, Doc knew Grifford's father and mother when Grifford was a child. Doc was an air force mechanic.

West, Glen - Pilot, Ghost One. Mechanic and owner of West's Ghost Ranch and airplane restoration business, Glen West's Restorations. In the race circuit: works in the pits and flies some competition. Grifford Montgomery's alias. Father deceased. Mother, Helen, living with Glen on the Ghost Ranch.

West, Charlie - Pilot, Ghost Two. Lead mechanic at the Ghost Ranch and Glen West's wife.

Williamson, Ralph - CEO and president of an East Coast multinational banking firm, Openlands Financials.

Williamson, Monte - Son of Ralph Williamson. Husband of Catherine (Cat) (Collingsworth) and father of son, Michael (Mike) (10), and daughter Melony (Mel) (11).

Williamson, Catherine - Wife of Monte Williamson by an arranged marriage when she was 17 (32). Called "Cat" by her family and friends.

Places and Things:

-A-

AGL - Above Ground Level. The term used when altitude is measured from the local terrain level.

-C-

Charlie's Airplanes - Cessna 180, work airplane she restored until it was destroyed in a ground accident in Denver.

Legacy, a rebuild project to replace the 180.

North American TF-51 rebuild project, a wedding gift from West.

Clock Positions - For directional referencing, the airplane is viewed from the top with the nose pointed at twelve o'clock on an imaginary clock face. A direction from the pilot's point of view is referred to by its associated direction, hour hand direction. Off the right wing is three o'clock, left wing is nine o'clock, tail is six o'clock, and so on. From the another airplane, the airplane's position is announced as simply being "on your Three," or "on your Six."

-F-

FBO - Fixed Base Operator. A business located on an airport.

-G-

Ghost Ranch, West's - Private ranch of Glenn West and his airplane restoration business. Structures consist of multiple semi-buried hangars and a refueling ramp.

Airstrip: Flying field concept with the hangars in the middle of the usable surface area, approx. 1.5 miles in radius. Mean elevation 5840 ft.

Ghost Ranch LLC Airplanes

Flying Utility:

Cessna T206

De Havilland Beaver - *Box Car*

Flying Fighters:

TF-51 Mustang * - *The Beautiful Lady* (07GW)

P-40D Kittyhawk - *Anxious Delivery*

P-51D Mustang - *Lucky Shot*

P-51D Mustang - *Hell Raiser*

SBD-5 Dauntless - *Deep Six*

F6F-5 Hellcat - *Steppin' Out*

Spitfire Mk XIVe - (Unnamed) (Griffon powered)

Spitfire Mk IIIB - (Unnamed) (Merlin powered)

F4U-5 Corsair** - *'Your' Bad Luck*

Airplanes in Restoration:

Legacy - Charlie's personal airplane

TF-51 Mustang * - Charlie's personal airplane. (*My Affair*, subtitled *Charlie's Other Man*.)

P-51C Mustang - (Unnamed)

AT-6B Texan - *Pistol Packin' Mama*

Customer Rebuild Projects:

P-51D Mustang - *Gold Rush*: Richard Mendelson

Available in Stores for Rebuild:

P-51D Mustang - (Unnamed)

P-51A Mustang - (Unnamed)

F4F-x Wildcat - (Unnamed)

P-38L Lightning - (Unnamed)

Typhoon Mk IB - (Unnamed)

Hurricane Mk IIA - (Unnamed)

Mosquito - (Unnamed)

SNJ-3 - (Unnamed)

Fw. 190A-3 - (Unnamed)

Bf. 109K-4 - (Unnamed)

A6M5 Reisen - Mitsubishi (Unnamed)

Fw. 190D-9 - (Unnamed)

* No fuselage fuel tank; 2 ea. 85-gal, wing & 2 ea. 110-gal, drop tanks; equals 390 gal, total.

** 233-gal, fuselage fuel tank & 2 ea. 170-gal, drop tanks; equals 573 Gal, total.

-M-

MSL - Mean Sea Level. A term used when altitude is measured from the mean elevation of sea level, worldwide.

-V-

vas a mantenerla? - Spanish for "you're going to keep it?"

-Y-

Yáʼátʼééh - Navajo for "good morning," "hello" or more correctly, "it is good, the morning."

Books by Aidan Red:

West's Ghost Ranch Series
Eight's Warning
(A tale in the world of high octane aviation fuel and restored warbirds)
Part 1: The Past Hunts
Part 2: The Past Attacks
Part 3: The Price of Escape

Paladin Shadows Series
Terran Assignment
Book 1: Things Are Not As They Seem
Book 2: When Luck Is Not Enough
Book 3: Fate Has A Different Idea
Terran Recruits
Book 4: In the Wake of Chaos
Book 5: Terran Talents Join Forces
Book 6: New Rules of Engagement
Operation Retribution
Book 7: The Training Phase
Book 8: Taking the Fight Off-World
Book 9: Luring the Prince Into the Open
Garda Nua
Book 10: The Proliferation of Talent
Book 11: When A Planet Is Stolen
Book 12: Right Does Not Ask Permission
Assignment: Casha-Six
Book 13: No Warning
Book 14: The Best Laid Plans
Book 15: A Change of Heart?

More Books by Aidan Red

Keeper and His Tiger Series

(After living homeless to find his parents murderer...)

Book 1: An Unexpected Complication

Book 2: Deadly Undercurrents

Book 3: The Trap

Fearin' the Banshee

About the Author

Aidan Red's passion for aviation and aircraft design, engineering, and a deep interest in space and space travel go back many years. An avid reader from an early age, Aidan, with great trepidation, ventured into the world of writing during college. With real world experience in business aviation, Aidan's creative side led him to create an alternate world where the beautiful Riggs Valley was born and Shara's life became chronicled in his epic science fiction series, Paladin Shadows.

Paladin Shadows consists of the five triptychs (three-part works), *Terran Assignment, Terran Recruits, Operation Retribution, Garda Nua* and *Assignment: Casha-Six*. In between the Paladin triptychs, Aidan has penned two, three book series, *Keeper and his Tiger Series,* and *Eight's Warning,* in West's Ghost Ranch Series and a novel, *Fearin' the Banshee.*

The unpublished books in his various series are scheduled for release on a regular basis in the coming months.

You can visit

www.RedsInkandQuill.com or

www.AdianRedBooks.com

for more information on Aidan Red's books and where to purchase them.

Made in the USA
Columbia, SC
23 July 2022

63839927R00139